EASTERN GHOSTS

WITHDRAWN

APR 2 0 2022

NAFC PUBLIC LIBRARY

NEW ALBANY-FLOYD COUNTY PUBLIC LIBRARY

33110003080502

Volumes in the American Ghosts series:

Dixie Ghosts
Eastern Ghosts
Ghosts of the Heartland
New England Ghosts
Western Ghosts

DEC 1 6 1993

EASTERN GHOSTS

Haunting, Spine-Chilling Stories
from
New York, Pennsylvania, New Jersey,
Delaware, Maryland, and the District of Columbia

Edited by
Frank D. McSherry, Jr., Charles G. Waugh,
and Martin H. Greenberg

Rutledge Hill Press
Nashville, Tennessee

Copyright © 1990 by Frank D. McSherry, Jr., Martin Harry Greenberg, and Charles G. Waugh

All rights reserved. Written permission must be secured from the publisher to use or reproduce any part of this book, except for brief quotations in critical reviews or articles.

Published in Nashville, Tennessee, by Rutledge Hill Press, Inc., 513 Third Avenue South, Nashville, Tennessee 37210

Typography by Bailey Typography, Nashville, Tennessee
Cover design by Harriette Bateman

Library of Congress Cataloging-in-Publication Data

Eastern ghosts : haunting, spine-chilling stories from New York,
    Pennsylvania, New Jersey, Delaware, Maryland, and the District of
    Columbia / edited by Frank D. McSherry, Jr., Charles G. Waugh, and
    Martin H. Greenberg.
        p.   cm.
    ISBN 1-55853-091-6
    1. Ghost stories, American—East (U.S.) 2. East (U.S.)—Fiction.
I. McSherry, Frank D.   II. Waugh, Charles.   III. Greenberg, Martin
Harry.
PS648.G48E28   1990   90-44724
813'.08733080974—dc20   CIP

Manufactured in the United States of America
1 2 3 4 5 6 7 8 — 96 95 94 93 92 91 90

Table of Contents

A Shade Treatise

In the last two hundred years, thousands of ghost stories have been written. Many of the earliest are just as entertaining as those written today. Why do they have such continuing popularity and staying power? There are several possible reasons.

Social views about death seem fairly constant, and death and the possibility of an afterlife are issues we all face. The existence of ghosts would give assurances that we would continue to exist, in some recognizable form, after death. Scary ghost stories also jolt us from mundane lives, providing momentary rollercoaster-like thrills to savor.

Eastern Ghosts is the last volume of the American Ghosts Series that covers the regions of the United States state-by-state. The others are *Dixie Ghosts, Western Ghosts, Ghosts of the Heartland,* and *New England Ghosts.* New York, New Jersey, Pennsylvania, Delaware, Maryland, and the District of Columbia comprise the Eastern, or mid-Atlantic, region. Though this region lacks the unified identity of New England, Dixie, the Heartland, or the West, it is the most urban region of the United States, the cultural and financial center of the world, and the nerve center of our government. It has great geographical importance, much industrial development, and immense historical importance, as G. J. A. O'Toole's story "Turn Down for Richmond," reminds us.

Edgar Allan Poe spent much of his short life in the Eastern region, often selling his now famous work for pennies. The ghastly (and ghostly) details behind a cache of Poe's unpublished masterpieces are exposed in Robert Bloch's "The Man Who Collected Poe." New Jersey, Delaware, and Maryland have long be famous for their seashore resorts, and Mario Martin, Jr.'s "A Seance in Summer," provides a gritty feel for honky-tonk summer life (and death) at the shore. Edward D. Hoch's "Remember My Name" reveals little known facts about the Miss America contest. New York's Yankee Stadium, the "house that Ruth built," is a part of Paul Gallico's "The Word of Babe Ruth," which gives one last glimpse of the great Bambino as he appears at the home of his greatest heckler.

Many of the four types of ghosts stories—the science fictional, the traditional, the bogus, and the Janus—are also included in this collection.

The science fictional ghost story depicts ghosts as fantastic but natural. Here ghosts are usually discovered to be aliens, robots, mutants, death rays, or new types of poison. The traditional ghost story depicts ghosts as fantastic and supernatural, usually responsible for "ghostly" phenomena, although such ghosts could also be exposed as werewolves, vampires, zombies, or any other supernatural entities. The bogus story reveals a ghost to be a prankster, madman, or criminal.

Finally, the Janus (or two-faced) story is ambiguous and often psychological. It leaves us guessing whether the story deals with the known world or the fantastic. Is, for example, Nancy Varien Berberick's colorful New Jersey story, "Ransom Cowl Walks the Road," about possession or mental illness? What about Burton Kline's Pennsylvania story, "The Caller in the Night"? Does the ghostly cry the protagonists hear actually exist, or is it imagined? We may choose an interpretation, but we never *know* for the author doesn't say.

All these stories and more, as the barker might say, are by some of America's most famous writers. All between these two covers. All you have to do is turn the page . . .

—Charles G. Waugh

Acknowledgments

"Double Vision" by Mary Higgins Clark. Copyright © 1989 by Mary Higgins Clark. From *The Anastasia Syndrome* by Mary Higgins Clark. Reprinted by permission of Simon & Schuster, Inc.

"The Man Who Collected Poe" by Robert Bloch. Copyright © 1951, 1979 by Robert Bloch. Reprinted by permission of the Scott Meredith Literary Agency, Inc., 845 Third Avenue, New York, New York 10022.

"Ransom Cowl Walks the Road" by Nancy Varian Berberick. Copyright © 1988 by Nancy Varian Berberick. Reprinted by permission of the author.

"Turn Down for Richmond" by G. J. A. O'Toole. Copyright © 1988 by G. J. A. O'Toole. From *The Encyclopedia of American Intelligence and Espionage* by G. J. A. O'Toole. Reprinted by permission of Facts On File, Inc.

"The Word of Babe Ruth" by Paul Gallico. Copyright © 1954 by the Curtis Publishing Company. Copyright renewed © 1982 by Virginia Gallico, Robert Gallico, and William Gallico. Reprinted by permission of Harold Ober Incorporated.

"A Séance in Summer" by Mario Martin, Jr. Copyright © 1974 by Arthur Tofte. Reprinted by permission of Larry Sternig Literary Agency, Inc.

"Little Note Nor Long Remember" by Henry T. Parry. Copyright © 1974 by Henry T. Parry. Reprinted by permission of the author.

"The Jest of Warburg Tantavul" by Seabury Quinn. Copyright © 1934 by *Weird Tales*. Reprinted by permission of the agents for the author's Estate, the Scott Meredith Literary Agency, Inc., 845 Third Avenue, New York, NY 10022.

"Remember My Name" by Edward D. Hoch. Copyright © 1990 by Edward D. Hoch. An original story, published by arrangement with the author.

"Author! Author!" by Isaac Asimov. Copyright © 1964 by Isaac Asimov. Reprinted by permission of the author.

EASTERN GHOSTS

When Jimmy Cleary killed the wrong twin, he knew he had to correct his mistake. What he didn't know was exactly how close identical twins can be.

ONE

Double Vision
Mary Higgins Clark

Jimmy Cleary crouched in the bushes outside Caroline's garden apartment in Princeton. His thick brown hair fell on his forehead and he pushed it back with the studied gesture that had become a mannerism. The May evening was unseasonably raw and chilly. Even so, perspiration soaked his sweat suit. He moistened his lips with the tip of his tongue. His whole body tingled with nervous exhilaration.

Five years ago tonight he had made the blunder of a lifetime. He had killed the wrong girl. He, the best actor in the entire world, had fouled up his ultimate scene. Now he was going to rectify that error. This time there would be no mistakes.

The back door of Caroline's apartment opened onto the parking lot. For the last few nights he'd been studying the area. Last night he'd unscrewed the light bulb outside her apartment, so now the back entrance was in deep shadows. It was 8:15; time to go in.

From his pocket he took out a spikelike tool, inserted it in the keyhole, and twisted it until he heard the click of the cylinder. With gloved hands he turned the knob and opened the door just wide enough to slip in. He closed and relocked it. There was an inside chain that she probably fastened at night. That was fine. Tonight she'd lock the two of them in. It gave Jimmy distinct pleasure to contemplate Caroline carefully securing the place. It would be like the ghost story that ended, "Now, we're locked in for the night."

He was in the kitchen, which opened directly from an

1

archway into the living room. Last night he'd hidden out-side the kitchen window and observed Caroline. There were plants on the sill, so the shade didn't go all the way down. At ten o'clock, she came out of the bedroom wearing red-and-white-striped pajamas. While she watched the news, she exercised, bending from the waist so that her blond hair flew from shoulder to shoulder.

She went back to her bedroom where she probably read for a while because the light stayed on for about an hour. He could just as easily have finished her then, but his sense of drama wanted him to wait for the exact anniversary.

The only light came from the outside streetlamps, but there weren't many places to hide in the apartment. He could fit under her bed, which had a velvet dust ruffle. It was an interesting idea: He could wait there, while she read, got sleepy, turned off the light; wait until she stopped mov-ing and her breath became even. Then he could silently ease his body out, kneel beside her, watch her the way he had watched the other girl, and then wake her up. But be-fore he decided, he'd check other possibilities.

When he opened the door of the bedroom closet, a light went on automatically. Jimmy caught a glimpse of an almost full traveling bag. Quickly he closed the door. There was no place to hide here.

Imagine a woman who has less than two hours to live. Does she sense it? Does she go about her normal routine? These were the hypothetical questions Cory Zola had thrown at the acting class one night. Cory was a famous teacher who only took on students he thought had the po-tential to become stars. He put me in his private class the first time I auditioned for him, Jimmy reminded himself now. He knows talent.

There was no place to hide in the living room. The front door, however, opened directly into it, and there was a closet at a right angle. The closet door was open a couple of inches. Swiftly he moved over to inspect it.

This closet didn't have an automatic light. He pulled a pencil-thin flashlight from his pocket and shone the beam on the interior, which was unexpectedly deep. A heavy dress bag, encased in voluminous layers of plastic, hung at the front. This was the reason the door wasn't closed. It would have squashed the dress. He'd bet anything it was her wedding gown. Last night when he'd followed her, she'd stopped at a bridal shop and stayed nearly half an hour, probably for a final fitting. Maybe they'd bury her in this dress.

The cascade of plastic created a perfect hiding place. Jimmy stepped into the closet, slid between two winter coats and pulled them together. Suppose Caroline went into his closet and found him? The worst that could happen would be that he couldn't kill her exactly as he'd planned. But those traveling bags in the other closet were almost full. She probably was just about packed. He knew she was flying to St. Paul in the morning. She was getting married next week. She *thought* she was getting married next week.

Jimmy eased out of the closet. At five o'clock, in his rented car, he'd been waiting for Caroline outside the State House in Trenton. She'd worked late. He'd followed her to the restaurant where she met Wexford. He'd stood outside, and didn't leave until, through the window, he'd seen them order. Then he came directly here. She wouldn't be back for another hour at least. He helped himself to a can of soda from the refrigerator and settled on the couch. It was time to prepare himself for the third act.

It had begun five and a half years ago, that last semester at Rawlings College of Fine Arts in Providence. He'd been in the theater program studying acting. Caroline had majored in directing. He'd been in a couple of the plays she directed. As a junior he'd played Biff in *Death of a Salesman*. He'd been so fantastic that half the school started calling him Biff.

Jimmy sipped the soda. In memory he was back at college on the set of the senior play. He had the lead. The president of the college had invited an old friend, a Paramount producer, as his guest for opening night, and the word was out that the producer was looking for new talent. From the beginning he and Caroline hadn't seen eye to eye on his interpretation of the part. Then two weeks before opening night, she'd taken the part from him and given it to Brian Kent. He could still see her, her blond hair in a Psyche knot, her plaid shirt tucked inside her jeans, her earnest, worried look. "You're just not quite right, Jimmy. But I think you'd be perfect as the second lead, the brother."

Second lead. The brother had about six lines. He'd wanted to plead, to beg, but had known it was useless. When Caroline Marshall made a casting change she couldn't be budged. And he'd known in his gut that somehow being the lead in that play was crucial to his career. In that split second he'd made up his mind to kill her, and right away started performing. He'd laughed, a lighthearted, chagrined chuckle, and said, "Caroline, I've been working up the courage to tell you I'm so far behind in term papers, I can't even think about acting."

She'd fallen for it. And looked relieved. The Paramount producer had come. He'd invited Brian Kent to the Coast to test for a new series. The rest, as we say in Hollywood, Jimmy thought, was history. After nearly five years, the series was still in the top-ten ratings, and Brian Kent had just signed to do a movie for three million bucks.

Two weeks after graduation Jimmy had gone to St. Paul. Caroline's family's home was practically a mansion, but he'd quickly found that the side door was unlocked. He'd made his way along the downstairs floor, up the wide, sweeping staircase, past the master bedroom suite. The door was ajar. The bed was empty. Then he'd opened the next bedroom door and seen her: lying there asleep. He could still see the outlines of her room, the brass four-poster bed, the silky sheen of the soft, expensive percale sheets. He remembered how he'd bent over her as she lay there curled up in bed, her blond hair gleaming on the pillowcase. He'd whispered, "Caroline," and she'd opened her eyes, looked at him, and said "No."

He'd thrown his arms over her and covered her mouth with his hands. She'd listened, her eyes panicking, while he whispered that he was going to kill her, that if she hadn't taken the lead from him, he'd have been seen by the Paramount producer instead of Brian Kent. Finally he'd said, "You're not going to direct anything anymore, Caroline. You've got a new role. You're the victim."

She'd tried to pull away from him, but he yanked her back and twisted the cord around her neck. Her eyes had widened, blazing out at him. Her hands had lifted, palms outstretched begging him, then had fallen limp on the sheet.

The next morning he couldn't wait to read the newspapers. "Daughter of Prominent St. Paul Banker Slain." He remembered how he'd laughed, then cried with frustration when he read the first few sentences. *The body of twenty-one-year-old Lisa Marshall was found by her twin sister this morning.*

Lisa Marshall. Twin sister.

The story continued: *The young woman had been strangled. The twins were alone in the family home. Police have been unable to question Caroline Marshall. At the sight of her sister's body, she went into profound shock and is under heavy sedation.*

He'd tell Caroline about that later on tonight. All these years in Los Angeles he'd had a subscription to the Minneapolis-St. Paul papers, watching for any news about the case. Then he read that Caroline was engaged and would be married on May 30—next week. Caroline Marshall, who was a lawyer on the staff of the Attorney General in Trenton, New Jersey, was marrying an associate professor from Princeton University, Dr. Sean Wexford. Wexford had been a graduate student when Jimmy was at Rawlings. Jimmy had him for a psychology course. He wondered when Caroline and Wexford got together. They weren't going around when Caroline was a student at Rawlings. He was sure of that.

Jimmy shook his head. He took the empty soda can out to the kitchen and tossed it in the wastebasket. Caroline might be coming along anytime now. He went into the bathroom and winced at the noisy flush of the toilet. Then with infinite care he stepped into the closet and pulled the winter coats around him. He felt for the length of cord in the pocket of his sweat suit. It was cut from the same roll of heavy fishing tackle he'd used on her sister. He was ready.

"Cappuccino, darling?" Sean smiled across the candlelit table. Caroline's dark blue eyes were pensive with that look of absolute sadness that sometimes came into them. Understandable tonight. It was the anniversary of the last night she'd spent with Lisa.

To try to distract her, he said, "I felt like a bull in a china shop when I picked up your gown this afternoon."

Caroline raised her eyebrows. "You didn't look at it? That's bad luck."

"They didn't let me get near it. The saleslady kept apologizing that they couldn't send it."

"I've been rushing around so much this last month I've lost weight. They had to take it in."

"You're too thin. We'll have to fatten you up in Italy. Pasta three times a day."

"I can hardly wait." Caroline smiled across the table. She loved the bigness of Sean, the way his sandy hair always looked a bit disheveled, the humor in his gray eyes. "My mother phoned this morning. She's still worried that my dress doesn't have sleeves. She reminded me twice that the joke in Minnesota is, 'Which day was summer?'"

"I volunteer to keep you warm. Your dress is in the front closet. By the way, I'd better give you back your extra keys."

"Keep them. If I forget anything, you can bring it out with you next week."

When they left the restaurant Caroline followed him to the roomy Victorian house that would be theirs when they returned from the honeymoon. She was leaving her car in the second garage while they were away. Sean drove his car into the driveway, parked it, and got into hers. She slid over and he drove her home, his arm around her.

Jimmy was proud that even after an hour of standing still, he felt fine. That was because he was in shape from the gym and all the dancing lessons.

He'd spent the past five years studying, knocking on doors, trying to see casting people, getting close and then shut out. To get a good agent, you needed to show you'd had some good roles. To get sent to the good casting people, you needed a hotshot agent. And sometimes he'd hear the ultimate killer: "You're a Brian Kent type, and that isn't helping you."

The memory infuriated Jimmy, and he shook his head.

And all of this after his mother had persuaded his father to stake him to a year of what he called "trying to act."

Jimmy felt the old anger again. His father had never liked what he did. When Jimmy was so great in *Death of a Salesman,* had his father been proud? No. He wanted to cheer for a son who was the quarterback, a Heisman Trophy contender.

Jimmy hadn't bothered to ask for more when the money from his father ran out. Every month or so his mother sent him whatever she could squeeze from the house money. The old man might have plenty, but he sure was tight. But boy, would he have loved it if James Junior had been the one to sign Brian Kent's three-million-dollar contract last week. "That's my boy," he'd be yelling.

That's the way the scene would have been played if five years ago Caroline hadn't yanked him from the part and given it to Brian Kent.

Jimmy stiffened. There was a sound of voices at the front door. Caroline. *She wasn't alone.* A man's voice. Jimmy shrank against the wall. As the door opened and the light was snapped on, he glanced down and froze. The light filtered into the closet. He was sure he couldn't be seen, but the tips of his beat-up running shoes, pointing outward, screamed their presence.

Caroline glanced around the living room as the light went on. Tonight, for some reason, the apartment seemed different, alien. But of course that was only because it was tonight. Lisa's anniversary. She put her arms around Sean and he gently kneaded the back of her neck. "You do know that all evening you've been miles away."

"I always hang on your every word." It was an attempt at lightheartedness that failed. Her voice broke.

"Caroline, I don't want you to be alone tonight. Let me stay with you. Look, I know why you want to be by yourself, and I understand. Go into the bedroom. I'll stretch out on the couch."

Caroline tried to smile. "No, I'm really okay." She wrapped her arms around his neck. "Just hold me tight for one minute and then get out of here," she said. "I'm setting the alarm for six-thirty. I'm better off doing final packing in the morning. You know me. Sharp in the A.M. Fade in the P.M."

"I hadn't noticed." Sean's lips caressed her neck, her forehead, found her lips. He held her, feeling the tension in her slender body.

Tonight she had told him, "Once the anniversary is over, I'm really okay. It's just that the couple of days before, it's as though Lisa is with me. It's a feeling that builds and builds. Like today. But I know it will be fine tomorrow, and I'll go home and get ready for the wedding and be happy."

Reluctantly, Sean released Caroline from his arms. She looked so tired now, and oddly that made her look so young. Twenty-six, and at this moment she could have passed for one of the kids in his freshman class. He told her that. "But you're much prettier than any of them," he concluded. "It's going to be awfully nice to wake up and look at you first thing in the morning for the rest of my life."

Jimmy Cleary's body was soaked with perspiration. Suppose she let Wexford spend the night here. They'd surely see him in the morning when Caroline took the wedding dress from the closet. They were wrapped up in each other less than a foot from where he was standing. Suppose one of them smelled the perspiration from his body. But Wexford was leaving.

"I'll be here at seven, love," he told Caroline.

And you'll find her the way she found her sister, Jimmy thought. That's how you'll envision her in the morning for the rest of your life.

Caroline bolted the door behind Sean. For an instant she was tempted to reopen it immediately, call out to him, tell him yes, stay with me. I don't want to be alone. But I'm not alone, she thought as she took her hand from the knob. Lisa is so close to me tonight. Lisa. Lisa.

She went into the bedroom and undressed quickly. A hot shower helped to relieve some of the tension she felt in the muscles of her neck and back. She remembered the way Sean's hands had kneaded those muscles. I love him so much, she thought. Her red-and-white-striped pajamas were on the hook on the bathroom door. She'd been shopping for lingerie and nightgowns in a Madison Avenue boutique when she'd spotted them. "If you like them, better

8

make up your mind fast," the salesgirl had said. "We only got in one pair in red. They're comfortable and awfully cute."

One pair. That had decided Caroline. One of the hardest things in these past five years was to break the habit of buying *two* of everything. For years if she saw something she liked, she'd automatically buy two. Lisa had done the same thing. They were exactly the same size, same height, same weight. Even their parents had trouble telling them apart. When they were juniors in high school, Mother had urged them to buy different gowns for the prom. They'd shopped separately in different stores and arrived home with exactly the same blue and white dotted-swiss gown.

The next year, they'd tearfully agreed with their parents and the school psychologist that they'd be doing themselves a favor if they attended different colleges and did not discuss being an identical twin. "Being close is wonderful," the psychologist had said, "but you've got to think of yourselves as individuals. You're not going to grow to your full capacity unless you give yourselves and each other space."

Caroline had gone to Rawlings, Lisa to Southern Cal. In college it secretly delighted Caroline that people thought she had inscribed her own picture, "To my best friend." They'd even graduated on the same day. Mother had gone to be with Lisa. Dad had come to Caroline's commencement.

Caroline went into the living room, remembered to fasten the chain on the back door, turned on the television, and halfheartedly began bending from side to side. A commercial for life insurance came on. "Isn't it a comfort to know that your family will be taken care of after you're gone?" Caroline snapped off the television. Turning off the livingroom light, she rushed into the bedroom and slipped under the covers. Lying on her side, she pulled her legs against her body and buried her face in her hands.

Sean Wexford could not shake off the feeling that he should have flatly refused to leave Caroline. He sat in the car for a few minutes looking at her door. But she needed to be alone. Shaking his head, Sean reached for the car keys.

On the drive home his emotions seesawed between his

concern for Caroline and anticipation that a week from to-morrow they'd be married. How astonished he'd been last year when he'd seen her jogging ahead of him on the Princeton campus. She'd been in only one of his classes in Rawlings. In those days he'd been working so hard on his doctoral thesis, he hadn't even thought about dating. That morning a year ago, she'd told him about going to Columbia Law School, clerking for a New Jersey Superior Court judge, and then going to work in the Attorney General's office in Trenton. And, Sean thought, as he steered the car into his driveway, *over that first cup of coffee we both knew what was happening to us.* He parked Caroline's car behind his own and went into the house smiling at the realization that soon their cars would always be together in the driveway.

Jimmy Cleary was surprised that Caroline had turned off the television so abruptly. He thought again of the questions Cory Zola had thrown at the acting class: *Imagine a woman who has less than two hours to live. Does she sense it? Does she go about her normal routine?* Caroline might be sensing danger. When he was back in class, he'd bring up that question again. "In my opinion," he would say, "there is a quickening of the spirit as it prepares to leave the body." He had a feeling that Zola would find his insight profound.

Jimmy felt a cramp in his leg. He wasn't used to standing perfectly still for so long, but he could do it for as long as necessary. If Caroline's intuition was warning her of danger, she'd be listening for even the smallest sound. These garden-apartment walls weren't thick. One scream and someone might hear her. He was glad she'd left the bedroom door open. He wouldn't have to worry about the door creaking when he went to her.

Jimmy closed his eyes. He wanted to duplicate the exact stance he'd been in when he woke her sister. One knee on the floor beside the bed, his arms ready to wrap around her, his hands in position to clamp over her mouth. Actually he'd knelt for a minute or two before he awakened the other girl. He probably wouldn't chance that luxury now. Caroline would be sleeping lightly. Her spirit would be pounding at her to beware.

Beware. A beautiful word. A word to whisper from the stage. He would have a stage career now. Broadway. Not nearly the pay you got for a film, but prestige. His name on the marquee.

Caroline was his jinx, and she was about to be removed.

Caroline lay curled up in bed, shivering. The soft down comforter could not stop the trembling. She was afraid. So terribly afraid. Why? "Lisa," she whispered, "Lisa, was this the way you felt? Did you wake up? Did you know what was happening to you?" *Did I hear you cry out that night and go back to sleep?*

She still didn't know. It was only an impression, a blurred, dreamy image that came to her in the weeks after Lisa's death. She and Sean had talked it through. "I think I might have heard her. Maybe if I had forced myself awake. . . ."

Sean had made her understand that her reaction was typical of families of victims. The "if only" syndrome. In this last year, through him and with him, she'd begun to experience peace, a healing. Except for now.

Caroline turned in the bed and forced herself to stretch out her legs and arms. "Irrational anxiety and profound sadness are symptoms of depression," she had read. Sadness, okay, she thought. It is the anniversary, but I won't give in to the anxiety. Think of the happy times with Lisa. That last evening.

Mother and Dad had left for a bankers' seminar in San Francisco. She and Lisa had ordered pizza with everything on it, drunk wine, and talked their heads off. Lisa's decision to go to law school. Caroline had taken the law school admittance exams too but still wasn't sure what she wanted to do.

"I really loved being in the theater group," she'd told Lisa. "I'm not a good actress but I can sense good acting. I think I could make a pretty fair director. The play went over well, and Brian Kent, who I just knew was right for the lead, was picked up by a producer. Still, if I get a law degree maybe we can open an office and tell people they're getting double their money's worth."

They'd gone to bed about eleven o'clock. Their rooms adjoined. Usually they left the door open, but Lisa wanted

11

to watch a television show and Caroline was sleepy, so they blew kisses and Caroline closed the door. If only I'd left it open, she thought. I would surely have heard her if she'd had a chance to cry out.

The next morning, she hadn't waked up until after eight. She remembered sitting up, stretching, thinking how good it felt to have college behind her. As a graduation present, she and Lisa had been given a trip to Europe that summer.

Caroline remembered how she'd jumped out of bed, deciding to get coffee and juice and bring it up on a tray to Lisa. She squeezed fresh juice while the coffee perked, then put the glasses and cups and coffeepot on a tray and went up the stairs.

Lisa's door was open a crack. She'd kicked it open and called, "Wake up, my girl. We've got a tennis date in an hour."

And then she'd seen Lisa. Her head slumped unnaturally, the cord biting her neck, her eyes wide open and filled with fear, her palms extended as though trying to push something back. Caroline had dropped the tray, splashing her legs with the coffee, had managed to stumble to the phone and dial 911 and then scream, scream until her throat broke into a harsh, guttural sound. She awakened in the hospital three days later. She was told that the police found her lying beside Lisa, Lisa's head on her shoulder.

The only clue, the muddied partial print of a running shoe just inside the side door. "And then," as the chief of detectives told them later, "he, or she, was polite enough to scrape the rest of the mud off on the mat."

If only they had found Lisa's murderer, Caroline thought as she lay in the darkness. The detectives all believed that it was someone who had known Lisa. There was no attempt at robbery. No attempt to rape. They'd exhaustively questioned Lisa's friends, her dates at college. There was one young man in her class who had been obsessed by her. He'd remained a strong suspect, but the police could never prove he was in St. Paul that night.

They'd looked into mistaken identity, especially when they learned that neither girl had told her college friends she had an identical twin. "At first we didn't tell because we promised not to. It became a game with us," Caroline said.

12

"How about friends from college visiting your home?"

"We just didn't bring college friends home. We were glad to have time together during holidays and school breaks."

Oh, Lisa, Caroline thought now. If I only knew why. If I only could have helped you that night. She was not sleepy but was suddenly weary.

At last her eyelids began closing on their own. Oh, Lisa, she thought, I wanted you to have happiness like mine too. If only I could make it up to you.

The window was open a few inches from the bottom. Protective side locks kept it from being raised higher. Now a sharp gust of wind made the shade rattle. Caroline jumped up, realized what had happened, and forced herself to lie back against the pillows. Stop it, she told herself, stop it. Deliberately she closed her eyes and after a while fell into a light dream-filled sleep, a sleep in which Lisa was trying to call her, trying to warn her.

It was time. Jimmy Cleary could sense it. The rustling of the sheets had stopped. There was absolutely no sound coming from the bedroom. He slipped between the garments that had concealed him and eased aside the bag containing Caroline's gown. The hinges gave off a faint rubbing noise when he pushed the closet door open, but there was no reaction from inside the bedroom. He made his way across the living room to the side of the bedroom door. Caroline had a night-light plugged into one of the sockets, and it threw off just enough light so that he could tell she was sleeping restlessly. Her breathing was even but shallow. Several times she turned her head from side to side as though she was protesting something.

Jimmy felt in his pocket for the cord. It was strangely satisfying to know it came from the same roll of tackle he'd used on the sister. This was even the same jogging suit he'd worn five years ago and the same running shoes. He'd known it was a little risky to keep them, just in case the cops ever questioned him, but he'd never been able to throw them away. Instead he'd put them with other stuff in a storage space he rented where nobody asked questions. Of course he'd used a different name.

He tiptoed to the side of Caroline's bed and knelt down.

He was able to savor a full minute of watching her before her eyes fluttered open and his hands snapped around her mouth.

Sean watched the ten o'clock news, realized he had absolutely no sleep in him, and opened a book he'd been wanting to read. A few minutes later he tossed it aside impatiently. Something was wrong. He could feel it as tangibly as though he could see smoke pouring from the next room and know that there was a fire blazing in the house. He'd phone Caroline. See how she was doing. On the other hand, maybe she'd managed to get to sleep. He walked over to the liquor cabinet and poured a generous amount of scotch into a tumbler. A few sips helped him to realize that he was probably acting like a nervous old biddy.

Caroline opened her eyes as she heard her name whispered. It's a nightmare, she thought, I've been dreaming. She started to cry out, then felt a hand clasped on her mouth, a hard, muscular hand that squeezed her cheekbones, that clamped her lips together, that half covered her nostrils. She gasped, fighting for breath. The hand slid down a fraction of an inch and she was able to breathe. She tried to pull away, but now the man was holding her with his other arm. His face was close to hers. "Caroline," he whispered, "I've come to correct my mistake."

The night-light sent eerie shadows onto the bed. That voice. She'd heard it before. The outline of his bold forehead, the square jaw. The powerful shoulders. Who?

"Caroline, the hotshot director."

Now she recognized the voice. Jimmy Cleary. Jimmy Cleary, and in that same instant she knew why. Like a scene from a movie, the moment when she'd told Jimmy he simply wasn't right for the part flashed through Caroline's mind. He'd taken it so well. Too well. She hadn't wanted to know he was acting. It had been easier to pretend that he agreed with her decision. *And he killed Lisa when he wanted to kill me. It's my fault.* A moan slipped past her lips, disappeared against his palm. My fault. My fault.

And then she heard Lisa's voice as clearly as though Lisa was whispering in her ear, telling secrets again, the way they had as children. *It's not your fault, but it's your fault if you let him kill again. Don't let this happen to Mother and Dad. Don't let it happen to Sean. Grow old for me. Have babies. Name one after me. You've got to live. Listen to me. Tell him he didn't make a mistake. Tell him you hated me too. I'll help you.*

Jimmy Cleary's breath was hot on her cheek. He was talking about the part, about Brian Kent being signed up by the producer, about Brian's new contract. "I'm going to kill you exactly the way I killed your sister. An actor keeps at his role until he has it perfect. You want to hear the last thing I said to your sister?" He lifted his hand a fraction so she could mouth an answer.

Tell him you're me.

For a split second Caroline was six again. She and Lisa were playing on the foundation of a house being built near theirs. Lisa, always more daring, always surefooted, was leading the way over the piles of cinder block. "Don't be a scaredy-cat," she'd urged. "Just follow me."

She heard herself whisper, "I'd love to hear all about it. I want to know how she died, so I can laugh. You did murder Caroline. I'm Lisa."

She felt the hand slap her mouth with savage force.

Someone had rewritten the script. Furiously, Jimmy dug his fingers into her cheekbones. Whose cheekbones? Caroline's? If he'd already killed her, why hadn't his luck changed? Without moving the arm that lay over her chest, he reached into the breast pocket of his sweat suit for the cord. Get it over with, he told himself. If they're both dead, you'll be sure you got Caroline.

But it was like being on stage in the third act without knowing how the play ended. If the actor didn't know the climax, how could you expect the audience to feel any tension? Because there was an audience, an invisible audience named fate. He had to be sure. "If you try to scream, you won't even get so far as a yelp," he told her. "That's all your sister got out."

She *had* heard Lisa that night.

"So nod if you promise not to scream. I'll talk to you. Maybe if you convince me, I'll let you live. Wexford wants

15

to look at you first thing in the morning for the rest of his life, doesn't he? I heard him say so."

Jimmy Cleary had been here when they came in. Caroline felt darkness close over her.

Do as he says! Don't you dare pass out. Lisa's bossy voice. "The Duchess has spoken," Caroline used to tell her, and they'd laugh together.

Jimmy angled the arm that lay across Caroline's body, yanked the cord around her neck, and tied it in a slipknot. It was twice the length of the section he'd used last time. It had occurred to him that this time he'd make a double knot, a grand final gesture as he exited from the spotlight of death.

The extra length gave him the ability to manipulate her. Calmly he told her to get out of bed, that he was hungry— he wanted her to fix him a sandwich and coffee—that he'd be holding the end of the cord and would pull it till she strangled if she raised her voice or tried anything funny.

Do as he says.

Obediently Caroline sat up as Jimmy lifted the weight of his arm from across her body. Her feet touched the cool wood of the floor. Automatically she fumbled for her slippers. I may be dead in seconds and I worry about bare feet, she thought. As she bent forward the cord bit into her neck. "No . . . please." She heard the panic in her voice.

"Shut up!" She felt Jimmy Cleary's hands on her neck, loosening the cord. "Don't move so fast and don't raise your voice again."

Side by side they walked through the living room and into the kitchen. His hand rested on the back of her neck. His fingers gripped the cord. Even loosened, she could feel its pressure, like a band of steel. In her mind she could see the grayish stripe embedded in Lisa's throat. For the first time she began to remember the rest of that morning. She'd dialed 911 and begun to scream. Then she'd dropped the receiver. Lisa's body was almost on the edge of the bed as though in that last moment she'd tried to escape. Her skin was so blue, I was thinking she was cold, I had to warm her, Caroline recalled as she opened the refrigerator door. I ran around the bed and got in and put my arms around her and began to talk to her and I tried to get the cord from around her neck and then I felt as though I was falling.

16

Now the cord was around her neck. In the morning would Sean find her as she had found Lisa?

No. It mustn't happen. Make the sandwich. Make him coffee. Act as though you two are playing a great scene. Tell him how bossy I was. Come on. Take all the good things and turn them around. Blame me the way he's blaming you.

Caroline looked inside the refrigerator and had a swift feeling of gratitude that she'd put off emptying it. She'd always kept sandwich makings for Sean on hand; the cleaning woman was coming in the morning to take them home. She pulled out ham and cheese and turkey, lettuce, mayonnaise, and mustard. She remembered that at school when the cast went out for a late snack Jimmy Cleary always ordered a hero.

How would I have known that? Ask him what he wants.

She looked up. The only light came from the refrigerator but her eyes were adjusting to the darkness. She could clearly see the unmistakable square jaw that toughened Jimmy Cleary's face, and the anger and confusion in his expression. Her mouth dry with fear, she whispered, "What kind of sandwich do you want? Turkey? Ham? I've got whole wheat bread or Italian rolls."

She could sense that she passed the first test.

"Everything. The works on a roll."

She felt the cord loosen slightly. She put the kettle on to boil. She made the sandwich swiftly, piling turkey and ham on top of cheese, spreading the lettuce, gobbing mayonnaise and mustard across the roll.

He made her sit next to him at the table. She poured coffee for herself, forced herself to sip. The cord was biting into her neck. She moved her hand to loosen it.

"Don't touch that." He released it slightly.

"Thank you." She watched him wolf the sandwich.

Talk to him. You've got to convince him before it's too late.

"I think you told me your name but I didn't really get it."

He swallowed the last bit of sandwich. "On the marquee it's James Cleary. My agent and my friends call me Jimmy."

He was gulping the coffee. How could she make him believe her, trust her? From where she was sitting Caroline

17

could see the outline of the front closet. It had been almost closed before. That was where he must have been hiding. Sean had wanted to stay with her. If only she had let him stay. In those first couple of years after Lisa's death, there had been times when it seemed too much of a struggle to get through the day. Only the harsh demands of law school had kept her from sinking into suicidal depression. Now she could see Sean's face, so inexpressibly dear. *I want to live,* she thought. *I want the rest of my life.*

Jimmy Cleary felt better. He hadn't realized how hungry he was. In a way this was better than last time. Now he was acting out a cat-and-mouse scene. Now he was the judge. Was this Caroline? Maybe he hadn't made a mistake last time. But if he'd wasted Caroline, why hadn't the jinx been lifted? He finished the coffee. His fingers curled around the end of the cord, drawing it a hairbreadth tighter. Reaching over, he turned on the table lamp. He wanted to be able to study her face. "So tell me," he said easily. "Why should I believe you? And if I believe you, why should I let you live?"

Sean undressed and showered. In the bathroom mirror he looked at himself intently. He'd be thirty-four in ten days. Caroline would be twenty-seven the next day. They'd celebrate their birthdays in Venice. It would be good to sit in St. Mark's Square with her, to sip wine and hear the sweet sounds of the violins and watch the gondolas glide by. It was an image that had occurred to him several times in the past few weeks. Tonight it was as though he was drawing a blank. That picture simply wouldn't form.

He *had* to talk to Caroline. Wrapping a thick bath towel around him, he went to the bedside phone. It was nearly midnight. Even so, he dialed her number. The blazes with making excuses, he thought. *I'll just tell her that I love her.*

"It's not easy to be a twin." Caroline tilted her head so she could look directly into Jimmy Cleary's face. "My sister and I fought a lot. I used to call her the Duchess. She was so bossy. Even when we were little, she'd do things and blame me. I ended up hating her. That's why we went to colleges at opposite ends of the continent. I wanted to get away from her. I was her shadow, her mirror image, a nonperson. That last night she wanted to watch television and her set was broken, so she made me change rooms. When I found her that morning, I guess I just collapsed. But you see, even my mother and father didn't realize the mistake."

Caroline widened her eyes. She dropped her voice, making it intimate, confidential. "You're an actor, Jimmy. You can understand. When I came to they were calling me Caroline. You know the first words my mother said when I woke up were 'Oh, Caroline, we thank God it wasn't you.' "

Very good. You're getting to him.

She was six again. They were playing on the foundation. Lisa was running faster and faster. Caroline had looked down and gotten dizzy. But she'd still tried to keep up with her.

Jimmy was enjoying himself. He felt like a casting agent telling a hopeful to give him a cold reading. "So just like that you decided to be Caroline. How did you get away with it? Caroline went to Rawlings. What happened when Caroline's friends from Rawlings showed up?"

Caroline finished her own coffee. She could see the glints of madness in Jimmy Cleary's eyes. "It really wasn't hard. Shock. That was the excuse. I pretended not to remember lots of people we both knew. The doctors called it psychological amnesia. Everyone was very understanding."

Either she was a darn good actress or she was telling the truth. Jimmy was intrigued. He started to feel some of his anger fading. This girl was different from Caroline. Softer. Nicer. He felt a kinship with her, a regretful kinship. No matter what, he couldn't let her live. The only trouble was that if he had killed Caroline, if she wasn't lying—and he still wasn't sure—why hadn't the jinx been lifted five years ago?

Those cute red-and-white pajamas she was wearing. He laid his hand on her arm, then withdrew it. He had a sudden thought. "How about Wexford? How come you got together with him?"

"We just bumped into each other. I heard him call 'Caroline,' and I knew it was someone I was supposed to know. He told me his name as soon as he caught up with me jogging and in the next breath said something about having me in class, so I just faked it."

Remind Jimmy that Sean didn't bother with the real Caroline at Rawlings. Point out that he fell for you right away.

Jimmy shifted restlessly. Caroline said, "I can't tell you how many times Sean has said that I'm a much nicer person now. That's because I'm not the same person. Don't you love it? I'm glad you're sharing my secret, Jimmy. For the last five years you've been my secret benefactor, and at last I'm getting to know you. Would you like more coffee?"

Was she trying to snow him? Did she mean it? He touched her elbow. "More coffee sounds fine." He stood behind her, slightly to the side, as she turned the heat under the kettle. A very pretty girl. But he realized he couldn't let her live. He'd finish the coffee, bring her back into the bedroom and kill her. First he'd explain to her about the jinx. He glanced at the clock. It was 12:30. He'd killed the other sister at 12:40, so the timing was perfect. An image came into his mind of how the other girl had reached out her hands as though she wanted to claw him, how her eyes had blazed and bulged. Sometimes he dreamed about that. In the daytime the memory made him feel good. At night it made him break into a sweat.

The phone rang.

Caroline's hand gripped the handle of the kettle convulsively. She knew it would be Sean. Other nights when he'd sensed that she was terribly down and probably not sleeping, he'd phoned.

Convince Jimmy you've got to answer the telephone. You've got to let Sean know that you need him.

The phone rang a second, a third time.

Sweat glistened on Jimmy's forehead and upper lip. "Forget it," he said.

"Jimmy, I'm sure it's Sean. If I don't answer he'll think there's something wrong. I don't want him here. I want to talk to you."

Jimmy considered. If that was Wexford she was probably telling the truth. The phone rang again. It was attached to an answering machine. Jimmy pushed the button that made the conversation audible, picked up the receiver and handed it to her. He tightened the cord so that it bit into her throat.

Caroline knew she could not allow her voice to sound

20

shaky. "Hello." She managed to sound sleepy and was rewarded by a slight relaxing of the pressure on her neck.

"Caroline, honey, you were asleep. I'm sorry. I was worried that you were feeling pretty low. I know what tonight means to you."

"No, I'm glad you called. I wasn't really asleep. I was just starting to drift off." *What can I tell him?* Caroline wondered desperately.

The dress. Your wedding dress.

"It's kind of late," she heard Sean say. "Did you finish packing tonight after all?"

Jimmy tapped her shoulder and nodded.

"Yes. I felt wide awake, so I finished it."

Jimmy was looking impatient. He signaled for her to cut it short. Caroline bit her lip. If she didn't carry this off, it was the end. "Sean, I love you for calling and I'm really fine. I'll be ready at seven-thirty. Just one thing. When they packed my dress, did you remember to ask them to be sure to put lots of tissue in the sleeves so they wouldn't wrinkle?" She thought, don't let Sean give me away.

Sean felt his fingers holding the receiver go clammy. The dress. Caroline's dress did not have sleeves. And there was something else. Her voice had a hollow sound. She wasn't in bed. She was on the kitchen phone and the conference button was on. She wasn't alone. With a supreme effort he kept his voice steady. "Honey, I can swear on a stack of Bibles that the saleslady said something about that. I think your mother had called to remind her too. Now listen, get some sleep. I'll see you in the morning and remember, I love you." He managed to put the receiver down without letting it bang, then dropped the towel and pulled his sweat suit from the closet. The keys to Caroline's apartment were on the dresser with his car keys. Should he take the time to call the police? The phone in his car. He'd call them while he was on the way. Dear God, he thought, please. . . .

Sean had understood. Caroline replaced the receiver and looked at Jimmy. "You did a good job," he told her. "And you know, I'm starting to believe you." He led her back into the bedroom and forced her to lie down. He laid his arm across her, exactly as he had held down the sister. Then he

21

explained what his teacher, Cory Zola, had told him about the jinx. "We were doing a dueling scene in class last week, and I guess I was pretty mad. I cut the other student. Zola really got upset with me. I tried to explain that I'd been thinking about this jinx someone put on me and how it's spoiling everything. He told me to stay away from class until I'd gotten rid of it. So, even if I believe you that I got Caroline last time, I still have to get rid of that feeling because I can't go back to class until I'm free of it. And in my book, Lisa—that's the real name, huh?—you inherited it."

His eyes glittered. The expression was vacant, cold. He is mad, Caroline thought. It will take Sean fifteen minutes to get here. Three minutes gone. Twelve minutes more. Lisa, help me.

Brian Kent is the jinx. Strangers on a Train.

Her mouth was so dry. His face was so near hers. She could smell the perspiration that was dripping from his body. She felt his fingers begin to pull the cord. She managed to sound matter-of-fact. "Killing me won't solve anything. Brian Kent is the jinx, not me. If he's out of the way, you'll have your chance. And if I kill him you'll have just as big a hold on me as I have on you."

The astonished sucking in of his breath gave her hope. She touched his hand. "Stop fooling with that cord, Jimmy, and listen to me for two minutes. Let me sit up." Again the memory of playing follow-the-leader on the foundation of that new house ran through her mind. At one point they'd come to a gaping space left for a window. Lisa had jumped over. Caroline, a few steps behind her, had hesitated, closed her eyes, and jumped, barely clearing the opening. She was taking a jump now. If she failed, it was all over. Sean was coming. She knew it. She had to stay alive for the next eleven minutes.

Jimmy released his arm, allowing her to sit up. She drew her legs against her body and locked her hands around her knees. The cord was digging against her neck muscles but she didn't dare ask him to ease it. "Jimmy, you told me that your big problem is that you're too much like Brian Kent. Suppose something happened to Brian? They'd need to have a replacement. So, become him. Replace him the way I became Caroline. He has a sudden accident, they'll be

22

frantic to find someone to step into that movie. Why shouldn't it be you?"

Jimmy shook the sweat from his forehead. She was suggesting a new interpretation of the role Brian was playing in his life. He'd always concentrated on becoming a star, becoming bigger than Brian, surpassing him, getting a better table in the restaurants, watching him fade. Never once had he thought about Brian just disappearing from the scene. And even if he killed this girl, this Lisa, because now he believed she was Lisa, Brian Kent would still be signing contracts, posing for spreads in *People* magazine. And worse, agents would still be telling him that he was a Brian Kent type.

Did he believe her? With her tongue, Caroline tried to moisten her lips. They were so dry it was hard to talk. "If you kill me now, they'll find you. Jimmy, the cops aren't dumb. They always questioned whether or not the wrong twin was killed."

He was listening.

"Jimmy, we can bring off *Strangers on a Train*. You remember the plot. Two people exchange murders. There's no motive. The difference is, we'll carry it off. You've already done your part. You got Caroline out of the way for me. Now let me get rid of Brian Kent for you."

Strangers on a Train. Jimmy had done a scene from that movie in class. He'd been great. Cory Zola had said, "Jimmy, you're a natural." His eyes flickered over her face. Look at her, smiling at him. She was a cool one. If she'd gotten away with convincing her family she was Caroline, she might be capable of setting up Brian Kent and pulling it off. But what insurance did he have that she wouldn't scream for the cops the minute he left her? He asked her that.

"Why, Jimmy, you have the best insurance in the world. You know I'm Lisa. They never checked Caroline's fingerprints against our birth records. You could give me away. Do you know what that would do to my parents, to Sean? Do you think they'd ever forgive me?" She looked directly into Jimmy's eyes, awaiting his judgment.

Sean ran from the house, then bit his lip in wild frustration. Caroline's car was blocking his. He wanted to be able to phone the police on the way. He ran back into the house, grabbed her car keys, pulled her car out of the way and got into his own. As he backed with furious speed onto the road, he ripped the car phone off its cradle and dialed 911.

Jimmy was experiencing a dazzling sense of rebirth. How many times in L.A. had he seen Brian Kent drive by in that Porsche of his? They'd gone to school together for four years, but Brian never gave him more than a cool nod if they bumped into each other. How much better if Brian didn't exist. And Lisa—she was Lisa, he was convinced of that—was right. He would have a hold on her. Deliberately he released his grip on the cord but did not remove it from her neck. "Let's say I believe you. How would you get him?"

Caroline fought to keep back the lightheaded sensation that came with hope. What could she tell him?

You'll go to the Coast. Look up Brian.

Desperately she searched for a plausible plot. Again she was six, skimming over the foundation. The gaping spaces between the cinder blocks were getting wider.

Poison. Poison.

"Sean has a friend, a professor who specializes in the history of medicine. Last week at dinner, he was talking about how many absolutely undetectable poisons there are. He described one of them, exactly how to prepare it from things you have in your medicine chest. A few drops is all it takes. Next month when I come back from my honeymoon, I have to go to California to depose a witness. I'll call Brian. After all, I—I mean Caroline gave him his big break. Right?"

Be careful.

She had slipped. But Jimmy didn't seem to notice. He was listening intently. The perspiration had caused his hair to curl so that it lay in damp ringlets on his forehead. She didn't remember that his hair was that curly. He must have had a body wave. Now it was cut exactly like the recent picture she'd seen of Brian Kent. "I'm sure he'd be glad to see me," she continued. As though stretching her legs from cramping, she eased them over the side of the bed.

His hand reached for and encircled the end of the cord. She slipped her hand over his. "Jimmy, there's a poison that

24

takes a week, ten days to act. The symptoms don't even begin for three or four days. Even if there's an inquiry, who would connect the fact that Brian had coffee with an old college friend, who just married a Princeton professor, with a murderer? It's the perfect scenario."

Jimmy realized he was nodding in assent. The night had turned into a dream, a dream that would start his whole life all over. He could trust her. With dazzling clarity he accepted the truth of what she had pointed out to him. As long as Brian Kent was alive, he, who was the greatest actor in the world, would go unnoticed. The night-light in the bedroom became a footlight. The darkened living room was the theater where the audience was sitting. He was standing on stage. The audience was clapping its approval. He savored the moment, then chucked Caroline—no, Lisa—under the chin. "I do believe you," he whispered. "When exactly are you coming to California?"

Hang on. You're almost safe.

They were running faster and faster over the foundation. She couldn't keep up. Caroline heard her voice crack as she answered, "The second week in July."

Jimmy's remaining doubts vanished. Kent was due to start his new movie the first of August. If he was dead by then, they'd be frantic looking for a replacement.

He stood up and pulled Caroline to her feet. "Let me get that thing off your neck. Just remember it's right here in my pocket in case I ever need it again. I'm leaving now. We've got a deal. But if you don't keep your part of the bargain, some night when your professor is away or some afternoon when you stop for a red light, I'll be there."

Caroline felt the cord loosen, felt him pull it over her head. Hysterical sobs of relief were breaking in her throat. "It's a deal," she managed to say.

He dug his fingers into her shoulders and kissed her on the mouth. "I don't seal agreements with handshakes," he said. "Too bad I haven't got more time. I could go for you." His caricature of a smile became a bemused, wide-toothed grin. "I feel like the jinx is lifted already. Come on." He walked her to the back door. He reached up his hand to unfasten the chain.

Caroline caught a glimpse of the clock on the kitchen

wall. It was twelve minutes since Sean had phoned. In the next thirty seconds Jimmy would be gone and she could chain and barricade the door. In the next few minutes Sean would be there.

Again the memory of being six, running on the foundation. She had glanced down. It was eight or ten feet to the ground. Jutting pieces of broken concrete were lying there. Lisa had made the last jump over a wide space left for a door. . . .

Jimmy opened the door. She could feel the cool rush of night air on her face. He turned to her. "I know you never had the chance to see me perform, but I am a truly great actor."

"I know you're a great actor," Caroline heard herself say. "After *Death of a Salesman,* didn't everyone in school call you Biff?"

On the foundation she had hesitated that one moment before she made the final jump after Lisa. She had lost momentum. She had tumbled and her forehead had smashed against the concrete. With sickening fear she knew she had once again failed to follow Lisa.

The door slammed shut. For a split second she and Jimmy stared at each other. "Lisa couldn't have known that," Jimmy whispered. "You've been lying to me. You *are* Caroline." His hands lunged for her neck. She tried to scream as she backed away from him, turned and stumbled toward the front door. But only a low moan came from her lips.

Sean raced through the quiet streets. The 911 operator was asking him his name, where he was calling from, what was the nature of the emergency. "Get a squad car to eighty-one Priscilla Lane, apartment one-A," he shouted. "Never mind how I know there's something wrong. Get a car there."

"And what is the nature of the emergency?" the operator repeated.

Jimmy's hand slammed onto the front door as she tried to turn the lock. Caroline ducked past him and ran around the club chair. In the shadowy light she caught a glimpse of herself in the mirror over the couch, his looming presence behind her. His breath was hot on her neck. If she could only live for a minute more, Sean would be here. Before she could complete the thought, Jimmy had vaulted over the club chair. He was in front of her. She saw the cord in his hands. He spun her around. She felt her hair pulled back, the cord on her neck, saw their reflection in the mirror over the couch. She dropped to her knees and the cord tightened. She tried to crawl away from him, felt him leaning over her. "It's all over, Caroline. It's really your turn to be the victim."

Sean turned into Caroline's street. The brakes screeched as he jammed them on in front of her house. From a distance he could hear sirens. He ran to the door and tried the knob. With one fist he pounded on the door while he groped in his pocket for her keys. He remembered that the damn security lock had not been installed properly. You had to pull the door toward you before it would turn. In his anxiety, he could not match up the cylinder and the lock. It took three turns of the key before the lock released. Then the other key for the regular lock. Please. . . .

She was on her knees, clawing at the cord. It was choking her. She could hear Sean pounding on the door, calling her. So close, so close. Her eyes widened as the cord cut off her breath. Waves of blackness were rolling over her. Lisa . . . Lisa . . . I tried.

Don't pull away. Lean backward. Lean backward, I tell you.

In a final effort to save her life, Caroline forced herself to bend backward, to slide her body toward Jimmy instead of pulling away from him. For an instant the pressure on her throat eased. She gulped in one breath before the cord began to tighten again.

Jimmy shut out the sounds of the pounding and shouting. Nothing in the whole world mattered except to kill this woman who had ruined his career. Nothing.

The key turned. Sean slammed the door open. His gaze fell on the mirror over the couch, and the blood drained from his face.

Her eyes were blazing, bulging, her mouth was open and

27

gaping, her palms extended, her fingernails like claws. A bulky figure in a sweat suit was bending over her, strangling her with a cord. For an instant Sean was rooted, unable to move. Then the intruder looked up. Their eyes met in the mirror. As Sean watched, in that one second, still unable to move, he saw the horrified expression that came into the other man's face, watched him drop the cord from his hands, throw his arms over his face.

"Stay away from me!" Jimmy screamed. "Don't come any nearer. Stay away."

Sean spun around. Caroline was on the floor, clawing at the cord that was choking her. Sean dove across the room, butted the man who had been attacking her. The force of the blow sent Jimmy back against the window. The sound of shattering glass mingled with his screams and the wail of sirens as patrol cars screeched to a halt.

Caroline felt hands yanking at the cord. She heard a low moaning sound come from her throat. Then the cord released and a rush of air filled her lungs. Darkness, sweet, welcome darkness, enveloped her.

When she awoke, she was lying on the couch, an icy cloth around her neck. Sean was sitting by her, chafing her hands. The room was filled with policemen. "Jimmy?" her voice was a harsh croaking sound.

"They took him away. Oh, my darling." Sean lifted her up, wrapped her in his arms, laid her head against his chest, smoothed her hair.

"Why did he start screaming?" she whispered. "What happened? In another few seconds I'd have been dead."

"He saw the same thing I did. You were reflected in the mirror over the couch. He's completely nuts. He thought that he was seeing Lisa. He thought she was coming for revenge."

Sean would not leave her. After the policemen were gone, he lay beside her on the roomy couch, pulled the afghan over them and held her close. "Try to get some sleep." Safe in his arms, beyond exhaustion, she did manage to drift off.

At 6:30 he woke her up. "You'd better start getting ready," he told her. "If you're sure you're okay, I'll run home and get showered and dressed." Brilliant sunlight spilled through the room.

Five years ago this morning, she had walked into Lisa's room and found her. This morning, she had awakened in Sean's arms. She reached up and held his face in her hands, loving the faint stubble on his cheeks. "I'm all right. Really."

When Sean left, she went into the bedroom. Deliberately she stared at the bed, remembering how it had felt to open her eyes and see Jimmy Cleary. She showered, letting the hot water run for long minutes over her body, her hair, wanting all trace of his presence to be washed away. She dressed in a khaki-colored jumpsuit, cinching a braided belt around her waist. As she brushed her hair, she saw the reddish-purple welt around her neck. Quickly she turned away.

It was as though time were in abeyance, waiting for her to complete what must be completed. She packed her suitcase, set it with her handbag near the door. Then she did what she knew she had to do.

She knelt on the floor just as she had been kneeling when Jimmy Cleary tried to strangle her. She arched her body backward and stared at the mirror. It was as she had expected. The bottom of the mirror was a fraction of an inch above her hairline. There was no way she could have been reflected there. Jimmy had been right: He had seen Lisa.

"Lisa, Lisa, thank you," she whispered. There was no feeling of an answer. Lisa was gone, as Caroline had known she would be gone. For the last time the thought that she had been the cause of Lisa's death filled her consciousness and then was vanquished. It had been an act of fate, and she would not insult Lisa's memory by dwelling on it. She stood up, and now she was reflected in the mirror. Tenderly she raised her fingertips to her lips and blew a kiss. "Goodbye. I love you," she said aloud.

In the street she heard a car pull up. Sean's car. Caroline hurried to the door, flung it open, pushed out her suitcase and purse, reached for the plastic-wrapped garment bag that enveloped her wedding gown, and carrying it cradled in her arms, slammed the door behind her and ran to meet him.

Mary Higgins Clark was born in New York in 1929, was educated at Ward Secretarial School and Forham University, and worked as a stewardess for Pan American Airways before starting as a radio writer. She produced her first novel, Where Are the Children? *in 1975, which—along with her other novels* A Cry in the Night *and* Stillwatch—*hit the best seller lists. She added the icy touch of the supernatural to her work in* The Anastasia Syndrome and Other Stories, *in which her heroines deal with murderous ghosts of the past.*

Launcelot Canning had the world's largest collection of Poe memorabilia, but there was one item he did not dare show to anyone.

TWO

The Man Who Collected Poe

Robert Bloch

Author's Introduction

Would Edgar Allan Poe be able to sell his stories if he were writing today? This is a question which has long intrigued editors, authors, readers, and critics of fantasy. It is a question I have sought to answer in the only possible way—by writing a story of Poe in the manner which Poe himself might have written it. I do not claim a tenth of his talent or a tithe of his genius . . . but I have proposed deliberately, insofar as possible, to recreate his style. Poe scholars will recognize my deliberate inclusion of sentences and sections from "The Fall of the House of Usher," and the casual reader will quite easily discover them. The result is, I believe, a "Poe story" in a rather unique and special sense . . . and one which it gave me great pleasure to write as a tribute to a figure to whom I, like every other writer of fantasy, must own indebtedness.

—Robert Bloch

During the whole of a dull, dark, and soundless day in the autumn of the year, when the clouds hung oppressively low in the heavens, I had been passing alone, by automobile, through a singularly dreary tract of country, and at length found myself, as the shades of the evening drew on, within view of my destination.

I looked upon the scene before me—upon the mere house, and the simple landscape features of the domain—upon the bleak walls—upon the vacant eye-like windows—upon a few rank sedges—and upon a few white trunks of

31

decayed trees—with a feeling of utter confusion commingled with dismay. For it seemed to me as though I had
visited this scene once before, or read of it, perhaps, in
some frequently rescanned tale. And yet assuredly it could
not be, for only three days had passed since I had made the
acquaintance of Launcelot Canning and received an invitation to visit him at his Maryland residence.

The circumstances under which I met Canning were simple; I happened to attend a bibliophilic meeting in Washington and was introduced to him by a mutual friend.
Casual conversation gave place to absorbed and interested
discussion when he discovered my preoccupation with
works of fantasy. Upon learning that I was traveling upon a
vacation with no set itinerary, Canning urged me to become
his guest for a day and to examine, at my leisure, his unusual display of memorabilia.

"I feel, from our conversation, that we have much in
common," he told me. "For you see, sir, in my love of fantasy I bow to no man. It is a taste I have perhaps inherited
from my father and from his father before him, together
with their considerable acquisitions in the genre. No doubt
you would be gratified with what I am prepared to show
you, for in all due modesty, I beg to style myself the world's
leading collector of the works of Edgar Allan Poe."

I confess that his invitation as such did not enthrall me, for
I hold no brief for the literary hero-worshiper or the scholarly collector as a type. I own to a more than passing interest
in the tales of Poe, but my interest does not extend to the
point of ferreting out the exact date upon which Mr. Poe first
decided to raise a moustache, nor would I be unduly intrigued by the opportunity to examine several hairs pre-
served from that hirsute appendage.

So it was rather the person and personality of Launcelot
Canning himself which caused me to accept his proffered
hospitality. For the man who proposed to become my host
might have himself stepped from the pages of a Poe tale.
His speech, as I have endeavored to indicate, was characterized by a courtly rodomontade so often exemplified in
Poe's heroes—and beyond certainty, his appearance bore
out the resemblance.

Launcelot Canning had the cadaverousness of complexion, the large, liquid, luminous eye, the thin, curved lips, the delicately modeled nose, finely molded chin, and dark, web-like hair of a typical Poe protagonist.

It was this phenomenon which prompted my acceptance and led me to journey to his Maryland estate, which, as I now perceived, in itself manifested a Poe-etic quality of its own, intrinsic in the images of the gray sedge, the ghastly tree-stems, and the vacant and eye-like windows of the mansion of gloom. All that was lacking was a tarn and a moat—and as I prepared to enter the dwelling I half-expected to encounter therein the carved ceilings, the somber tapestries, the ebon floors and the phantasmagoric armorial trophies so vividly described by the author of *Tales of the Grotesque and Arabesque.*

Nor upon entering Launcelot Canning's home was I too greatly disappointed in my expectations. True to both the atmospheric quality of the decrepit mansion and to my own fanciful presentiments, the door was opened in response to my knock by a valet who conducted me, in silence, through dark and intricate passages to the study of his master.

The room in which I found myself was very large and lofty. The windows were long, narrow, and pointed, and at so vast a distance from the black oaken floor as to be altogether inaccessible from within. Feeble gleams of encrimsoned light made their way through the trellised panes, and served to render sufficiently distinct the more prominent objects around; the eye, however, struggled in vain to reach the remoter angles of the chamber or the recesses of the vaulted and fretted ceiling. Dark draperies hung upon the walls. The general furniture was profuse, comfortless, antique, and tattered. Many books and musical instruments lay scattered about, but failed to give any vitality to the scene.

Instead they rendered more distinct that peculiar quality of quasi-recollection; it was as though I found myself once again, after a protracted absence, in a familiar setting. I had read, I had imagined, I had dreamed, or I had actually beheld this setting before.

Upon my entrance, Launcelot Canning arose from a sofa on which he had been lying at full length, and greeted me with a vivacious warmth which had much in it, I at first thought, of an overdone cordiality.

Yet his tone, as he spoke of the object of my visit, of his earnest desire to see me, and of the solace he expected me to afford him in a mutual discussion of our interests, soon alleviated my initial misapprehension.

Launcelot Canning welcomed me with the rapt enthusiasm of the born collector—and I came to realize that he was indeed just that. For the Poe collection he shortly proposed to unveil before me was actually his birthright.

Initially, he disclosed, the nucleus of the present accumulation had begun with his grandfather, Christopher Canning, a respected merchant of Baltimore. Almost eighty years ago he had been one of the leading patrons of the arts in his community and as such was partially instrumental in arranging for the removal of Poe's body to the southeastern corner of the Presbyterian Cemetery at Fayette and Green streets, where a suitable monument might be erected. This event occurred in the year 1875, and it was a few years prior to that time that Canning laid the foundation of the Poe collection.

"Thanks to his zeal," his grandson informed me, "I am today the fortunate possessor of a copy of virtually every existing specimen of Poe's published works. If you will step over here"—and he led me to a remote corner of the vaulted study, past the dark draperies, to a bookshelf which rose remotely to the shadowy ceiling—"I shall be pleased to corroborate that claim. Here is a copy of *Al Aaraaf, Tamerlane and other Poems* in the 1829 edition, and here is the still earlier *Tamerlane and other Poems* of 1827. The Boston edition, which, as you doubtless know, is valued today at fifteen thousand dollars. I can assure you that Grandfather Canning parted with no such sum in order to gain possession of this rarity."

He displayed the volumes with an air of commingled pride and cupidity which is ofttimes characteristic of the collector and is by no means to be confused with either literary snobbery or ordinary greed. Realizing this, I remained patient as he exhibited further treasures—copies of the *Philadelphia Saturday Courier* containing early tales, bound ʿmes of *The Messenger* during the period of Poe's editorship, *Graham's Magazine,* editions of the *New York Sun* and the *New York Mirror* boasting, respectively, of "The Balloon Hoax" and "The Raven," and files of *The Gentleman's Magazine.* Ascending a short library ladder, he handed down to me the Lea and Blanchard edition of *Tales of the Grotesque and Arabesque,* the *Conchologist's First Book,* the Putnam *Eureka,* and, finally, the little paper booklet, published in 1843 and sold for twelve and a half cents, entitled *The Prose Romances of Edgar A. Poe;* an insignificant trifle containing two tales which is valued by present-day collectors at fifty thousand dollars.

Canning informed me of this last fact, and, indeed, kept up a running commentary upon each item he presented. There was no doubt but that he was a Poe scholar as well as a Poe collector, and his words informed tattered specimens of the *Broadway Journal* and *Godey's Lady's Book* with a singular fascination not necessarily inherent in the flimsy sheets or their contents.

"I owe a great debt to Grandfather Canning's obsession," he observed, descending the ladder and joining me before the bookshelves. "It is not altogether a breach of confidence to admit that his interest in Poe did reach the point of an obsession, and perhaps eventually of an absolute mania. The knowledge, alas, is public property, I fear.

"In the early seventies he built this house, and I am quite sure that you have been observant enough to note that it in itself is almost a replica of a typical Poe-esque mansion. This was his study, and it was here that he was wont to pore over the books, the letters, and the numerous mementos of Poe's life.

"What prompted a retired merchant to devote himself so fanatically to the pursuit of a hobby, I cannot say. Let it suffice that he virtually withdrew from the world and from all other normal interests. He conducted a voluminous and lengthy correspondence with aging men and women who had known Poe in their lifetime—made pilgrimages to Fordham, sent his agents to West Point, to England and Scotland, to virtually every locale in which Poe had set foot during his lifetime. He acquired letters and souvenirs as gifts, he bought them, and—I fear—stole them, if no other means of acquisition proved feasible."

Launcelot Canning smiled and nodded. "Does all this sound strange to you? I confess that once I, too, found it almost incredible, a fragment of romance. Now, after years spent here, I have lost my own objectivity."

"Yes, it is strange," I replied. "But are you quite sure that there was not some obscure personal reason for your grandfather's interest? Had he met Poe as a boy, or been closely associated with one of his friends? Was there, perhaps, a distant, undisclosed relationship?"

At the mention of the last word, Canning started visibly, and a tremor of agitation overspread his countenance.

"Ah!" he exclaimed. "There you voice my own inmost conviction. A relationship—assuredly there must have been one—I am morally, instinctively certain that Grandfather Canning felt or knew himself to be linked to Edgar Poe by ties of blood. Nothing else could account for his strong initial interest, his continuing defense of Poe in the literary controversies of the day, and his final melancholy lapse into a world of delusion and illusion.

"Yet he never voiced a statement or put an allegation upon paper—and I have searched the collection of letters in vain for the slightest clue.

"It is curious that you so promptly divine a suspicion held not only by myself but by my father. He was only a child at the time of my Grandfather Canning's death, but the attendant circumstances left a profound impression upon his sensitive nature. Although he was immediately removed from this house to the home of his mother's people in Baltimore, he lost no time in returning upon assuming his inheritance in early manhood.

"Fortunately being in possession of a considerable income, he was able to devote his entire lifetime to further research. The name of Arthur Canning is still well known in the world of literary criticism, but for some reason he preferred to pursue his scholarly examination of Poe's career in privacy. I believe this preference was dictated by an inner sensibility; that he was endeavoring to unearth some information which would prove his father's, his, and for that matter, my own, kinship to Edgar Poe."

"You say your father was also a collector?" I prompted.

"A statement I am prepared to substantiate," replied my

host, as he led me to yet another corner of the shadow-shrouded study. "But first, if you would accept a glass of wine?"

He filled, not glasses, but veritable beakers from a large carafe, and we toasted one another in silent appreciation. It is perhaps unnecessary for me to observe that the wine was a fine old amontillado.

"Now, then," said Launcelot Canning. "My father's special province in Poe research consisted of the accumulation and study of letters."

Opening a series of large trays or drawers beneath the bookshelves, he drew out file after file of glassined folios, and for the space of the next half-hour I examined Edgar Poe's correspondence—letters to Henry Herring, to Dr. Snodgrass, Sarah Shelton, James P. Moss, Elizabeth Poe—missives to Mrs. Rockwood, Helen Whitman, Anne Lynch, John Pendleton Kennedy—notes to Mrs. Richmond, to John Allan, to Annie, to his brother, Henry—a profusion of documents, a veritable epistolary cornucopia.

During the course of my perusal my host took occasion to refill our beakers with wine, and the heady draught began to take effect—for we had not eaten, and I own I gave no thought to food, so absorbed was I in the yellowed pages illumining Poe's past.

Here was wit, erudition, literary criticism; here were the muddled, maudlin outpourings of a mind gone in drink and despair; here was the draft of a projected story, the fragments of a poem; here was a pitiful cry for deliverance and a paean to living beauty; here was a dignified response to a dunning letter and an editorial pronunciamento to an admirer; here was love, hate, pride, anger, celestial serenity, abject penitence, authority, wonder, resolution, indecision, joy, and soul-sickening melancholia.

Here was the gifted elocutionist, the stammering drunkard, the adoring husband, the frantic lover, the proud editor, the indigent pauper, the grandiose dreamer, the shabby realist, the scientific inquirer, the gullible metaphysician, the dependent stepson, the free and untrammeled spirit, the hack, the poet, the enigma that was Edgar Allan Poe.

Again the beakers were filled and emptied.

I drank deeply with my lips, and with my eyes more deeply still.

For the first time the true enthusiasm of Launcelot Canning was communicated to my own sensibilities—I divined the eternal fascination found in a consideration of Poe the writer and Poe the man; he who wrote Tragedy, lived Tragedy, was Tragedy; he who penned Mystery, lived and died in Mystery, and who today looms on the literary scene as Mystery incarnate.

And Mystery Poe remained, despite Arthur Canning's careful study of the letters. "My father learned nothing," my host confided, "even though he assembled, as you see here, a collection to delight the heart of a Mabbott or a Quinn. So his search ranged further. By this time I was old enough to share both his interest and his inquiries. Come," and he led me to an ornate chest which rested beneath the windows against the west wall of the study.

Kneeling, he unlocked the repository, and then drew forth, in rapid and marvelous succession, a series of objects each of which boasted of intimate connection with Poe's life.

There were souvenirs of his youth and his schooling abroad—a book he had used during his sojourn at West Point—mementos of his days as a theatrical critic in the form of playbills, a pen used during his editorial period, a fan once owned by his girl-wife, Virginia, a brooch of Mrs. Clemm's; a profusion of objects including such diverse articles as a cravat-stock and—curiously enough—Poe's battered and tarnished flute.

Again we drank, and I own the wine was potent. Canning's countenance remained cadaverously wan—but, moreover, there was a species of mad hilarity in his eye—an evident restrained hysteria in his whole demeanor. At length, from the scattered heap of curiosa, I happened to draw forth and examine a little box of no remarkable character, whereupon I was constrained to inquire its history and what part it had played in the life of Poe.

"In the *life* of Poe?" A visible tremor convulsed the features of my host, then rapidly passed in transformation to a grimace, a rictus of amusement. "This little box—and you will note how, by some fateful design or contrived coincidence it bears a resemblance to the box he himself conceived of and described in his tale 'Berenice'—this little box is concerned with his death, rather than his life. It is, in fact, the selfsame box my grandfather Christopher Canning clutched to his bosom when they found him down there."

Again the tremor, again the grimace. "But stay, I have not yet told you of the details. Perhaps you would be interested in seeing the spot where Christopher Canning was stricken; I have already told you of his madness, but I did no more than hint at the character of his delusions. You have been patient with me, and more than patient. Your understanding shall be rewarded, for I perceive you can be fully entrusted with the facts."

What further revelations Canning was prepared to make I could not say, but his manner was such as to inspire a vague disquiet and trepidation in my breast.

Upon perceiving my unease he laughed shortly and laid a hand upon my shoulder. "Come, this should interest you as an *aficionado* of fantasy," he said. "But first, another drink to speed our journey."

He poured, we drank, and then he led the way from that vaulted chamber, down the silent halls, down the staircase, and into the lowest recesses of the building until we reached what resembled a donjon-keep, its floor and the interior of a long archway carefully sheathed in copper. We paused before a door of massive iron. Again I felt in the aspect of this scene an element evocative of recognition or recollection.

Canning's intoxication was such that he misinterpreted, or chose to misinterpret, my reaction.

"You need not be afraid," he assured me. "Nothing has happened down here since that day, almost seventy years ago, when his servants discovered him stretched out before this door, the little box clutched to his bosom; collapsed, and in a state of delirium from which he never emerged. For six months he lingered, a hopeless maniac—raving as wildly from the very moment of his discovery as at the moment he died—babbling his visions of the giant horse, the fissured house collapsing into the tarn, the black cat, the pit, the pendulum, the raven on the pallid bust, the beating heart, the pearly teeth, and the nearly liquid mass of loathsome— of detestable putridity from which a voice emanated.

"Nor was that all he babbled," Canning confided, and

here his voice sank to a whisper that reverberated through the copper-sheathed hall and against the iron door. "He hinted other things far worse than fantasy; of a ghastly reality surpassing all of the phantasms of Poe.

"For the first time my father and the servants learned the purpose of the room he had built beyond this iron door, and learned too what Christopher Canning had done to establish his title as the world's foremost collector of Poe.

"For he babbled again of Poe's death, thirty years earlier, in 1849—of the burial in the Presbyterian cemetery—and of the removal of the coffin in 1874 to the corner where the monument was raised. As I told you, and as was known then, my grandfather had played a public part in instigating that removal. But now we learned of the private part—learned that there was a monument and a grave, but no coffin in the earth beneath Poe's alleged resting place. The coffin now rested in the secret room at the end of this passage. That is why the room, the house itself, had been built.

"I tell you, he had stolen the body of Edgar Allan Poe—and as he shrieked aloud in his final madness, did not this indeed make him the greatest collector of Poe?

"His ultimate intent was never divined, but my father made one significant discovery—the little box clutched to Christopher Canning's bosom contained a portion of the crumbled bones, the veritable dust that was all that remained of Poe's corpse."

My host shuddered and turned away. He led me back along that hall of horror, up the stairs, into the study. Silently, he filled our beakers and I drank as hastily, as deeply, as desperately as he.

"What could my father do? To own the truth was to create a public scandal. He chose instead to keep silence; to devote his own life to study in retirement.

"Naturally the shock affected him profoundly; to my knowledge he never entered the room beyond the iron door, and, indeed, I did not know of the room or its contents until the hour of his death—and it was not until some years later that I myself found the key among his effects.

"But find the key I did, and the story was immediately and completely corroborated. Today I am the greatest collector of Poe—for he lies in the keep below, my eternal trophy!"

This time I poured the wine. As I did so, I noted for the first time the imminence of a storm; the impetuous fury of its gusts shaking the casements, and the echoes of its thunder rolling and rumbling down the time-corroded corridors of the old house.

The wild, overstrained vivacity with which my host hearkened, or apparently hearkened, to these sounds did nothing to reassure me—for his recent revelation led me to suspect his sanity.

That the body of Edgar Allan Poe had been stolen—that this mansion had been built to house it—that it was indeed enshrined in a crypt below—that grandsire, son, and grandson had dwelt here alone, apart, enslaved to a sepulchral secret—was beyond sane belief.

And yet, surrounded now by the night and the storm, in a setting torn from Poe's own frenzied fancies, I could not be sure. Here the past was still alive, the very spirit of Poe's tales breathed forth its corruption upon the scene.

As thunder boomed, Launcelot Canning took up Poe's flute, and, whether in defiance of the storm without or as a mocking accompaniment, he played; blowing upon it with drunken persistence, with eerie atonality, with nerve-shattering shrillness. To the shrieking of that infernal instrument the thunder added a braying counterpoint.

Uneasy, uncertain, and unnerved, I retreated into the shadows of the bookshelves at the farther end of the room, and idly scanned the titles of a row of ancient tomes. Here was the *Chiromancy* of Robert Flud, the *Directorium Inquisitorum,* a rare and curious book in quarto Gothic that was the manual of a forgotten church; and betwixt and between the volumes of pseudo-scientific inquiry, theological speculation, and sundry incunabula, I found titles that arrested and appalled me. *De Vermis Mysteriis* and the *Liber Eibon,* treatises on demonology, on witchcraft, on sorcery moldered in crumbling bindings. The books were old, but the books were not dusty. They had been read—

"Read them?" It was as though Canning divined my inmost thoughts. He had put aside his flute and now approached me, tittering as though in continued drunken defiance of the storm. Odd echoes and boomings now sounded through the long halls of the house, and curious grating sounds threatened to drown out his words and his laughter.

"Read them?" said Canning. "I study them. Yes, I have gone beyond grandfather and father, too. It was I who procured the books that held the key, and it was I who found the key. A key more difficult to discover, and more important, than the key to the vaults below. I often wonder if Poe himself had access to these selfsame tomes, knew the selfsame secrets. The secrets of the grave and what lies beyond, and what can be summoned forth if one but holds the key."

He stumbled away and returned with wine. "Drink," he said. "Drink to the night and the storm."

I brushed the proffered glass aside. "Enough," I said. "I must be on my way."

Was it fancy or did I find fear frozen on his features? Canning clutched my arm and cried, "No, stay with me! This is no night on which to be alone; I swear I cannot abide the thought of being alone, I can bear to be alone no more!"

His incoherent babble mingled with the thunder and the echoes; I drew back and confronted him. "Control yourself," I counseled. "Confess that this is a hoax, an elaborate imposture arranged to please your fancy."

"Hoax? Imposture? Stay, and I shall prove to you beyond all doubt"—and so saying, Launcelot Canning stooped and opened a small drawer set in the wall beneath and beside the bookshelves. "This should repay you for your interest in my story, and in Poe," he murmured. "Know that you are the first other person than myself to glimpse these treasures."

He handed me a sheaf of manuscripts on plain white paper; documents written in ink curiously similar to that I had noted while perusing Poe's letters. Pages were clipped together in groups, and for a moment I scanned titles alone.

"'The Worm of Midnight,' by Edgar Poe," I read, aloud. "'The Crypt,'" I breathed. And here, "'The Further Adventures of Arthur Gordon Pym'"—and in my agitation I came close to dropping the precious pages. "Are these what they appear to be—the unpublished tales of Poe?"

My host bowed.

"Unpublished, undiscovered, unknown, save to me—and to you."

"But this cannot be," I protested. "Surely there would have been a mention of them somewhere, in Poe's own letters or those of his contemporaries. There would have been a clue, an indication, somewhere, someplace, somehow."

Thunder mingled with my words, and thunder echoed in Canning's shouted reply.

"You dare to presume an imposture? Then compare!" He stooped again and brought out a glassined folio of letters. "Here—is this not the veritable script of Edgar Poe? Look at the calligraphy of the letter, then at the manuscripts. Can you say they are not penned by the selfsame hand?"

I looked at the handwriting, wondered at the possibilities of a monomaniac's forgery. Could Launcelot Canning, a victim of mental disorder, thus painstakingly simulate Poe's hand?

"Read, then!" Canning screamed through the thunder. "Read, and dare to say that these tales were written by any other than Edgar Poe, whose genius defies the corruption of Time and the Conqueror Worm!"

I read but a line or two, holding the topmost manuscript close to eyes that strained beneath wavering candlelight; but even in the flickering illumination I noted that which told me the only, the incontestable truth. For the paper, the curiously *unyellowed* paper, bore a visible watermark; the name of a firm of well-known modern stationers, and the date—1949.

Putting the sheaf aside, I endeavored to compose myself as I moved away from Launcelot Canning. For now I knew the truth; knew that one hundred years after Poe's death a semblance of his spirit still lived in the distorted and disordered soul of Canning. Incarnation, reincarnation, call it what you will; Canning was, in his own irrational mind, Edgar Allan Poe.

Stifled and dull echoes of thunder from a remote portion of the mansion now commingled with the soundless seething of my own inner turmoil, as I turned and rashly addressed my host.

"Confess!" I cried. "Is it not true that you have written

43

these tales, fancying yourself the embodiment of Poe? Is it not true that you suffer from a singular delusion born of solitude and everlasting brooding upon the past; that you have reached a stage characterized by the conviction that Poe still lives on in your own person?"

A strong shudder came over him and a sickly smile quivered about his lips as he replied. "Fool! I say to you that I have spoken the truth. Can you doubt the evidence of your senses? This house is real, the Poe collection exists, and the stories exist—they exist, I swear, as truly as the body lying in the crypt below!"

I took up the little box from the table and removed the lid. "Not so," I answered. "You said your grandfather was found with this box clutched to his breast, before the door of the vault, and that it contained Poe's dust. Yet you cannot escape the fact that the box is empty." I faced him furiously. "Admit it, the story is a fabrication, a romance. Poe's body does not lie beneath this house, nor are these his unpublished works, written during his lifetime and concealed."

"True enough." Canning's smile was ghastly beyond belief. "The dust is gone because I took it and used it—because in the works of wizardry I found the formulae, the arcana whereby I could raise the flesh, re-create the body from the essential salts of the grave. Poe does not *lie* beneath this house—he *lives!* And the tales are *his posthumous works!*"

Accented by thunder, his words crashed against my consciousness.

"That was the end-all and the be-all of my planning, of my studies, of my work, of my life! To raise, by sorcery, the veritable spirit of Edgar Poe from the grave—reclothed and animate in flesh—set him to dwell and dream and do his work again in the private chambers I built in the vaults below—and this I have done! To steal a corpse is but a ghoulish prank; mine is the achievement of true genius!"

The distinct, hollow, metallic, and clangorous yet apparently muffled reverberation accompanying his words caused him to turn in his seat and face the door of the study, so that I could not see the workings of his countenance—nor could he read my own reaction to his ravings.

His words came but faintly to my ears through the

thunder that now shook the house in a relentless grip; the wind rattling the casements and flickering the candle flame from the great silver candelabra sent a soaring sighing in an anguished accompaniment to his speech.

"I would show him to you, but I dare not; for he hates me as he hates life. I have locked him in the vault, alone, for the resurrected have no need of food or drink. And he sits there, pen moving over paper, endlessly moving, endlessly pouring out the evil essence of all he guessed and hinted at in life and which he learned in death.

"Do you not see the tragic pity of my plight? I sought to raise his spirit from the dead, to give the world anew of his genius—and yet these tales, these works, are filled and fraught with a terror not to be endured. They cannot be shown to the world, he cannot be shown to the world; in bringing back the dead I have brought back the fruits of death!"

Echoes sounded anew as I moved toward the door—moved, I confess, to flee this accursed house and its accursed owner.

Canning clutched my hand, my arm, my shoulder. "You cannot go!" he shouted above the storm. "I spoke of his escaping, but did you not guess? Did you not hear it through the thunder—the grating of the door?"

I pushed him aside and he blundered backward, upsetting the candelabra, so that flames licked now across the carpeting.

"Wait!" he cried. "Have you not heard his footstep on the stair? *Madman, I tell you that he now stands without the door!*"

A rush of wind, a roar of flame, a shroud of smoke rose all about us. Throwing open the huge, antique panels to which Canning pointed, I staggered into the hall.

I speak of wind, of flame, of smoke—enough to obscure all vision. I speak of Canning's screams, and of thunder loud enough to drown all sound. I speak of terror born of loathing and of desperation enough to shatter all my sanity.

Despite these things, I can never erase from my consciousness that which I beheld as I fled past the doorway and down the hall.

There without the doors there *did* stand a lofty and enshrouded figure; a figure all too familiar, with pallid features, high, domed forehead, moustache set above a mouth. My glimpse lasted but an instant, an instant during which the man—the corpse—the apparition—the hallucination, call it what you will—moved forward into the chamber and clasped Canning to his breast in an unbreakable embrace. Together, the two figures tottered toward the flames, which now rose to blot out vision forevermore.

From that chamber, and from that mansion, I fled aghast. The storm was still abroad in all its wrath, and now fire came to claim the house of Canning for its own.

Suddenly there shot along the path before me a wild light, and I turned to see whence a gleam so unusual could have issued—but it was only the flames, rising in supernatural splendor to consume the mansion, and the secrets, of the man who collected Poe.

Robert Bloch is the author of more shivery tales of the supernatural than any other living writer. Born in Chicago in 1917, he sold his first story two months after high school graduation. His most famous short story, "Yours Truly, Jack the Ripper," appeared in 1943. His novel, Psycho, *was made into the famous Alfred Hitchcock film and led to a screen and television writing career that continues today. His best short works of horror are collected in* The Opener of the Way; *his novel,* Night of the Ripper, *deals with his old friend Red Jack again.* Screams, *his latest book, is a collection of three mystery novels.*

Karen thought the skip-rope rhyme about mass murderer Ransom Cowl was just part of a child's game—until the night someone dug up his grave.

THREE

Ransom Cowl Walks the Road

Nancy Varian Berberick

Dre: my husband's name has always held the magic to make me smile. Bowdre Carson. I can still hear his mother calling him. She would stand at the back door of the enormous old house. "Bowdre!" she would call, pause, and then louder: "Bowdree!" The *dreee!* would rise, skirling into the summer blue sky, losing none of its demand for distance. Dre would stop what he was doing at once. He'd grin sheepishly, and shrug, then scramble off to answer the summons. And always, before he left, he would stop to pull one of my long black braids and then dance away laughing. I didn't know it then, of course, but I probably loved Dre even in those golden days when being eight made the summer last forever.

I never longed, as many of my friends did, to leave our little town in the hills of western New Jersey. For me there were no bigger and better things to find than Dre and little Petersons Run. The years spent away at college were obligatory and I quickly put them behind me. Returning to Petersons Run to teach seemed right. I like completed circles. And after my first year at the grammar school "Karen Keller" became "Karen Carson" and I was happy.

My days moved to the songs of children, skip-rope rhymes, and learning tunes. *"A" my name is Alice and my husband's name is Al*—and *Lincoln, Lincoln, I've been thinkin', what's that stuff that you been drinkin'*—or *I before E except after C.* And, still, as it had been during the time

47

that Dre and I watched the years move along outside the wide classroom windows: *Ransom Cowl walks the road, Ransom Cowl can see! Ransom Cowl walks the road, and he comes for thee!* and the *thee!* would rise, high, almost hysterically high, and end in giggles and gasps.

Ransom Cowl was Petersons Run's own mass murderer.

He haunted the nights of the town's children with a delicious fear, mitigated by the nearness of parents murmuring in soft conversation, and the completed ending of the terrible story. Ransom Cowl had met justice. Strapped into a huge, ungainly wooden chair he went, assisted by killing voltage, to a quicker death than any of his victims had met. And each child knew that when a story is ended, it is ended. No one seemed to remember that the little rhyme chanted in schoolyards to the cadence of a skip rope was the curse of Beckon Cowl, spat out into the hot July dust the day her grandson was executed.

Jason's Meadow was named for Dre's maternal great-grandfather. The house, one hundred fifty years old and still in good condition, had been in his family since it was built to hold his great-grandfather's brood of seven children. It was a large, neatly laid-out clapboard at the edge of the four acres of Jason's Meadow that remained to Dre's family. The house came to Dre in the normal course of things, and both of us were happy to continue our lives together in this place where we'd played during our childhood. Another circle complete, I would think, as I went about cleaning the many rooms. Our children would grow up here, and theirs. My roots, when they are set, are set deeply.

I listened to the sighing of the snow in December, the insistent piping of cardinals in May, and the winding *chirrrr* of cicadas in July. These were the songs of my life until dirges came to replace them.

That year, though I was grateful for the summer school classes that provided extra money, I was also grateful that they would soon be over. Two more weeks, I thought as I took the steps of the front porch. Two more weeks!

I could sense Dre's mood before I saw him. I knew he was in the kitchen at the back of the house, brooding over a beer, before I called out. "Too many years together," he used to say when I did what he called reading his mind. He'd laugh and shake his head and swear that there was no use keeping secrets from me. I didn't read his mind, of course, and we both knew it. It was just cumulative knowledge. He could do the trick, too, but didn't very often.

"Dre?"

"Back here, honey." His voice was flat, dull, empty of anything that would tell me his mood. Still, I knew.

"You're home early." I dropped my book bag onto the sofa in the living room, scooped up the mail from the coffee table, and went through into the kitchen. July sunlight splashed soft squares of gold across the wide planked floor. The earthy scents of basil, thyme, and oregano interlaced under the sun's heat with the marigolds' musk and drifted in from the kitchen garden.

Dre pushed his beer aside and sat back. His dark thick hair was rumpled, his wide mouth, usually so generous with his smile, was a grim, hard line.

"Bad day," he sighed.

It was a standing joke between us: how bad could a day be on a police force of four men when two of them took turns napping from boredom? But there was no laughter in Dre's green eyes today.

"What happened, hon?"

"The cemetery's been vandalized."

"Oh, no."

"Yeah." His eyes were filled now with disgust.

"Badly?" I filled a tall glass with ice and poured myself a soda.

"One grave's been dug up."

"Ugh! Any ideas?"

"Not a one. That's why I'm home early. Just stopped in to get a bite to eat. I'll be out late tonight, Karen."

"Why?"

Dre shook his head. "It's not going to be fun, but Pete and I have drawn what you might call a graveyard shift tonight." For the first time a smile, wry at his own bad pun, lighted his face.

"I'll fix you a sandwich. Want something to take for tonight?"

49

"I don't think I could eat a thing tonight. Coffee would be nice, though."

I didn't know where the thermos was, but I got to my feet, determined to root through attic and cellar until I found it.

"Thanks, Karen."

"Sure." I paused in the doorway. "Which one? Which grave?"

Dre pulled in a chest full of air and let it out in a gusting sigh. "Ransom Cowl's."

I didn't say "ugh" this time. Chills crawled up my arms, my stomach was suddenly too tight and full of an old childhood fear. I heard, in my mind, the rhythmic slap-slap-slap of a school yard skip rope and the voices of young girls singing an old song that was peculiar to Petersons Run alone.

My determination to search through the dark attic and the musty cellar flagged a little, but I would not send him out into the night without his coffee. Dre must have seen the squaring of my shoulders because his "atta girl" followed me down the hall.

A lovely New Jersey night can turn threatening and ugly in only an hour. The dusk's promise of a clear evening went unfulfilled. Grey clouds hung, leaden and sulking, over Jason's Meadow. The approaching storm's power breathed in the air. The potent humidity of a steamy night crept into the house. In the hall the old Regulator clock groaned once and struck three times.

Startled by the weighty, echoing bongs, I realized that the volume of Shakespeare had fallen, unnoticed, from my hand. Though the night was warm, I shivered. I was listening. I had been listening, though not consciously, through the last scenes of the fourth act of Hamlet. The words, lovely, amusing, intricately woven, had passed through my mind, leaving little mark. My breathing had become soft, cautious. Polonius went to his death unremarked by me, and Hamlet made his discourse with his uncle about the fate of men and worms unheeded by me.

I was listening, and now I knew what it was that I listened for. Dre was not due back yet from his cemetery stakeout.

But like the night waiting for the storm, I waited and listened for his return.

Even as I realized this, I heard his car, the soft hum of the Volvo's engine on the long driveway that wound from the road to the house. Relief gusted through me and my breath came in a choppy sigh. I closed the book and went to the front door to watch the swinging arc of the Volvo's headlights sweep the elms that huddled near the garage.

The car's door chunked closed. A moment later I heard Dre's feet crunching on the driveway's gravel, the only sound in the thick, hot night.

"Honey?" I called.

He was a dark patch of night, moving closer to the house, his head down, his shoulders hunched.

"Dre?"

A cicada started up its whirring somewhere nearby. I gasped; my hand flew to my throat. A cricket piped its monotonous song, high, higher, high, under the front porch. My pulse jerked and thumped under my fingertips. The insects sounded too loud in the waiting stillness.

"How'd you make out, Dre?" Thunder growled in the western sky, lightning flashed, throwing the garage and the elms into startling silhouette. Close on that flash came another, and I saw Dre's face, pale and drawn. His eyes were dark pits of shadow. This time I could not read his mood. I shivered again in the hot night air and stepped out onto the porch.

"Come on in, honey, I'll fix you some coffee."

"I'm tired, Karen. I just want to go to bed."

He did look tired. His feet were dragging, his shoulders slumped. When he passed me I heard the soft slither of dirt dropping from his shoes. He smelled of dark earth and sunless places; the pungent scent of crushed weeds clung to him.

I followed him up to bed and didn't think to ask why he had abandoned his graveyard shift early.

The voice was high and thin, an echo of voices I had heard drifting in from the playground through the open windows of my classroom.

"Ransom Cowl walks the road! Ransom Cowl can see!"

In my dream I shuddered. Cold sweat traced clammy paths down my neck, between my breasts.

"Ransom Cowl walks the road!" Now the tinny echoing quality of the voice was gone. The words were spoken in a quavering old voice filled with groaning and hatred. I could not breathe. It was as though a hand pressed down upon my chest.

"And he comes for *theeeee!*"

I screamed. And behind my scream I heard the crackling old voice tell me that I could scream until my throat bled, I could scream until my eyes, clenched against the dread and terror, threatened to burst. It makes no difference; Ransom Cowl still comes.

He was filthy with evil, he wore it like a shroud, bore it like a shield. He laughed, and that laughter was the knell of church bells, tolling in mourning. He howled, and the howling was the sound of Death triumphant.

Putrid and stinking of hopeless, midnight places, rotting grave clothes still clinging to his wasted body, he shambled to the bed. His lifelessness chilled me to the bone, sucking from me all that was warm and alive. My heart slammed hard against my ribs, a terrified rabbit in a cage of bones. My ears were filled with the sound of my own racing blood. His scabrous hand, scraps of decayed flesh shivering on the white bones of his fingers, touched my lips.

"Lovely," he said. I heard the word as a doom pronounced, a sentence handed down. Nausea twisted my stomach and bile burned a searing path to my throat.

Thunder growled in the distance. A storm prowled close to the valley.

His face came close to mine and I could smell the rotten stench that gusted from his decaying, gap-toothed mouth. It was the stink of something long dead in the bushes, moldering and putrefying. Then I saw, the shock of the sight racing through me like an electrical current, that he had only empty, gaping sockets where his eyes should have been.

"Oh, God, no!" I screamed, and I was, at last, awake.

As though my scream had been the power that called it, lightning danced at the window, tossing huge, unrecognized shadows across the walls of my familiar bedroom.

There was a hand on my face.

"Karen." Dre's voice was soft, inquiring. His fingers stroked my cheek, moved up to brush my hair back from my face.

"Dre—I—it was—"

"It's all right," he whispered, leaning closer to me, curling his leg over mine beneath the sheet. "It's all right, it's all right."

"A—a nightmare—" I shivered, trembling hard as if from a bone freezing cold.

"I know. It's all right." He tucked his chin over my shoulder and buried his face in my hair, offering the comfort of his nearness, of his body. But when his hand moved up to my breast, when his lips brushed gently against my ear as he murmured, "Lovely," my blood turned to ice.

"Dre."

"Lovely Karen." He sighed.

"No. No, Dre." I turned away from him and felt his leg move away, his hand draw back to my shoulder.

"It was just a dream, Karen."

"I know," I said, my voice a quivering whisper. I did know. And he had always called me "lovely" just before his lips moved from my ear to my neck, to my shoulder. But "lovely" had new echoes that I hated and feared.

I told myself that the dream would be gone in the morning, leaving not even a shadow of fear to be remembered by. I apologized silently to Dre, knowing that he would understand.

And he must have understood, for I heard his even, gentle breathing before long. I did not sleep that night, but listened to the rolling progress of the storm as it marched into our little valley.

When the phone rang my mouth was full of toothpaste. "Dre?" I called through clenched teeth. He didn't answer me, but must have answered the phone because it went silent after three rings. I finished brushing my teeth, washed up quickly, and pulled my robe closer around me. As I racketed down the stairs, I cursed the alarm clock I hadn't heard and decided that Dre and I were getting no better a breakfast than juice and cold cereal this morning. He was already in the kitchen, slouched in a chair. His elbows were on the table, his hands covered his eyes. It was not an unfamiliar pose: Dre tried to protect himself from the morning for as long as possible.

"OJ, honey?" I asked.

"No."

"Cereal?"

"No."

"Who was on the phone?"

"Pete's wife."

"Clare? What's up?" Yet even as I asked the question, I recalled, from some odd tangent of memory, that I hadn't asked Dre why he'd come home so early last night. I nudged the refrigerator door closed behind me and put the orange juice on the table. "Sure you won't have any juice, honey?"

"No!" The word was a bullet fired through the morning silence. Startled, I dropped the glass I'd been holding. The little bright shards scattered across the wooden floor, glittering in the sunlight. I held my breath and watched them spin and tumble.

"I'm sorry, Karen. I'm sorry."

He might have been, but I saw nothing of it in his eyes. They were dark holes in a face that was too pale. There wasn't enough room for apology in those eyes, crowded as they were with confusion and a haunted fear. Quietly, I swept the broken glass from the floor.

"Dre? What is it?"

"Pete didn't get home last night."

"Well, but—didn't you drop him off?"

His answer came fast. "Yes, of course I did."

"At the house?"

"At the road. He wanted to walk in."

"But—" I shook my head and took another tack. "You guys didn't stay very late last night."

"I think the wrong one of us is the cop in this house," Dre said coldly. He didn't look at me when he spoke. His eyes, those pits of confusion, were riveted to the table. The forefinger of his right hand traced the ancient pattern of some child's homework, engraved long ago into the soft pine planking.

"Dre."

"Leave me alone, will you, Karen? I'm tired, and I don't know where Pete is. Clare is upset. Will you stop by to see her on your way to school?"

I was late already, and for a moment my conscience warred between declaring a convenient illness so that I could spend the day with Clare, and the fact that my students would be dismissed early today because I couldn't find a substitute teacher at this hour. Clare—or perhaps it was the students—won.

"I'll call in sick, Dre. They can spare me for a day, I'm sure."

His "atta girl" was perfunctory, barely grunted. I put it down to his concern for Pete and kissed him briefly on the top of his head. He moved his hand as though to touch mine, but the gesture died with his sigh.

Clare hadn't immediately fallen into the "My God, He's Dead" syndrome. She worked her way toward it through the "My God, He's Cheating on Me" syndrome first.

By the time she'd reached the point of aggressively asserting that Pete was "a good man, a wonderful husband, he'd never cheat on me—*never!*—he loves me, loves the kids—" we'd gone through too many pots of coffee and eaten too many cookies. The evening sun slanted in through her kitchen windows, seven o'clock mellow. There was nothing left to face now but the fear that Pete was dead. When she finally acknowledged that fear, Clare's voice was a cracked whisper from which hope leaked fast.

"He's *not* dead, Clare."

"But where is he then? Where?"

I didn't know. I didn't know where Dre was either. He hadn't called at all that day. I snatched at this and patted Clare's trembling hand with an assurance I hardly felt.

"We haven't heard from Dre yet. Surely we'd have heard if something were wrong. Come on, come on, now."

She'd sent the two children to stay with her mother. I didn't know whether or not she'd told them that their father hadn't come home the night before. I thought now that the children would be just the comfort she needed. But when I

55

offered to pick them up and drop them off she only shook her head.

"No, Karen, not now. Not yet."

Her thick blonde hair was a tumbled mess. She'd piled it carelessly atop her head this morning and it fell now, in fits and straggles about her face and neck. She'd been plowing her fingers through it all day. Her face, one I'd always thought of as pretty and plump, looked haggard and bloated now. Without her makeup, in fear's harsh light, she appeared far older than forty-two.

"Karen, call the station for me? Call them to see what's going on? I can't stand this waiting anymore."

I didn't want to do it. I didn't want to hear the dispatcher's patient kindness. But I couldn't watch Clare gnawing at herself, either, poised to leap for a phone that hadn't rung all day.

The dispatcher's voice sounded like that of a mother who assures her frightened child that it was only a dream, only a nightmare, that there's really nothing to worry about. She hadn't heard from Dre all day, but, yes, he'd been out with the others looking for Pete.

"There are lots of people looking for him, Clare," I assured her as I hung up the phone. "The police, the whole auxiliary staff." It didn't make her feel better. Though Clare hadn't wept all day, tears threatened now in eyes bruised from exhaustion. Her lips trembled, her hands moved in unconscious jerks through her hair. I made a quick decision.

"Come with me,"

She looked puzzled. "Where?"

"Home. We'll wait there."

"No."

"Clare."

"No! I want to be *here*."

"Then I'm going to run home and leave a note for Dre. I'll get a few things and spend the night."

She didn't refuse that. Her gratitude poured from her eyes in the first tears I had seen all day.

The storm was a terrible one. Between the house-shaking blasts of thunder I heard rain lashing against the window of Clare's guest room. Lightning splashed the room with a baleful glare, threw the furniture into huge silhouette. Shadows staggered across the walls. I'd asked Clare if she wanted me to sleep with her, thinking she would want the comfort of another person nearby. I regretted her refusal more for my own sake than hers. It was a long time before I slept.

"Ransom Cowl walks the road."

The dream was upon me, smothering me like a thick woolen blanket. The tremorous old voice whispered in my ears, drifted around in my sleeping mind.

"Ransom Cowl can see."

In my dream I moaned.

It had been on all the local news stations, even the national news had carried the story for one day. *In the small New Jersey town of Petersons Run a local man is accused of murdering six women.* A serious, grim voice, newscaster-perfect in its enunciation, rolled through the dream.

And yet, how did I know this? How could the words of a broadcast that was older than I am whisper now in my dream?

My dream world began to rumble, to shake, like the quavering old voice that spoke the rhyme. "Ransom Cowl walks the road."

The six women had been butchered. It was a term too frequently used these days to mean brutally murdered. These women *had* been butchered. Like heifers for market, they had been neatly, cleanly taken apart. There had been no evidence of a killing wound. They'd been butchered alive.

"And he comes for *theee!*"

Death-awkward, he staggered across the guest room and stopped at the bedside. His fingers were ice upon my face. His nails, longer in death than they should have been in life, rested lightly on my cheek. A relentless, dread-filled ache seeped through me as his lifeless chill passed through skin and blood and bone. It touched deep inside me, reaching for the core of who I was.

Ransom Cowl scratched against the surface of my soul, chipped away shards of reality. I could not have screamed had I wanted to. And I did not want to this time. It seemed then that everything within me, my heart, my lungs, my mind, everything that *was* me, halted, paused, listened. Horror was crouched, ready, waiting to burst the boundaries of the thing I call my soul. It never did. My pent breath, ready to erupt in a ranting scream, sighed tremblingly away.

"Lovely," he said, his voice a grating rasp. "Lovely." He leaned nearer, filling my whole dream with the stench of his breath, and the rotting stink of his body. The white bone of his skull gaped in places through the putrefying flesh that had once been his face. Then, as on the night before, I did scream.

And, as on the night before, I was suddenly awake. My husband stood at my bedside.

"Dre!"

"Right here, Karen."

"How—how did you get here?"

His smile was slow and familiar. "I found your note, of course. I didn't want to spend the night alone."

I couldn't blame him. I sat up and reached for his arms. The storm had passed, leaving behind a sweet, clean breeze. It plucked now at the curtains, made their yellow rosebud pattern dance like a field of flowers in the wind.

"How did you get in?"

"Pete had his key."

"Pete! You found him!"

"Sure did."

"Where?"

"Tomorrow, Karen. It's late and I'm tired."

"What time is it?"

He sat on the edge of the bed, pulled off his shoes, and rose to unzip his pants. "Four. Now hush and let me in."

I moved over in the little double bed, made room for him, and cuddled next to him. I had turned away from his comfort the night before. I wouldn't tonight.

But he made no advance, simply settled down beneath the sheets and turned his back to me. "Good night," he mumbled.

Fair is fair, I thought wryly, and turnabout, they say, is fair play. I kissed the back of his head. "Good night."

I dreamed again, and heard only whispering, murmuring, and laughing. Snatches of the old rhyme drifted in and around these sounds, but I didn't wake until morning.

*　　*　　*

Bacon sizzled and spat in the pan. Coffee sent its familiar comfortable smell throughout the house. Despite the hour he'd arrived, Dre was up and humming around the kitchen, lurking near the stove for the first cup of coffee.

"You must be exhausted," I said, giving the bacon a final shake.

"Too wired to sleep."

I could understand that. It was why I was awake, rambling around in an unfamiliar kitchen, making breakfast. "I've made enough for Clare and Pete. Should I wake them?"

Dre shrugged.

"Where did you finally find Pete?"

Dre poured his coffee and took a seat at the table. "It's a long story, Karen. Wait until he's had a chance to explain to Clare. I'll tell you when we get home."

Had Pete been with some woman? Had he been cheating on Clare? I felt a sudden flare of anger, remembering her torment of fear. The anger must have shown on my face because Dre chuckled a little.

"Don't go jumping to conclusions, Karen."

"No, you're right." I smiled at him, feeling suddenly sheepish, and noticed that there was a smear of mud near the counter where he stood. "Dre, you're tracking up Clare's kitchen."

He glanced down at his feet and shrugged again. "Sorry."

His shoes were filthy, and dark stains smeared the legs of his pants. Where had he found Pete, anyway? "Oh, Dre, what a mess! See if you can find a broom. I'm going to see if Clare and Pete are awake."

My light tap at the bedroom door went unanswered. I knocked a little harder and waited. There was no sound from within. Maybe we should just have breakfast, I thought, leave a note, and call them later. I was anxious to get home anyway. But I tried one more time.

"Clare?"

I tapped again at the door. "Pete?" Nothing, not even snoring. The door was ajar, and as I turned to go back down the stairs my shoulder brushed against it. It opened with a creak and a sigh. A yellow line of sunlight from the bedroom window widened on the floor at my feet.

"Anybody awake?"

No one stirred. Shrugging, I reached for the doorknob, thinking to pull the door shut. I caught a glimpse of the room and saw only Clare lying still in the middle of the large bed, her hand flung over the side.

Was Pete up already? I listened, but heard no sound from the bathroom. "Clare?"

She didn't move. The morning breeze stirred at her window, fluttering the curtains. I wondered, suddenly, if she was all right. I'd made enough noise out here to wake the—

"Clare?"

I stepped into the room, not caring now that I was invading private territory. The white shag carpet was splashed with mud and something red.

"My God." My throat was tight and dry, my blood hummed and pounded in my head. Clare's blood was splattered all over the carpet. She was not all right.

The room spun around me, nausea churned in my stomach. The once-good smells of bacon and coffee drifted up from the kitchen, sickening me. I clamped my hands across my mouth as vomit rushed up against my teeth with its acid sting.

No one part of Clare was connected to another. The pieces of her lay on the bed, like parts of a toy ready for assembly. Everything was laid out neatly, arms near the torso, legs where they should be, her head upon the pillow. Her lovely blonde hair splayed across sheets that were crimsoned with her blood.

I wailed. "Dre! Dre! Dreeeee!"

I bolted from the room, gasping, moaning, a "no-no-no" chant of denial. I dashed my knee against the door. Pain burst like a fireball and raced along my leg but I did not stop. I scrambled for the stairs and took them running, stumbling twice. My leg screamed pain from my ankle to my knee but I righted myself, still gasping "No-no-no!" I could not think about what I had just seen, I could not allow those pictures back into my mind. My only thought was to get to the kitchen and Dre.

"Dreee!" I gasped, falling to my knees at the bottom of

the stairs. *No-no-no!* My mind coughed the words over and over, stuck in a groove of repetition. *No-no-no!*

His back was to me when I staggered into the kitchen. I fell against the table, grasping its edge as though it were the edge of a cliff. I heard the fat spattering in the frying pan, smelled the acrid stink of bacon burning.

"Dre! My God, my God, Dre! She's dead!"

When he turned he was Dre. And yet he was not Dre.

"I know." His voice was hollow, deep and cold. His eyes, Dre's eyes, were pits, holes, empty of any emotion. Even as fear's icy finger skipped up my spine my stomach clenched against a sudden flood of adrenaline. His face was changing before my eyes, shifting, wavering.

"Dre—"

The flesh of his face thinned. His jaw became more square now, his face longer. Dre's dark hair turned, before my horrified eyes, to slatey grey. His straight white teeth became ravaged by decay. I could smell the stink of his breath from across the kitchen.

I'd seen the pictures, grainy black and white newspaper photos. Every child in Petersons Run had sought them out at one time or another. When I was young it was almost a rite of passage: find a picture of Ransom Cowl, look at it, and try to suppress the giggling squeal of fear that you hoped your friends thought was only pretended. But I'd seen more than pictures. I'd seen him two nights running in my dreams.

No-no-no! The chant started up in my mind again. Breathless and terrified, it was a child's denial.

"Yes," he said, his voice as cold as winter's ice. His fingers gently caressed the shining edge of a carving knife. "Yes, yes."

He did not shamble now. He had the strength of Dre's body, Dre's strong legs, powerful and muscled. He leaped for me, throwing himself across the table, the knife gleaming silver in the sunlight.

I scrambled around the table, keeping it between him and me. "No! Dre! Dre!"

But he was no longer my Dre, and there was no emotion to respond to my pleading. There was only Ransom Cowl,

61

muttering "Lovely, lovely, lovely," and a voice, ghostly and cracked with age, whispering that Ransom Cowl could see.

My knee throbbed where I had smashed it against Clare's bedroom door. My hands shook, palsied with fear. Breathing in short, panting gasps, I wrapped my fingers around the back of a chair and took two retreating steps until the small of my back touched the counter. Fat from the burning bacon spattered against my arm, bit my skin with needle-sharp, fiery teeth.

"Lovely, lovely."

Dre's prelude to love, growled from the rotting throat of the thing before me, made me furious. It was violation, a rape of moments that had been beautiful. My fury gave me the strength I needed to act. Clutching the chair with one hand, I reached for the frying pan with the other.

The thing laughed, a guttural sound, and lunged around the table.

No-no-no! my mind gibbered. *No-no-no!* I hurled the spitting frying pan at the thing's face, laughed and screamed to hear its howl of pain. It could be hurt! My heart cringed at the knowledge. Of course it could be hurt; it was, in some awful way, Dre.

It still had the knife, grasped in fingers that were rotting before my eyes. It leaped from where it was crouched on the floor, hitting me low. I crashed to the floor, my elbow smashed against the stove, my head thumped against the floor.

No-no-no! I clawed at its face and pieces of skin came off in my hands. Bile rushed up my throat. I spat it out and forced my heaving stomach to calm. The Dre-thing lay across me full length, its face touching mine, its knees thrusting in attenuated kicks against my ribs. The knife in its right hand caught the light. The gleaming blade was all that I could see.

"Lovely, lovely, lovely."

It was going to kill me and my death would be a horrible one.

I thrust upward with all my strength but I could not move the thing. I twisted, screamed, kicked, but I could not free myself. My hand, in its flailing, found the frying pan. I clutched at its handle, raised it, and brought it crashing down on the thing's skull. The stinking face snapped away from mine, the body sagged and rolled off me. It was stunned, and I scrambled to my feet.

The knife! It lay a few inches from the creature's hand. *No-no-no!* It seemed that the screaming child in my mind already knew what I was about to do. *No-no-no!*

But I couldn't listen to it now. I couldn't take the time to consider what I was about to do. I simply did it.

The knife made horrible thudding sounds when I plunged it into the Dre-thing's chest, and wet, sucking sounds when I pulled it out. I did not butcher it—though the word would later be used to describe what I did. I killed it. I sent it back to the unholy grave it had come from, howling and screaming like a sidhe wailing across Irish moors.

And when I was done, it was not Ransom Cowl who lay beneath my hands. It was Dre. My Dre whom I'd loved from childhood, who had been all I'd ever asked from life. His head was smashed, his eyes seemed to stare, still frozen with terror, at my hands. His blood spattered in sticky drops from my fingers, tapping the first faint beat of a dirge that would haunt me all my days.

I wept for him, and wept for myself. Then I climbed to my feet. I staggered across the blood-smeared kitchen, moving numbly to the phone. *Police,* I thought, *I must call the po-lice—*. Victim, bereaved, and killer, I did not know what else to do.

I lifted the receiver. The dial tone sounded like the first whimpering echo in a long, black tunnel of loneliness.

Born in New Jersey in 1951 and educated there, Nancy Varian Berberick began writing full time in 1984. Her first novel, Storm-blade, *was published in 1988, and a grim tale, "Cairn and Pyre," appeared in* Amazing Stories *in 1989. "My work," she says, "is essentially optimistic and mystical." Her novel,* The Jewels of Elvish, *is available from Berkley, and two more will follow—* Shadow of the Seven Moons *in 1991 and* Children of Smoke, *a sequel to* The Jewels of Elvish, *in 1992.*

The old telegraph sounder was just another interesting piece of junk, until it started trying to send a message that had never been received.

FOUR

Turn Down for Richmond

G. J. A. O'Toole

What do you think of when you fly into a city like Washington, D.C., and look down on all those thousands of rooftops? Maybe you think of the thousands of human dramas simultaneously unfolding beneath them, the pains and passions of the people who live out their lives in the shelter of those slates and shingles and tarpaper. But I don't. I think about all those attics, and I wonder what the hell might be tucked away in some of them. In other words, I think about junk. If you don't think that's romantic, maybe you just haven't considered it, because junk can be very poignant.

Sometimes it can even be a little eerie.

Pedigreed junk is too rich for my budget, so I stay away from antique shops. Even those specialized varieties of trivia like baseball cards and comic books have become "collectable," hence pricy. I couldn't afford to indulge my taste for junk if it weren't for that wonderful new American institution, the garage sale.

Most Saturdays, bright and early, my wife, Jean, and I climb into the car and drive up and down the streets of some residential neighborhood, and I always find what I'm looking for in a few minutes—a hand-lettered sign saying "Tag Sale, Saturday and Sunday," and an address, tacked to a tree or telephone pole.

I always go on Saturday because by Sunday the assortment of junk for sale has been pretty well picked over, and I hate to think what I may have missed. And I go early. Often I pull up just as the hopeful junk dealer is setting up his or her card table or getting out the cash box.

What's that, sir or madam, as the case may be? The sale doesn't begin for another half-hour? Fine, I'll wait. Oh, may I come in and look around now? Thank you so much!

Jean always comes along, which might seem strange because she doesn't care for garage sales. That's just it: she hates junk—most of it, anyway. And she's afraid if she lets me go to the sales by myself, I'd come home with some enormous load of trash. She doesn't understand that junk is romantic.

"But, it's just—just junk!" she tells me.

"It's history," I reply. "It's been locked away in an attic. Most of these attics were here when Pearl Harbor was bombed. Many were here when McKinley was shot. Some stand today exactly as they stood when Fort Sumter was fired on. And a few are almost as old as the Republic. And all that time people have been cramming them full of the flotsam of life in the Nation's Capital."

"To you, it's flotsam; to me, it's junk."

We have that same conversation, word for word, every Saturday morning from April to October, which is the garage sale season. This year it started right on time, two weeks ago. April Fool's Day, as Jean remarked for some reason.

We set out right after breakfast, and I knew exactly where I wanted to look for a sale. I drove up Wisconsin Avenue above Georgetown, then headed east. It's a fairly old part of town, and a fairly affluent one. A year or so ago you wouldn't see any garage sales in that neighborhood. But times have gotten tough, and even pretty comfortable families are starting to feel the pinch. I guessed some of them might think of emptying out their attics and picking up a few dollars. I was right.

It was a big Victorian frame house, with lots of bay windows, turrets, and ivy on the walls. The sale wasn't actually in the garage; it was on a big screened porch that ran round three sides of the house. Two women, one elderly, the other middle-aged, were the proprietors. It turned out they were aunt and niece.

"Oh, I'm sorry," said the niece. "The sale doesn't start for another half-hour."

I went into my routine, and two minutes later Jean and I were wandering around the porch, picking through the treasure. I felt like the Count of Monte Cristo.

There was a clown bank; you pushed a lever and it stuck out its tongue to take a coin. And an ear trumpet, the hearing aid of a lost age innocent of transistors. There was a coffee mug with the Trylon and Perisphere of the 1939 New York World's Fair. There was an assortment of hand bells, two railroad oil lanterns, and a folding curtain stretcher. There were old 78 RPM records, and the labels bore the names of quaint and obscure ballads sung by forgotten voices—music that had not been heard in decades. There were books and bottles and boxes and—

Forgive me. Let's just say there was a gigantic and beautiful collection of junk. I bought a cut glass inkwell, a toy cannon, and a copy of *Don Sturdy in the Temples of Fear* before Jean began tugging me in the direction of the porch steps. That's when I saw it.

"Wait a minute!" I said.

It was a rectangle of polished wood, a few inches long and wide, set on a black metal base with a pair of holes at either end so it could be screwed to a table. A pair of black cylinders, each about an inch long and a half-inch in diameter, were fastened to the wood by a shiny brass housing. A T-shaped armature rested between a pair of set-screws. I grabbed it.

"How much?" I asked.

"Ten dollars," said the niece. "We'd ask more for it, but the spring is missing."

"What is it?" Jean demanded.

"A telegraph sounder," I replied.

"A what?"

"Back in the old days, when they sent telegrams by Morse Code, this was a receiver. It clicks." I jiggled the armature to demonstrate.

"It clicks," Jean echoed. "But what good is it?"

"Look," I answered patiently, "this thing is very old, maybe a hundred years, maybe more. It sat in some Western Union office, day in and day out for who knows how long, clicking out God knows what! Millions of messages, maybe; important ones, trivial ones! Maybe it reported the sinking of the *Maine*. Maybe it carried J. P. Morgan's instructions to his broker. Maybe it clocked out the dispatch that President Garfield was shot! Think of it!"

"It clicks," Jean repeated. "Ten dollars, and it's even got a spring missing. I think you've got a spring missing."

She stalked out while I paid for it. She didn't speak to me when we drove off, not until we turned onto Wisconsin Avenue.

"What? No more junk sales?"

"Not today," I said. "I want to get this home." I picked up the sounder from the seat. "This is something special."

"Thank Heaven for small favors!" she said. "What are you going to do with it?"

"First I'm going to clean it. Then I'm going to see if I can't scrounge up a spring somewhere in the cellar and fix it. Then I'm going to hook it up to a battery and see if it works."

"Goody! Click, click, click."

It shined up very nicely with a little furniture polish, metal cleaner, and elbow grease. I found a spring about the right size inside the latch from an old screen door. I attached one end to the little hook on the armature, and the other end to a knob on the end of the sounder that seemed to be the place where it was supposed to go. I had to go out to a hardware store to get a lantern battery to provide enough juice to work the magnets, and I also picked up a single-pole knife switch to use as a makeshift sending key. I already had enough wire.

It didn't take long to hook it up. There were a pair of screw-down terminals in the wood, connected under the base to the magnets. I attached the leads from the battery, after connecting the switch into the circuit. I drew a deep breath, then closed the switch.

Click.

I opened the switch.

Clack.

I closed and opened the switch rapidly.

Clickity clack, clickity, clickity, clack.

It was the music of history. I closed my eyes and conjured

67

up the image of some telegrapher in eyeshade and sleeve garters scribbling down the letters by gaslight.

"Clickity clack," said Jean from the doorway of the study. "Isn't there something about the difference between men and boys being nothing but the price of their toys? Are you ready for dinner, or do you want to play with that some more?"

After dinner I went back to my study and looked at the sounder again. I wondered how old it was. I'd have to go to the library and see if I could find a history of telegraphy. Maybe there'd be one with photographs. Maybe I'd see one just like mine.

I took some things off a shelf, set the sounder in their place, looked at it once more, and turned off the light and went into the living room. Jean was watching television, and there was supposed to be a good movie on at nine.

At nine-thirty, during the second bunch of commercials, I got up and went into the kitchen to get a beer. That's when I heard it.

Clickity, clickity, clack. Clickity, clickity, clack.

The sound stopped. I went into the study and turned on the light. The telegraph sounder sat there just as I left it. The battery was still connected, but the switch was open. It was silent.

"Jean?"

"What?"

"Did you hear anything just now?"

"Just the TV."

"Was there a clickity clack?"

"No. Are you still playing with that thing? Come on, the picture's started again."

It didn't happen again for more than a week. Then one night I heard it for the second time. It was about nine-thirty, just like before.

Clickity clack.

I ran into the study. Jean followed me.

"What's the matter?" she asked.

"Did you hear that?"

"Yes. It clicked. Isn't that what it's supposed to do?"

"Not if the switch isn't being opened and closed."

"Well, if it's not working right, why don't you take it back to those women and see if you can get a refund?"

I was about to reply when the sounder came to life.

Clickity, clickity, clack. Clickity clack.

It clicked and chattered like crazy.

"This is impossible," I said. "This can't be happening."

The sounder stopped. Jean had gone back to watch TV. I stood and stared at the thing for a long time. No more clicks. I picked it up, shook it. Maybe there was a loose connection, maybe it was getting triggered by some vibration from the street. No more clicks. I set it down, looked at it for a while longer, then turned out the light and went to watch TV.

I couldn't sleep that night. I kept thinking about what had happened, kept wondering about it. Then, about three in the morning, I got a very weird idea.

What if those clicks meant something?

I didn't know Morse Code. If I did, if I knew it well enough to decipher it by ear, would I have heard an intelligible message coming out of that old sounder? I chewed on that one for a couple of hours. Then, just before dawn, I knew what I was going to do.

When I came home from work that night, I had a tape recorder and a copy of the Morse Code. I got the first in a discount store and the second out of a book at the public library.

"What's all that for?" Jean asked.

"Wait and see."

I was ready at nine-thirty. I had been ready since nine. The microphone was right next to the sounder, the recorder was set to record at the push of a button. At nine-thirty the sounder sprang to life, right on schedule. I pushed the record button.

Clickity clack, clickity clack.

It went on furiously for about twenty seconds, then it stopped. Then it started up again for another twenty seconds and stopped. It did the same thing three more times, and I began to recognize a certain familiar rhythm in the clicks, as though it was repeating the same pattern each time. Then it went dead.

I rewound the recorder, set the speed back by a half, got paper and pencil ready, and played back the tape. I was

69

right, the same sequence of dots and dashes, over and over again, five times. I got out the Morse Code table and laboriously deciphered the dots and dashes.

I guess I must have expected it to be gibberish, because I was pretty damned shocked when it turned out that it wasn't.

"Turn down for Richmond," it read.

I went into the living room.

"Jean, do the words 'Turn down for Richmond' mean anything to you?"

"Sounds like the title of a Country and Western song. Why?"

"Oh, nothing." I wasn't going to try to explain what I didn't understand and could hardly believe. I waited until the next morning, then I called my friend Harvey. He's an electronics engineer, and I thought he might be able to explain what was happening.

"Any of your neighbors hams?" he asked.

"What?"

"Amateur radio operators," he said. "That must be what it is. Some guy down the block is sending Morse on his rig. Must have a damned powerful transmitter if he's activating those old electromagnets in your telegraph set. It's a wonder you're not picking it up in the fillings in your teeth. It's probably illegal. You could report him to the FCC."

"But why would he be sending out the same message over and over? What does that mean, 'Turn down for Richmond'?"

"Search me."

I searched the library instead. The local branch had a couple of books on telegraphy. I read them cover to cover, but I didn't find a clue to what the message might mean. The next day was Friday, almost two weeks since this crazy business started. I left work early and went to the Library of Congress. After a few hours I found what I was looking for. I slammed the book shut, turned it in, and headed home.

"Where have you been?" Jean demanded. "I've been waiting dinner for an hour and a half."

"Never mind that. I found out what it meant!"

"What what meant?"

" 'Turn down for Richmond.' See, back in the early days

of the telegraph, when a message had to go a long distance, the electrical impulses in the wires got very weak, hardly enough to energize the magnets in the sounder. So the telegraphers along the line would relay a 'turn down' message on ahead, and the telegraphers near the end of the line would turn the little knob on their sounders to ease the tension on the armature spring. That way the weak signals could click the sounder and the message would get through."

"I don't understand a word you've said. Do you feel all right?"

"I'm fine. Look, this is what it means. The spring I put on the sounder is wound too tight. If I loosen it, I'll get the rest of the message!"

"Dear, I think your spring is wound too tight. Why don't you have some dinner and go to bed early?"

"What time is it?"

"Almost nine-thirty."

I ran into my study and got the tape recorder ready. The digital clock on my desk read 9:29:59 P.M.

I hit the record button just as the telegraph sounder started clicking. There it was again, the now so familiar pattern that meant "Turn down for Richmond."

I reached over and turned the knob until the spring was almost hanging loose against the armature. The sounder came to life again, but there was a new pattern of clicks this time. No more twenty-second bursts. It chattered away furiously for five minutes. Then it stopped. When I was sure there was no more, I rewound the tape and began the laborious process of deciphering what I had recorded. It took me almost forty-five minutes.

This is what it read:

Richmond
April 14, 1865—9:30 P.M.

Major A. C. Richards,
Department of the Metropolitan Police,
483 Tenth Street,
Washington City.
Most urgent you take every measure to se-

cure the person of President Lincoln. Reports of informers here disclose plot to assassinate him in a public place in Washington City this evening.

Stover

I looked at the clock. 10:20:01 P.M. Today was Friday, April 14, the anniversary of Lincoln's assassination, and it was now almost the exact minute historians say Booth pulled the trigger. The message had finally arrived, more than a century overdue.

I never found out who Stover was. It doesn't really matter.

Do you believe in ghosts? Maybe the unquiet spirit of Detective Stover was haunting my old telegraph sounder, but I don't think so. After all, he did his job. It wasn't his fault others didn't do theirs. No, I don't think Stover's spirit is uneasy.

Maybe we all have some important thing we must do in life, some reason for being born, growing up, and dying. And maybe, for most of us, it's some little thing that we're supposed to do, something that doesn't seem very important at the time we're supposed to do it. For that nameless telegrapher, it must have been to turn down the tension on his armature spring on that April evening so long ago.

At last that's been done. I've heard no more clicking from the old sounder.

I turned down for Richmond, and that telegrapher, whoever he was, may rest in peace.

Since George J. A. O'Toole is the former head of the C.I.A.'s Problems Analysis Branch, it is no surprise that most of his books are mysteries or that little information about him is available. He was born in New York and turned to writing articles and fiction for such varied markets as Harpers, Playboy, *and* Mystery. *His first novel,* An Agent on the Other Side, *appeared in 1973. The* Cosgove Report *was about a Pinkerton agent who looks into the mystery of who really killed Abraham Lincoln; his* The Encyclopedia of Spies and Spying *was published in 1989.*

Mrs. Pollard knew the ruins of a nearby cabin held a terrible secret. She never expected to be the one to find out what it was.

FIVE

The Caller in the Night
Burton Kline

By the side of a road which wanders in company of a stream across a region of Pennsylvania farmland that is called "Paradise" because of its beauty, you may still mark the ruins of a small brick cabin in the depths of a grove. In summertime ivy drapes its jagged fragments and the pile might be lost to notice but that at dusk the trembling leaves of the vine have a way of whispering to the nerves of your horse and setting them too in a tremble. And the people in the village beyond have a belief that three troubled human beings lie buried under those ruins, and that at night, or in a storm, they sometimes cry aloud in their unrest.

The village is Bustlebury, and its people have a legend that on a memorable night there was once disclosed to a former inhabitant the secret of that ivied sepulchre.

All the afternoon the two young women had chattered in the parlor, cooled by the shade of the portico, and lost to the heat of the day, to the few sounds of the village, to the passing hours themselves. Then of a sudden Mrs. Pollard was recalled to herself at the necessity of closing her front windows against a gust of wind that blew the curtains, like flapping flags, into the room.

"Sallie, we're going to get it again," she said, pausing for a glance at the horizon before she lowered the sash.

"Get what?" Her visitor walked to the other front window and stooped to peer out.

73

Early evening clouds were drawing a black cap over the fair face of the land.

"I think we're going to have some more of Old Screamer Moll this evening. I knew we should, after this hot—"

"There! Margie, that was the expression I've been trying to remember all afternoon. You used it this morning. Where did you get such a poetic nickname for a thunder— O-oh!"

For a second, noon had returned to the two women. From their feet two long streaks of black shadow darted back into the room, and vanished. Overhead an octopus of lightning snatched the whole heavens in its grasp, shook them, and disappeared.

The two women screamed, and threw themselves on the sofa. Yet in a minute it was clear that the world still rolled on, and each looked at the other and laughed at her fright—till the prospect of an evening of storm sobered them both.

"Mercy!" Mrs. Pollard breathed in discouragement. "We're in for another night of it. We've had this sort of thing for a week. And tonight of all nights, when I wanted you to see this wonderful country under the moon!"

Mrs. Pollard, followed by her guest, Mrs. Reeves, ventured to the window timidly again, to challenge what part of the sky they could see from under the great portico outside, and learn its portent for the night.

An evil visage it wore—a swift change from a noon day of beaming calm. Now it was curtained completely with blue-black cloud, which sent out mutterings, and then long brooding silences more ominous still in their very concealment of the night's intentions.

There was no defense against it but to draw down the blinds and shut out this angry gloom in the glow of the lamps within. And, with a half hour of such glow to cozen them, the two women were soon merry again over their reminiscences, Mrs. Pollard at her embroidery, Mrs. Reeves at the piano, strumming something from Chopin in the intervals of their chatter.

"The girl" fetched them their tea. "Five already!" Mrs. Pollard verified the punctuality of her servant with a glance at the clock. "Then John will be away for another night. I do hope he won't try to get back this time. Night before last he left his assistant with a case, and raced his horse ten miles in the dead of the night to get home," Mrs. Pollard proudly reported, "for fear I'd be afraid in the storm."

"And married four years!" Mrs. Reeves smilingly shook her head in indulgence of such long-lived romance.

In the midst of their cakes and tea the bell announced an impatient hand at the door.

"Well, 'speak of angels!'" Mrs. Pollard quoted, and flew to greet her husband. But she opened the door upon smiling old Mr. Barber, instead, from the precincts across the village street.

Mr. Barber seemed to be embarrassed. "I—I rather thought you mought be wanting something," he said in words. By intention he was making apology for the night. "I saw the doctor drive away, but I haven't seen him come back. So I—I thought I'd just run over and see—see if there wasn't something you wanted." He laughed uneasily.

Mr. Barber's transparent diplomacy having been rewarded with tea, they all came at once to direct speech. "It ain't going to amount to much," Mr. Barber insisted. "Better come out, you ladies, and have a look around. It may rain a bit, but you'll feel easier if you come and get acquainted with things, so to say." And gathering their resolution the two women followed him out on the portico.

They shuddered at what they saw.

Night was at hand, two hours before its time. Nothing stirred, not a vocal chord of hungry, puzzled, frightened chicken or cow. The whole region seemed to have caught its breath, to be smothered under a pall of stillness, unbroken except for some occasional distant earthquake of thunder from the inverted Switzerland of cloud that hung pendant from the sky.

Mr. Barber's emotions finally ordered themselves into speech as he watched. "Ain't it grand!" he said.

The two women made no reply. They sat on the steps to the portico, their arms entwined. The scene beat their more sophisticated intelligences back into silence. Some minutes they all sat there together, and then again Mr. Barber broke the spell.

"It do look fearful, like. But you needn't be afraid. It's better to be friends with it, you might say. And then go to bed and fergit it."

They thanked him for his goodness, bade him goodby, and he clinked down the flags of the walk and started across the street.

He had got midway across when they all heard a startling sound, an unearthly cry.

It came out of the distance, and struck the stillness like a blow.

"What is it? What is it, Margie?" Mrs. Reeves whispered excitedly.

Faint and quavering at its beginning, the cry grew louder and more shrill, and then died away, as the breath that made it ebbed and was spent. It seemed as if this unusual night had found at last a voice suited to its mood. Twice the cry was given, and then all was still as before.

At its first notes the muscles in Mrs. Pollard's arm had tightened. But Mr. Barber had hastened back at once with reassurance.

"I guess Mrs. Pollard knows what that is," he called to them from the gate. "It's only our old friend Moll, that lives down there in the notch. She gets lonesome, every thunderstorm, and lets it off like that. It's only her rheumatiz, I reckon. We wouldn't feel easy ourselves without them few kind words from Old Moll!"

The two women applauded as they could his effort toward humor. Then, "Come on, Sallie, quick!" Mrs. Pollard cried to her guest, and the two women bolted up the steps of the portico and flew like girls through the door, which they quickly locked between themselves and the disquieting night.

Once safe within, relief from their nerves came at the simple effort of laughter, and an hour later, when it was clear that the stars still held to their courses, the two ladies were at their ease again, beneath the lamp on the table, with speech and conversation to provide an escape from thought. The night seemed to cool its high temper as the hours wore on, and gradually the storm allowed itself to be forgotten.

Together, at bed time, the two made their tour of the house, locking the windows and doors, and visiting the pantry on the way for an apple. Outside all was truly calm and still, as, with mock and exaggerated caution, they peered through one last open window. A periodic, lazy flash from the far distance was all that the sky could muster of its earlier wrath. And they tripped upstairs and to bed, with that hilarity which always attends the feminine pursuit of repose.

But in the night they were awakened.

Not for nothing, after all, had the skies marshalled that afternoon array of their forces. Now they were as terribly vociferous as they had been terrifyingly still before. Leaves, that had drooped melancholy and motionless in the afternoon, were whipped from their branches at the snatch of the wind. The rain came down in a solid cataract. The thunder was a steady bombardment, and the frolic powers above, that had toyed and practiced with soundless flashes in the afternoon, had grown wanton at their sport, and hurled their electric shots at earth in appallingly accurate marksmanship. Between the flashes from the sky, the steady glare of a burning barn here and there reddened the blackness. The village dead, under the pelted sod, must have shuddered at the din. Even the moments of lull were saturate with terrors. In them rose audible the roar of waters, the clatter of frightened animals, the rattle of gates, the shouts of voices, the click of heels on the flags of the streets, as the villagers hurried to the succor of neighbors fighting fires out on the hills. For long afterward the tempest of that night was remembered. For hours while it lasted, trees were toppled over, and houses rocked to the blast.

And for as long as it would, the rain beat in through an open window and wetted the two women where they lay in their bed, afraid to stir, even to help themselves, gripped in a paralysis of terror.

Their nerves were not the more disposed to peace, either, by another token of the storm. All through the night, since their waking, in moments of stillness sufficient for it to be heard, they had caught that cry of the late afternoon. Doggedly it asserted itelf against the uproar. It insisted upon being heard. It too wished to shriek relievingly, like the inanimate night, and publish its sickness abroad. They heard it far off, at first. But it moved, and came nearer. Once the two women quaked when it came to them, shrill and clear, from a point close at hand. But they bore its invasion along

77

with the wind and the rain, and lay shameless and numb in the rude arms of the night.

They lay so till deliverance from the hideous spell came at last, in a vigorous pounding at the front door.

"It's John!" Mrs. Pollard cried in her joy. "And through such a storm!"

She slipped from the bed, threw a damp blanket about her, and groped her way out of the room and down the stair, her guest stumbling after. They scarcely could fly fast enough down the dark steps. At the bottom Mrs. Pollard turned brighter the dimly burning entry lamp, shot back the bolt with fingers barely able to grasp it in their eagerness, and threw open the door.

"John!" she cried.

But there moved into the house the tall and thin but heavily framed figure of an old woman, who peered about in confusion.

In a flash of recognition Mrs. Pollard hurled herself against the intruder to thrust her out.

"No!" the woman said. "No, you will not, on such a night!" And the apparition herself, looking with feverish curiosity at her unwilling hostesses, slowly closed the door and leaned against it.

Mrs. Pollard and her friend turned to fly, in a mad instinct to be anywhere behind a locked door. Yet before the instinct could reach their muscles, the unbidden visitor stopped them again.

"No!" she said. "I am dying. Help me!"

The two women turned, as if hypnotically obedient to her command. Their tongues lay thick and dead in their mouths. They fell into each other's arms, and their caller stood looking them over, with the same fevered curiosity. Then she turned her deliberate scrutiny to the house itself.

In a moment she almost reassured them with a first token of being human and feminine. On the table by the stairs lay a book, and she went and picked it up. "Fine!" she mused. Then her eye traveled over the pictures on the walls. "Fine!" she said. "So this is the inside of a fine house!" But suddenly, as her peering gaze returned to the two women, she was recalled to herself. "But you wanted to put me out—on a night like this! Hear it!"

For a moment she looked at them in frank hatred. And on an impulse she revenged herself upon them by sounding, in their very ears, the shrill cry they had heard in the afternoon, and through the night, that had mystified the villagers for years from the grove. The house rang with it, and with the hard peal of laughter that finished it.

All three of them stood there, for an instant, viewing each other. But at the end of it the weakest of them was the partly sibylline, partly mountebank intruder. She swayed back against the wall. Her head rolled limply to one side, and she moaned, "O God, how tired I am tonight!"

Frightened as they still were, their runaway hearts beating a tattoo that was almost audible, the two other women made a move to support her. But she waved them back with a suddenly returning air of command. "No!" she said. "You wanted to put me out!"

The creature wore some sort of thin skirt whose color had vanished in the blue-black of its wetness. Over her head and shoulders was thrown a ragged piece of shawl. From under it dangled strands of grizzled gray hair. Her dark eyes were hidden in the shadows of her impromptu hood. The hollows of her cheeks looked deeper in its shadows.

She loosed the shawl from her head, and it dropped to the floor, disclosing a face like one of the Fates. She folded her arms, and there was a rude majesty in the massive figure and its bearing as she tried to command herself and speak.

"I come here—in this storm. Hear it! Hear that! I want shelter. I want comfort. And what do you say to me! Well, then I take comfort from you. You thought I was your husband. You called his name. Well, I saw him this afternoon. He drove out. I called to him from the roadside. 'Let me tell your fortune! Only fifty cent!' But he whipped up his horse and drove away. You are all alike. But I see him now—in Woodman's Narrows. It rains there, same as here. Thunder and lightning, same as here. Trees fall. The wind blows. The wind blows!"

The woman had tilted her head and fixed her eyes, shining and eager, as if on some invisible scene, and she half intoned her words as if in a trance.

"I see your husband now. His wagon is smashed by a

tree. The horse is dead. Your husband lies very still. He does not move. There!"—she turned to them alert again to their presence—"there is the husband that you want. If you don't believe me, all I say is, wait! He is there. You will see!"

She ended in a peal of laughter, which itself ended in a weary moan. "Oh, why can't you help me!" She came toward them, her arms outstretched. "*Don't* be afraid of me. I want a woman to know me—to comfort me. I die to-night. It's calling me, outside. Don't you hear?

"Listen to me, you women!" she went on, and tried to smile, to gain their favor. "I lied to you, to get even with you. You want your husband. Well, I lied. He isn't dead. For all you tried to shut me out. Do you never pity? Do you never help? O-oh—"

Her hand traveled over her brow, and her eyes wandered.

"No one knows what I need now! I got to tell it, I got to tell it! Hear that?" There had been a louder and nearer crash outside. "That's my warning. That says I got to tell it, before it's too late. No storm like this for forty years—not since one night forty years ago. My God, that night!" Another heavy rumble interrupted her. "Yes, yes!" she turned and called. "I'll tell it! I promise!"

She came toward her audience and said pleadingly, "Listen—even if it frightens you. You've got to listen. That night, forty years ago"—she peered about her cautiously— "I think—I think I hurt two people—hurt them very bad. And *ever* since that night—"

The two women had once again tried to fly away, but again she halted them. "Listen! You have no right to run away. You got to comfort me! You hear? Please, please, don't go."

She smiled, and so seemed less ugly. What could her two auditors do but cling to each other and hear her through, dumb and helpless beneath her spell?

"Only wait. I'll tell you quickly. Oh, I was not always like this. Once I could talk—elegant too. I've almost forgotten now. But I never looked like this then. I was not always ugly—no teeth—gray hair. Once I was beautiful too. You laugh? But yes! Ah, I was young, and tall, and had long black hair. I was Mollie, then. Mollie Morgan. That's the first time I've said my name for years. But that's who I was. Ask Bruce—he knows."

She had fallen back against the wall again, her eyes roaming as she remembered. Here she laughed. "But Bruce is dead these many years. He was my dog." A long pause. "We played together. Among the flowers—in the pretty cottage—under the vines. Not far from here. But all gone now, all gone. Even the woods are gone—the woods where Bruce and I hunted berries. And my mother!"

Again the restless hands sought the face and covered it.

"My mother! Almost as young as I. And how *she* could talk! A fine lady. As fine as you. And oh, we had good times together. Nearly always. Sometimes mother got angry—in a rage. She'd strike me, and say I was an idiot like my father. The next minute she'd hug me, and cry, and beg me to forgive her. It all comes back to me. Those were the days when she'd bake a cake for supper—the days when she cried, and put on a black dress. But mostly she wore the fine dresses—all bright, and soft, and full of flowers. Oh, how she would dance about in those, sometimes. And always laughed when I stared at her. And say I was Ned's girl to my fingertips. I never understood what she meant—then."

The shrill speaker of a moment before had softened suddenly. The creature of the woods sniffed eagerly this atmosphere of the house, and faint vestiges of a former personage returned to her, summoned along with the scene she had set herself to recall.

"But oh, how good she was to me! And read to me. And taught me to read. And careful of me? Ha! Never let me go alone to the village. Said I was too good for such a place. Some day we would go back to the world—whatever she meant by that. Said people there would clap the hands when they saw me—more than they had clapped the hands for her. Once she saw a young man walk along the road with me. Oh, how she beat my head when I came home! Nearly killed me, she was so angry. Said I mustn't waste myself on such trash. My mother—I never understood her then.

"She used to tell me stories—about New York, and Phil'delph. Many big cities. There they applaud, and clap the hands, when my mother was a queen, or a beggar girl, in the theatre, and make love and kill and fight. Have grand supper in hotel afterward. And I'd ask my mother how soon I too may be a queen. And she'd give me to learn the words they say, and I'd say them. Then she'd clap me on the head again and tell me, 'Oh, you're Ned's girl. You're a blockhead, just like your father!' And I'd say, 'Where is my father? Why does he never come?' And after that my mother would always sit quiet, and never answer when I talked.

"And then she'd be kind again, and make me proud, and tell me I'm a very fine lady, and have fine blood. And she'd talk about the day when we'd go back to the world, and she'd buy me pretty things to wear. But I thought it was fine where we were—there in the cottage, I with the flowers, and Bruce. In those days, yes," the woman sighed, and left them to silence for a space,—for silent seemed the wind and rain, on the breaking of her speech.

A rumble from without started her on again.

"Yes, yes! I'm telling! I'll hurry. Then I grow big. Seventeen. My mother call me her little giantess, her handsome darling, her conceited fool, all at the same time. I never understood my mother—then.

"But then, one day, it came!"

The woman pressed her fingers against her eyes, as if to shut out the vision her mind was preparing.

"Everything changed then. Everything was different. No more nights with stories and books. No more about New York and Phil'delph. Never again.

"I was out in the yard one day, on my knees, with the flowers. It was Springtime, and I was digging and fixing. And I heard a horse's hoofs on the road. A runaway, I thought at first. I stood up to look, and—" She faltered, and then choked out, "I stood up to look, and the man came!" And with the words came a crash that rocked the house.

"Hear that!" the woman almost shrieked. "That's him— that's the man. I hear him in every storm!

"He came," she went on more rapidly. "A tall man— fine—dressed in fine clothes—brown hair—brown eyes! Oh, I often see those brown eyes. I know what they are like. He came riding along the bye-road. When he caught sight of my mother he almost fell from his horse. The horse nearly fell, the man pulled him in so sharp. 'Good God!' the man said. 'Fanny! Is this where you are! Curse you, old girl, is this where you are!' Funny, how I remember his words. And then he came in.

"And he talked to my mother a long time. Then he looked round and said, 'So this is where you've crawled to!' And he petted Bruce. And then he came to me, and looked into my face a long time, and said, 'So this is his girl, eh? Fanny junior, down to the last eyelash! Come here, puss!' he said. And I made a face at him. And he put his hands to his sides and laughed and laughed at me. And he turned to my mother and said, 'Fanny, Fanny, what a queen!' I thought he meant be a queen in the theatre. But he meant something else. He came to me again, and squeezed me and pressed his face against mine. And my mother ran and snatched him away. And I ran behind the house.

"And by-and-by my mother came to find me, and said, 'Oho, my little giantess! So here you are! What are you trembling for!' And she kicked me. 'Take that!' she said.

"And I didn't understand—not then. But I understand now.

"Next day the man came again, and talked to my mother. But I saw him look and look at me. And by-and-by he reached for my hand. And my mother said, 'Stop that! None of that, my little George! One at a time, if you please!' And he laughed and let me go. And they went out and sat on a bench in the yard. And the man stroked my mother's hair. And I watched and listened. They talked a long time till it was night. And I heard George say, 'Well, Fanny, old girl, we did for him, all right, didn't we?' I've always remembered it. And they laughed and they laughed. Then the man said, 'God, how it does scare me, sometimes!' And my mother laughed at him for that. And George said, 'Look what I've had to give up. And you penned up here! But never mind. It will blow over. Then we'll crawl back to the old world, eh, Fanny?'"

All this the woman had rattled off like a child with a recitation, as something learned long ago and long rehearsed against just this last contingency and confession.

"Oh, I remember it!" she said, as if her volubility needed an explanation. "It took me a long time to understand. But one day I understood.

"He came often, then—George did. And I was not afraid of him any more. He was fine, like my mother. Every time I saw him come my stomach would give a jump. And I liked to have him put his face against mine, the way I'd seen him do to mother. And every time he went away I'd watch him from the hilltop till I couldn't see him any more. And at night I couldn't sleep. And George came very often—to see me, he told me, and not my mother.

"And my mother was changed then. She never hit me again, because George said he'd kill her if she did. But she acted very strange when he told her that, and looked and looked at me. And didn't speak to me for days and days. But I didn't mind—I could talk to George. And we'd go for long walks, and he'd tell me more about New York and Phil'delph—more than my mother could tell. Oh, I loved to hear him talk. And he said such nice things to me—such nice things to me! Bruce—I forgot all about Bruce. Oh, I was happy! But that was because I knew nothing.

"Yes, I pleased George. But by-and-by he changed too. Then I couldn't say anything that he liked. 'Stupid child!' he called me. I tried, ever so hard, to please him. But it was like walking against a wind, that you can't push aside. You women, you just guess how I felt then! You just guess! You want your husband. It was the same with me. I want George. But he wouldn't listen to me no more."

The woman seemed to sink, to shrivel, under the weight of her recollection. Finding her not a monster but a woman after all, her two hearers were moved to another slight token of sympathy. They were "guessing," as she commanded. But still, with a kind of weary magnanimity, she waved them back, away from the things she had yet to make clear.

"But one day I saw it. One day I saw something. I came home with my berries, and George was there. His breath was funny, and he talked funny, and walked funny. I'd seen people in the village that way. But—my mother was that way, too. She looked funny—had very red cheeks, and talked very fast. Very foolish. And her breath was the same as George's. And she laughed and laughed at me, and made fun of me.

"I said nothing. But I didn't sleep that night. I wondered what would happen. Many days I thought of what was hap-

84

pening. Then I knew. My mother was trying to get George away from me. That was what had happened.

"Another day I came back with my berries, and my mother was not there. Neither was George there. So! She had taken George away. My George. Well! I set out to look. No rest for me till I find them. I knew pretty well where they might be. I started for George's little brick house down in the hollow. That's where he had taken to living—hunting and fishing. It was late—the brick house was far away—I was very tired. But I went. And—"

She had been speaking more rapidly. Here she stopped to breathe, to swallow, to collect herself for the final plunge.

"I heard a runaway horse. 'George's horse!' I said. 'George is coming back to me, after all! George is coming back to me! She can't keep him!' And, yes, it was George's horse. But nobody on him. I was so scared I could hardly stand. Something had happened to George. Only then did I know how much I wanted him—when something had happened to him. I almost fell down in the road, but I crawled on. And presently I came to him, to George. He was walking in the road, limping and stumbling and rolling—all muddy—singing to himself. He didn't know me at first. I ran to him—to my George. And he grabbed me, and stumbled, and fell. And he grabbed my ankle. 'Come to me, li'l' one!' he said. 'Damn the old hag!' he said. 'It's the girl I want— Ned's own!' he said. 'Come here to me, Ned's own. I want you!' And he pinched me. He bit my hand. And—and I— all of a sudden I was afraid.

"And I snatched myself loose. 'George!' I screamed. 'No!' I said—I don't know why. I was very scared. I was wild. I kicked away—and ran—ran, ran—away—I don't know where—to the woods. And oh, a long time I heard George laugh at me. 'Just like the very old Ned!' I heard him shout. But I ran, till I fell down tired. And there I sat and thought.

"And all of a sudden I understood. All at once I knew many things. I knew then what my mother had said about Ned sometimes. He was my father. He was dead. Somebody had killed him, I knew—I knew it from what they said. George knew my father, then, too. What did he know? That was it! He—he was the man that killed my father. He was after my mother then—he had been after her before, and made her breathe funny, made a fool of her. That was why my beautiful mother was so strange to me sometimes. That's why there was no more New York and Phil'delph. George did that—spoiled everything. Now he was back— making a fool of her again—my mother! And wanted to make a fool of me. Oh, then I knew! That man! And I had liked him. His brown hair, his brown eyes! But oh, I understood, I understood.

"I got up from the ground. Everything reeled and fell apart. There was nothing more for me. Everything spoiled. Our pretty cottage—the stories—all gone. Spoiled. So I ran back. Maybe I could bring my mother back. Maybe I could save something. Oh, I was sick. The trees, they bent and rolled the way George walked. The wind bent them double. They held their stomachs, as if they were George, laughing at me. They seemed to holler 'Ned's girl!' at me. I was dizzy, and the wind nearly blew me over. But I had to hurry home.

"I got near. No one there. Not even George. But I had to find my beautiful little mother. All round I ran. The brambles threw me down. I fell over a stump and struck my face. I could feel the blood running down over my cheeks. It was warmer than the rain. No matter, I had to find my mother. My poor little mother.

"Bruce growled at me when I got to the house. He didn't know me. That's how I looked! But there was a light in the house. Yes, my mother was there! But George was there, too. That man! They had bundles all ready to go away. They weren't glad to see me. I got there too soon. George said, 'Damn her soul! Always that girl of Ned's! I'll show her!' And he kicked me.

"George kicked me!

"But my mother—she didn't laugh when she saw me. She was very scared. She shook George, and said, 'George! Come away, quick! Look at her face! Look at her eyes!' she said.

"Oh, my mother, my little mother. She thought I would hurt her. Even when she'd been such a fool. I was the one that had to take care of her, then. But she wanted to go away—with that man! That made me wild.

"'You, George!' I said, 'You've got to go! You've—

The Caller in the Night

you've done too much to us!' I said. 'You go!' And 'Mother!' I said. 'You've got to leave him! He's done too much to us!' I said.

"She only answered, 'George, come, quick!' And she dragged George toward the door. And George laughed at me. Laughed and laughed—till he saw my eyes. He didn't laugh then. Nor my mother. My mother screamed when she saw my eyes. 'Shut up, George!' she screamed. 'She's not Ned's girl now!' And George said, 'No, by God! She's *your* brat now, all right! She's the devil's own!'

"And they ran for the door. I tried to get there first, to catch my little mother. My mother only screamed, as if she were wild. And they got out—out in the dark. 'Mother!' I cried. 'Mother! Come back, come back!' No answer. My mother was gone.

"Oh, that made me feel, somehow, very strong. 'I'll bring you back!' I shouted. 'You, George! I'll send you away. Wait and see!' They never answered. Maybe they never heard. The wind was blowing, like tonight.

"But I knew where I could find them. I knew where to go to find George. And I ran to my loft, for my knife. But, O my God, when I saw poor Mollie in the glass! Teeth gone. I wasn't beautiful any more. And my eyes!—they came out of the glass at me, like two big dogs jumping a fence. I ran from them. I didn't know myself. I ran out of the door, in the night. I went after that man. He had done too much. That storm—the lightning that night! Awful! But no storm kept me back. Rain—hail—but I kept on. Trees fell—but I went on. I called out. I laughed then, myself. I'll get him! I say, 'Look out for Ned's girl! Look out for Ned's girl!' I say—

Unconsciously the woman was re-enacting every gesture, repeating every phrase and accent of her journey through the night, that excursion out of the world, from which there had been no return for her. "Look out for Ned's girl!"—the house rang with the cry. But this second journey, of the memory, ended in a moan and a faint.

"I said I would tell it! Help me!" she said.

In some fashion they worked her heavy bulk out of its crazy wrappings and into a bed. John arrived, to help them. Morning peered timidly over the eastern hills, as if fearful of beholding what the night had wrought. In its smiling calm

87

the noise of the storm was already done away. But the storm in the troubled mind raged on.

For days it raged, in fever and delirium. Then they buried the rude minister of justice in the place where she commanded—under the pile of broken stones and bricks among the trees in the hollow. And it is said that the inquisitive villagers who had a part in the simple ceremonies stirred about till they made the discovery of two skeletons under the ruins. And to this day there are persons in Bustlebury with a belief that at night, or in a storm, they sometimes hear a long-drawn cry issuing from that lonely little hollow.

Little seems to be known about Burton Kline, but he was a frequent contributor to magazines in the early 1900s. Many of his stories appeared in O'Brien's Best Short Stories of the Year *volumes. They often dealt with the supernatural, as in "In the Open Code" and "The Caller in the Night."*

Harry Murphy had to make his grandson understand how important baseball was. If only he had some help . . .

SIX

The Word of Babe Ruth
Paul Gallico

I don't say you should believe this story. Maybe the whole thing is just the imaginings of an old man who ain't got much more time left to sit in the sun in the grandstand behind third base and listen to that sweet sound when the ash is applied to the middle of the old horsehide and you know the ball is heading for Railroad Avenue the other side of the fence.

Could be I just dreamed it all, or maybe it was Jimmy, Jr.'s, dream that I got into somehow. But I know I seen and talked with a real saint. I seen him just as plain as you're looking at this page, that night a year ago when I went into Jimmy, Jr.'s, room feeling licked and lower than a snake's piazza. I had come to New York because Jimmy's mother asked me to live with them and help make a man out of the boy, but I wasn't getting anywhere. You see, the kid didn't care about baseball. That was a terrible thing. Twelve years old and he don't know Mickey Mantle's or Ralph Kiner's batting average, and can't tell you who's leading the league in R.B.I.'s.

How bad it is, he don't even know or care who's leading the League, American or National. His teacher in school said he was a natural pull hitter and could make the team if he cared. But all the kid wanted to do was read about space rockets and trips to Mars, and look at Captain Universe on the television.

What made it worse is who his father was. And his grandfather. That's me, Harry Murphy.

89

So this night I am going to tell you about. I'd come back from a night game at the Yankee Stadium, which was just across the way from where Janet, Jimmy, Jr.'s, mother, had her flat on the Grand Concourse, and I couldn't sleep. Vic Raschi beats the Detroits six to five and Mantle hits one in the clutch; I sat alone back of third base. Used to be a time when I'd dreamed of sitting there with my grandson. But the kid stayed behind to look at a television show. And it wasn't baseball.

That Yankee Stadium was like home to me. I let out a couple of blasts at the Yanks, but it wasn't the same like the old days when the Babe and Lou Gehrig was there and everybody knew me.

I lay there thinking about what the kid was missing, and what I could do about it. Maybe I did ask for help. You wouldn't want to see any boy of yours grow up without caring how the home team made out, would you? Why, sometimes that's all that holds the country together when things get tough.

The next thing I know, it's two o'clock in the morning and I thought I heard a noise in Jimmy, Jr.'s, room next door. So I got up to look, figuring maybe he wasn't well or wanted something.

But when I came in, I could see he was sleeping peacefully, for there was a moon over Coogan's Bluff, lighting up the Polo Grounds on the other side of the river, and it came in the window. Then I saw the stranger sitting by his bedside.

He was a great big guy, built like a beer barrel. I should'a' jumped a mile high from scare, but right away I saw there was something familiar about him. He was wearing a big camel's-hair polo coat and a tan camel's-hair cap. His head was turned and he was looking down at Jimmy, Jr., but when I came into the room he switched around so that the moon lit up his face and I saw who it was. I'd of known that big ugly mug with the little piggy eyes and the nose spread all over his face anywhere in the world.

And at that moment I didn't even stop to think that he'd been dead five years. I said, "Hello, Babe!"

He said, "Hello, keed. How's things?" but didn't get up or

offer to shake hands. He just sat there, his jaws moving on a big plug of tobacco he had in his mouth.

I couldn't think of anything to say but "The Yanks won tonight, six to five. Mantle got hold of one in the eighth."

He nodded. "Yeah, I know. I was there. That's a good kid, that Mantle, but he ought to stick to one side or the other. Them switch hitters ain't never consistent."

"Boy," I said, "Babe Ruth. Am I glad to see you!" All of a sudden it come home to me who I was talking to. "Hey," I whispered so as not to wake Jimmy, Jr., "what's going on? You're dead, aren't you?"

The Babe grunted, "Uh-huh!"

"Then what are you doing here?"

The Babe chewed on his plug for a while before replying. "You sent for me, didn't you?"

"Me?" I was so mixed up by this time I couldn't remember.

"I dunno," the Babe said. "You oughta know what's cooking. We got a call about a half hour ago. The Manager told me to get my pants off the bench and take a look in here."

It came back then, what I'd been doing a half hour ago. I ain't much of a religious man, but when it comes down to it and a member of my family is in trouble, like Jimmy, Jr., was, I ain't ashamed to pray.

I said, "I remember now. I asked the saints to help me."

"O.K.," the Babe said. "What's on your mind, keed?"

Much as I loved the big monkey, I couldn't help letting out a snort. "Hey! What are you giving me? You a saint?"

The Babe for a second actually managed to look modest, which was never one of his long points, though maybe "sheepish" was a better way to describe it, and he said hastily, "I know, I know. I done all kinds of fatheaded things when I was around here, didn't I? Women, liquor, horsing around. But They got a way of overlooking those, if you say you're sorry when you get there. So, after I'd been there a couple of years and kept my nose clean, They made me a saint."

I couldn't figure it out. I said, "I thought you had to be made a saint from down here."

The Babe's ugly puss busted into a big grin. He replied, "Up there They don't always wait. Particularly when They got use for a guy."

I asked, "How did it happen, Babe?"

He chawed a while and then replied, "I dunno. One day one of Them came along and says, 'Hey, Babe. What about that time you got up at that dinner to Jimmy Walker and promised to turn over a new leaf for the sake of the dirty-faced kids in the street?' I says, 'What about it?' He says, 'Were you on the level? Did you really mean it?' I says, 'What do you think? Ain't you never seen a kid with his heart broke because something or somebody he believed in went sour?' He says, 'O.K., Babe. That's all I wanted to know. You come along with me. We got work for you to do.' So They put me on the roster."

I said, "Well, what do you know? What are you saint of? What do I call you?"

He shifted his chew and said, affably, 'Call me Babe. Up there I'm known as Saint Bambino, but I don't go much for that stuff. Baseball, of course. It's the biggest thing in the world, ain't it?"

I started to say, "You're tellin' me—" when he continued:

"There's millions of kids in this country to whom baseball's mighty important. They worry, and snivel themselves to sleep because they can't hit a curve ball, stop pulling back from a fast one inside or hold a hot liner with the meat hand. Sometimes it's a matter of timing. Others, it's moxie. I'm in charge of that."

"Yeah, is that right? What do you do?"

"Oh, I dunno. Take a look around and maybe ask Number One, the Manager, to give 'em a hand. Unless they ask for me personally, like some do." He grinned again. "There was that kid last week in Biloxi, Mississippi, he threw wild to home plate from left field, let two runs in and lost the game. All the other kids picked on him. That night he asked me if I'd ever pulled one like that? He kept bellerin', 'Babe, I bet you never did that. Babe, I'm no good. I wanna die. Help me.'"

"So what did you do?"

"So I reminded the kid about that time in Cleveland in

1923 when we were two games out of first place for the pennant the last week in August."

I said, "What happened? I don't remember that one."

The Babe laughed that big, old, deep, rumbling laugh of his. "We're leading six-five in the last of the ninth. The Indians got two on and two out. What's-His-Name, their shortstop, comes up, and I figure him for a short single between first and second if he hits, and come in to take it on the first hop."

"And does he?"

"Sure. And I got the runner for home out by a mile, only I'm still full of beer from the night before and throw the ball right over the top of the press box. Boy, Hug was sore. He slapped a hundred-dollar plaster on me. I told him to keep his shirt on, I'd get the games back for him."

"And did you?"

"Sure. I got hold of two the next day. Day after, I clobbered 'em. I got a single, a double and two triples, and threw Who's-is, their second baseman, out at the plate with the tying run from the right-field fence. Hug took the plaster off."

"What about the kid from Biloxi?"

"He quit blubberin'. He'll go out and try to win the next three games and make 'em forget his error."

I moved so that the light from the moon through the window fell onto my face. The Babe suddenly took a good gander at me.

"Say," he said, "I seen you before some place. Hey, wait a minute! Ain't you that red-faced turkey used to sit back of the boxes behind third base in the Stadium and ride me all the time in the old days? I can't remember the name—"

Babe never could remember anybody's name, not even the guys on his own team. But I could of busted with pride and almost cried to think he knew me.

"Murphy," I said, "Leather-Lung Murphy!"

The Babe slapped his knee. "That's the son-of-a-sailor," he said. "Boy, that brass voice of yours used to get under my skin."

How it all came back to me then, those years when I used to give it to him back in the old days. The Babe would come up to bat, and I'd holler, "Strike out, ya bum! Oh, what a bum!" And if he'd hit one, I'd bawl, "Oh, you lucky stiff!"

They said my voice would carry all the way down to the 138th Street Harlem River Bridge. The crowd would whoop and holler and laugh and turn around and point me out, saying, "That's Leather-Lung Murphy from Detroit. He always rides the Babe." The papers wrote pieces about me and the kids would come up and ask for my autograph. I was as famous as any of 'em.

It was like I could close my eyes and be back there more than twenty-five years ago and see the Yankee Stadium on a summer afternoon with the Babe up to bat. He had a body shaped like a pear and he'd stand up on those thin, pipestem ankles of his with the number "3" on his back, leaned over and waving his big bat a little. I remember how the elevated trains would slow down as they passed the Stadium, so the motorman could see whether the Babe got hold of one. Nobody could make any mistake, no matter from how far, who it was up.

He'd have his big paws wrapped around that bat handle so it looked like a matchstick in his fingers. The pitch would come; he'd miss it with an almighty swipe and wrap himself around so his legs was twisted like a pretzel. A roar would go up, and on top of it would be me, like a brass trumpet, yelling, "Strike out, ya bum!"

There'd be another throw and he'd be taking a backswing before the ball got out of the pitcher's grip. Then you'd hear a click—it wasn't a crack, or a bang, or a thud, but a click like no other sound you ever hear. It was never different, and it always meant the ball was out of the park over the right-field fence.

Boy, that roar! And that big ape trotting around the bases on them too-small dogs of his, tipping his cap. And maybe giving me a grin when I handed him the bird as he rounded third base.

Pretty soon the game'd be over, the fans would be streaming across the diamond. I'd go home to a big thick steak my good wife, Ellen, would have cooked for me and tell my Jimmy, who was eight then, what his big hero, the Babe, had done that day. That was the life. It was never so good, before or after.

94

The Babe shifted in his chair next to Jimmy, Jr.'s, bed and said, "What was it you had it in for me for, in them days, Murph?"

"Nothing personal, Babe," I replied. "I come from Detroit, so there was only one ballplayer in the world for me—Ty Cobb."

It was true. I was born and raised in Detroit. After you'd watched the Georgia Peach play, you couldn't see no other diamond jockey for dust. When I come out of the Army in 1919, I stayed in New York and got a job as a mechanic. Afterward I got into the garage business and made my pile. But I'm always a Tiger rooter because that's how I was born.

Babe was scratching his head like he was trying to think back on something. Finally it come to him.

"What made you quit riding me, Murph? Seemed like one day all of a sudden you wasn't there any more. I missed you, keed. You used to get my goat so I'd want to bust that apple clear out to Hunt's Point."

I said, "On the level, don't you remember, Babe?"

He looked at me with surprise. "Naw," he replied. "What happened, keed?"

"Don't you remember little Jimmy Murphy in St. Agatha's Hospital—the kid who was so sick the doctors give him up?"

The Babe still looked blank. Me, I could hardly choke down the lump in my throat. Ever since I come into the room and see him sitting there by Jimmy, Jr.'s, bedside, I got another scene in my mind just like it, when my boy Jimmy was dying back in 1926. Some sports writer got wind of it and fixed up a visit from the Babe because my kid was as crazy a fan for Babe Ruth as I was for Ty.

I can still see it like yesterday, the big monkey sitting next to my Jimmy's bed in the hospital. It was God come down from heaven in a tan polo coat and go-to-hell cap, holding an autographed baseball. He said, "You listen to the game on the radio tomorrow, keed. I'm gonna bust one for you."

He did too. I was with Jimmy and seen the glaze go out of his eyes and the color come back to his cheeks. After that, am I going to razz the Babe any more? To me, he's just the greatest man in the world.

"Yeah?" said Saint Bambino. "So what happened?"

I said, "You come to the hospital, autographed a baseball for him and promised to hit a home run for him."

"Yeah?" said Saint Bambino. "Did I? How'd he make out?"

He didn't remember. I suppose he visited a lot of kids in hospitals in his career. There was that Johnny Sylvester for whom he hit a home run in the World Series, and a boy in New Jersey, one in Chicago, and another in Boston.

I said, "He got well. But he wouldn't of if it hadn't been for you."

"That's good," Saint Bambino said. "He must be a big guy now. Whatever become of him?"

I swallowed so I would steady my voice. "He was leading a company in the Hürtgen Forest in the last war," I said. "A Heinie threw a potato masher. He covered it with his body to keep his men from being clobbered."

Saint Bambino chewed his wad for a considerable time before he nodded and said, "That's bad."

I nodded toward Jimmy, Jr., asleep next to him. "That's his kid there."

The Saint looked down at him. I never would have thought such tenderness could spread over that ugly mush. For the first time I noticed a faint glow that seemed to surround or come from the wide-brimmed camel's-hair cap on the big head.

"Is it now?" he said. "What would be his trouble? What made you send for me?"

I had to swallow again hard before I spoke. "Saint," I said finally, "he don't care about baseball."

The Babe chewed and let another stream out the window. When he spoke again, it was to say, "That's real bad. How did that happen?"

"After his father was killed, his mother never remarried," I explained. "Women don't understand about baseball like men. The kid's father was the greatest Yankee fan in the world, but Jimmy, Jr., grew up without a man around the house. All he wants to do is look at television shows and read space comics."

"That's terrible," Saint Bambino said. "Comics is O.K. if a game is rained out and you got nuthin' else to do."

"A year or so ago, his mother smarted up to what was

going on," I continued. "The boy was pale and didn't eat good. He should 'a' been out with the other kids, running the bases, beltin' that apple, and have his head full of something worth while instead of them bum television jokes. I was back in Detroit, where I had a string of garages. When the good wife, Ellen, died six months ago, I sold out and retired. Janet—that's Jimmy, Jr.'s, mother—telephoned me to come here and live with them and work on the boy. But it's too late. He just don't care."

So we sat there a minute, looking down at Jimmy, Jr. He was a good-put-together kid, with his mother's mouth and his father's fighting chin, but he was thin and his color wasn't right.

Saint Bambino leaned forward a little in his chair and began to talk in a low, deep voice. Only he wasn't talking to me any longer but to the kid.

"Jimmy, Jr., listen to me," he said. "Don't you make no mistake. Baseball's the greatest game in the world, and any man can be proud to have a connection with it, no matter what, even if it's only sitting in the grandstand and keeping a box score and yelling for the home team to git out and get them runs."

I thought Jimmy, Jr., would wake up, but he don't. He just moved a little in his sleep.

"Do you know what baseball can do, Jimmy, Jr.?" the Saint continued. "It can take a nobody out of the gutter, maybe somebody that's seen the inside of a jail or a reform school, and make him a bigger man than the President of the United States. Now you tell me any other game that can do that and I'll kiss your fist."

The moon was starting to slide past the open window now, and it seemed like the glow coming from the camel's-hair cap on the big dark head was brighter.

"Don't kid yourself, Jimmy, Jr.," the Saint went on. "You gotta be a man to play baseball. It's the toughest game in the world, because you gotta have everything. You gotta have condition, co-ordination, speed, science, know-how, hustle and moxie. Plenty of moxie, son, because if you ever show a yellow streak, the pitchers'll dust you, the base runners'll cut you to ribbons and the bench jockeys will ride you right out of the league.

"You can't let up for a minute, keed. You got to give it everything you got and use the old bean besides. You let one get by you in April, and maybe you find out it's the error that's cost you the pennant in September. You can't slack off or ease up. When you're in there at bat or running the bases, you got nine guys working against you, and a big brain sitting on the bench as well, figuring how to make a monkey out of you."

I never heard such earnestness in any man's voice as in the Saint's. He leaned a little farther forward and went on:

"Keed, there never was a game figured out prettier to test a man for speed and guts and the old whip; whether the runner gets to the bag first or the ball beats him. Ninety feet between bases, and guys like Ty Cobb was fast enough to steal home while the pitcher is winding up and letting it go. Sixty feet six inches from the pitcher's mound to home plate, and you got maybe a half a second while the ball is in the air to pick out whether you're going to be a hero or a bum. It takes real men to put together a double play and make it look easy and graceful-like.

"Why do you suppose so many millions of people— grown-up men and women as well as kids, Jimmy, Jr.— love baseball? Why, for so many reasons I could sit here all night long and tell ya. Some of the finest men that ever breathed the air of our country has been in baseball, men everybody can look up to and be proud of because they never give anything but the best they had.

"It's a game, and yet it's like life, keed, and it gets you ready for it. Maybe the score is six to nothing against you in the ninth with two out. Half the crowd is heading for the exits because they figure you ain't got a chance. But you know you ain't dead until there's three out, so you go up there to the plate and take your cut, and next thing you know the pitcher is walking to the showers, the new one ain't warmed up good and you clobber him. The fans stop walking out and five minutes later you got the game in the bag. Nobody ever played baseball, keed, or followed them that did, that wasn't the better for it."

His voice dropped even lower, until it was just like a deep, soft, friendly growl, "It's a team game, Jimmy, and it's ours. It come out of the guts of this country. That's why we're so hard to lick when the chips are down, because when we get into a jam, we play it like a team instead of every man for his self. A soldier or a sailor or an airman will back up his buddy because maybe he's learned somewhere on some sand lot or inside a stadium that a pitcher can throw his heart out, but you gotta spear those liners and pick those drives off the fences and then go out and get him some runs, or it don't do no good. It's like you're a family or a lot of brothers working together. It's the only game you don't have to play to feel the good in it and learn the lessons that are gonna help you sometime when you're in need."

The Saint paused for a moment, then gently patted Jimmy, Jr., on the shoulder.

"That's all for now, keed," he said. "Think it over. Good luck. I may be seeing you again sometime." I thought that Jimmy, Jr., seemed to smile in his sleep. The Saint turned to me, "O.K., Murph. I guess I won't be needed around here any longer, so I'll be beating it. The kid'll be O.K. If you ever need me again, holler. I'll be keeping an eye on him."

I was all choked up, but I managed to say, "Is there anything I can do for you, Babe—I mean Saint Bambino?"

He thought for a moment, and then got up from the chair. The moon was gone, but from the glow on his cap I could see a kind of sheepish grin on his big mug.

"Yeah," he said, "maybe there is. Things are kind of quiet-like where I am. Just for old-time's sake, gimme the old razz. I'd like to hear the old leather lung just once more."

"Which one?" I asked. "I hate to do it to you, Babe."

He grinned again. "The strike-out one. It used to keep me on my toes."

I saw he was on the level, so I let him have it just like I used to, with all the brass and steam I had left.

"Strike out, ya bum!"

For a moment I thought I could hear the roar of the crowd again, and the sharp click that meant the management was out another baseball.

Jimmy, Jr., woke up with a start, but when he saw me, he quieted right down. "Oh, Granddad!" he said. "Was that you? I was having a dream about Babe Ruth and baseball."

I started to say that the Babe, or rather Saint Bambino,

was right there, but when I looked to where he had been, he was gone.

Instead, Jimmy, Jr.'s, mother came hustling into the room in her dressing gown, saying, "Land's sakes! What's happened, Dad, you yelling fit to wake the dead?"

I said, "I was only showing Jimmy, Jr., how I used to holler at the Babe in the old days."

"At this time of morning, when the child ought to be getting some rest! I declare, you men—"

But Jimmy, Jr., just lay there looking up at the ceiling. After a little, he said, "That was a funny dream, but I liked it. Granddad, can I go to the ball game with you tomorrow?"

Yeah, there's one more part to the story, and you don't got to believe that either.

Last week Jimmy's school nine is playing in the crucial game, with Jimmy, Jr., catching and batting in the clean-up position. It's two out in the ninth; Jimmy is up. The bases are loaded and we need those runs. In a couple of seconds, the pitcher, a big, tough kid was a nasty eye, has breezed two strikes past my Jimmy, Jr., and one of 'em is a duster that almost took the P.S.A.L. lettering off his chest. Two and none, and I can see the boy is shaken by the duster. We're in a bad hole.

All of a sudden I hear a familiar voice say, "Move over, keed." I look up, and it's the big guy in the tan polo coat and go-to-hell cap. He sits down next to me.

"Babe," I said, "you got here just in time. The kid's in a spot."

The Saint laughs his deep, rumbling laugh. "Take it easy, keed," he says. "Just you watch him."

I look. And there's Jimmy, Jr., standing at the plate, his bat over one shoulder, and with his free hand he's pointing out to the center-field fence just like the Babe did that day in the World Series in Chicago. It rattles the tough kid just enough. He lets the pitch go. Smack!

No, it wasn't a homer, but for what was needed, just as good, a triple to deep center that clears the bases.

The Saint laughs again, deeper and more satisfied. "The old trade-mark," he says, and grins out to where Jimmy, Jr., is roosting on third base. "That's the keed. Didn't get enough of the old back porch into that one. A little more meat on your piazza and it's over the fence. Gotta work on them wrists of yours too. Ain't quite cocking them enough on the backswing. Well, so long, keed."

I heard that big laugh again as he vanished, then it was lost in the noise of the crowd cheering for Jimmy, Junior.

Sportswriter-novelist-screenwriter Paul Gallico was born in New York City in 1897 and educated at Columbia University. After Navy service during World War I, he was a sports reporter for the New York Daily News; *turning to fiction full time, he wrote several hundred short stories as well as forty books. Bestsellers like* The Snow Goose *took him to Hollywood, and film versions of books such as* The Poseidon Adventure *made him rich enough to spend the rest of his life traveling. He died in 1976.*

Amy felt there was something wrong with Aunt Charlotte's fake séances. She didn't know how right she was.

SEVEN

A Séance in Summer

Mario Martin, Jr.

Aunt Charlotte had always been the strangest person in the family. Ever since Amy could remember, someone was always talking about the odd things Aunt Charlotte did. Like the time she took up raising snakes. Not just garter snakes, but real poisonous ones, like cobras. Once she took up trapeze work, too, and said she was going to join a circus. But everyone told her she'd probably get herself killed, and finally she didn't join a circus. Aside from Aunt Charlotte's odd ways, Amy liked being with her. She told good stories, and she delighted in taking Amy to Nutley's Ice Cream Parlor and to play miniature golf.

One of Aunt Charlotte's favorite interests was the supernatural, and this was reflected in the decorations which filled her quaint little house on the boardwalk at Ocean City. Her parlor was filled with musty old books, human skulls, crystal balls, and other scary things. When Amy arrived for her annual summer visit, she wasn't surprised, then, to see a new sign outside the house.

MADAME CHARLOTTE. MEDIUM AND SPIRITUALIST
READINGS, FORTUNES, AND SÉANCES

Amy guessed that Aunt Charlotte was just carrying her newest interest further than usual and was going to try to make money off the crowds of beach tourists during the summer.

Aunt Charlotte explained the whole thing. "Of course," she said. "Séances (she pronounced it 'say-ahnces') are the

102

latest thing. Everyone's talking about them this year, Amy. You'd be surprised how many people want to get in touch with some dead relative!"

Amy was surprised at the light tone in which Aunt Charlotte spoke of communicating with dead people. "But can you really do that for them?" she asked doubtfully, brushing a wisp of blond hair from her face.

"Why of course not, child" Aunt Charlotte laughed. "It's not real. It's just a game. People enjoy it—*and* they pay good money for it."

Amy studied her aunt's features. she looked pretty old to Amy—maybe she was as much as forty. Her hair was tinged with gray, and she wore it in a big bun at the back of her neck. Her eyes were blue and small and caked with makeup. And she wore lots of long, printed dresses with puffy sleeves and lace cuffs, which accented her thin, delicate hands. She had never married, and Amy wondered why. Maybe it was because nobody could fall in love with someone who tried all the weird, crazy things Aunt Charlotte had.

Finally Amy spoke again, her voice registering her doubt about Aunt Charlotte's new game. "You mean you're going to fool the people who come to you? Take their money?"

"Amy, you're too young to understand. Everyone has to make money to live," said Aunt Charlotte. "Don't you worry. Your Aunt Char knows what she's doing."

Amy nodded, feeling a bit guilty, for she still didn't really agree with what Aunt Charlotte planned to do.

"Look, I'll show you there's no harm in it," Aunt Charlotte continued in a bubbly voice. "Tonight I'm having my first séance of the summer. You sit in the alcove off the parlor and watch. All right? Then you'll see."

That evening after dinner, Aunt Charlotte dressed herself in a flowing robe of deep purple covered with crescent moons, stars, and planets. On her head she wore a satin turban, and large earrings dangled from her ears like ornaments on a Christmas tree. Amy thought she looked kind of silly.

In the alcove, peeking through a small slit in the black curtains, Amy watched her aunt prepare for the séance. Aunt Charlotte covered the table with a purple, fringed cloth. She placed a large crystal ball in the center of the table and pushed chairs into place around it. And then she went around the room turning out all the lamps and lighting candles in their place. Soon the room was lit only by a faint, eerie light.

Around eight o'clock, most of the people arrived. Amy recognized several of them as Aunt Charlotte's friends, who also lived and worked in Ocean City. Two others she didn't know came, too. They must have strolled in off the boardwalk just out of curiosity. Aunt Charlotte asked them all to be seated around the table.

"Dear friends," she said in a solemn voice. "We are gathered at this séance to speak with the spirits of our departed loved ones. Which of you here tonight would like to begin?"

An older woman raised her hand. "I suppose I would. My husband, Arthur—poor Arthur. I haven't been the same since he's been gone." The woman produced a handkerchief to mop up tears that had now appeared.

Aunt Charlotte nodded gravely and instructed the guests to place their hands on the table. "If everyone will think very hard about Arthur's wandering spirit, perhaps he will hear us and come to us," she said. "As a sign of his coming, this table will rise off the floor."

Amy watched in the dim, flickering light as they closed their eyes and concentrated on calling up Arthur's spirit. The room was deathly still, and several people coughed nervously. Suddenly, as Amy held her breath in astonishment, the table stirred. Then it rose, stopped momentarily and shook, and continued to move upward. She wasn't imagining it! It was actually happening!

Up—up—up went the table until it floated motionless about a foot off the floor. There were gasps and cries of surprise from the people around the table. Only Aunt Charlotte remained unruffled. She spoke calmly. "Ah, good. Arthur has answered our calls. He is near us now."

Arthur's wife broke into tears, sobbing openly. "Oh, no!" she cried. "Oh, Arthur! Are you really here?"

Suddenly a cold breeze blew through the darkened parlor, accompanied by an eerie howling, whistling sound. The candles flickered, casting weird shadows on the walls. The people around the table stiffened, and several of them began to perspire.

"The spirit wind has entered this room," said Aunt Charlotte. "Arthur is now among us. Be silent, all. Arthur will speak to us if you but ask him a question."

A frost was crawling up Amy's backbone, and she could feel goose pimples forming on her bare arms and on the back of her neck. She shuddered, wanting to run from the room, wishing only to escape these strange happenings. But she couldn't without upsetting everyone. She forced herself to remain seated on the stool behind the curtains.

"What would you ask of the dear departed?" Aunt Charlotte asked the crying woman.

"Oh, I don't know—I don't know—I can't believe this is really happening." The woman was very upset. All the others stared straight ahead, afraid to look at her, shifting uneasily in their chairs.

The howling spirit wind increased in intensity, and Amy covered her ears.

"Arthur grows impatient," said Aunt Charlotte. "Perhaps I should speak for you?"

The woman, reduced to a skaking mass of fear, nodded mutely.

"Arthur, do you hear me?" called Aunt Charlotte.

Yes, I can hear you. The deep, hollow-sounding voice echoed throughout the room. Everyone, including Amy, jumped, filled with the fear of the unknown.

"Arthur," called Aunt Charlotte. "Are you happy where you are? Mildred has come to speak with you."

I am quite happy here. Again, the strange voice.

The woman wailed. "Oh, that's Arthur! I know it is. I'd recognize his voice anywhere!" After a sobbing pause, she added, "Please tell him I miss him and ask him if there's anything he wants me to do for him."

Aunt Charlotte frowned at the woman's words, but she repeated the question to the spirit.

The spirit world is not a lonely place. Yes, I can see all of you. I know what takes place on the earth.

The spirit's answer didn't seem to have anything to do with the woman's question, but apparently that didn't bother her. She simply nodded and wiped her eyes with a handkerchief.

Several more questions were directed to the spirit, and Amy thought the answers were vague and disconnected. But nobody else seemed to notice. And she was so tense and scared, maybe she wasn't hearing things just right.

A rumble of thunder filled the room, and the wind noises raised in intensity. *It is time that I leave your world once more. Perhaps I can return at another appointed hour. Goodbye.* The last word was nearly drowned out by more thunder and wind, and then there was silence.

"Close your eyes," said Aunt Charlotte, ignoring the strange sounds. "The end of the séance is at hand. Concentrate and be thankful that the spirits have been good to us."

Keeping their hands on the table, everyone closed his eyes. The table gradually began to descend, until it settled firmly on the floor with a solid thump. The sound seemed to stir everyone. They opened their eyes and looked at Aunt Charlotte.

"Thank you, everyone, for coming," she said, standing up. "Perhaps I shall see you again next week?" Firmly, she ushered them out of the room. All went, heads bowed, as if they were leaving church.

The front door closed, and Aunt Charlotte came back into the parlor. She pulled off her turban and dropped it on the table. "Oh, the fools!" she laughed. "The utter fools! It went so perfectly."

She pulled the alcove curtains aside. "You can come out now, child. C'mon out here."

As Amy entered the parlor, Aunt Charlotte was already turning on the lamps and blowing out candles. She looked at Amy and laughed at her puzzled expression. "What's the matter, Amy? You weren't frightened, were you?" And then she laughed again.

"Aunt Charlotte, I don't understand. What's so funny? How did you do it all?" Amy ran her fingers over the table, as if to test its weight and movability.

"Promise you won't tell anyone my secrets?" Aunt Charlotte looked at her sternly.

Amy nodded.

"Come here and look." Aunt Charlotte pointed to the

chair she had sat in during the séance. Amy looked. There was a row of buttons on the arm of the chair. "Push that first one," said Aunt Charlotte.

Amy pressed the button, and suddenly the table began to rise. Surprised, she dropped to her knees and lifted the tablecloth. A large pillar, on which the table rested, rose out of the floor. "What is it!" she gasped. "How does it work?"

Aunt Charlotte smiled. "An electric motor in the cellar. I had it built by a company over in Watson last winter. Now, push that next button."

Amy did as she was told, and the howling, wailing wind began to shift through the parlor.

"A simple electric fan with a whistle, up there," explained Aunt Charlotte, pointing to a lamp hanging on the wall. Behind it was a small fan. "And others there—and there—and there." Fans were concealed all around the room!

Without asking, Amy pushed the next button, and a now-familiar voice filled the room. *Yes, I can hear you.*

"Tape recorder," said Aunt Charlotte. "I also have a tape of a woman's voice." She laughed lightly as she brushed Amy's hand away from the chair and turned off all the buttons.

"It's all just tricks!" said Amy.

"Didn't I *tell* you I was only going to fool these people?" asked Aunt Charlotte.

And so she had. "But it all seemed so real," said Amy.

"That's just it, child. It's supposed to be real. You saw how they acted. They wanted to believe there was a ghost here. They didn't mind that the voice wasn't answering their questions."

Amy shivered. "Well, it's all kind of tricky. And somebody might catch you, you know."

"I don't think they will," said Aunt Charlotte. "Here, let me change out of this silly thing, and we'll go get some ice cream."

The weeks passed as June turned into July, and somehow or other the summer wasn't turning out to be much fun. Amy and Aunt Charlotte hardly ever went down to Nutley's for ice cream after the first week of vacation. And Aunt

Charlotte's stories were different, somehow, than they used to be—scarier, maybe. But there was something more.

Aunt Charlotte continued to hold her séances for audiences of surprised and shocked visitors. She collected her money and kept it in an ornate, gilded box on her perfume-laden dresser. As the money piled up, something seemed to happen to her. She changed. Amy didn't know quite how to put it, but Aunt Charlotte seemed to get kind of—oh—hard, like. She took to calling the visitors "marks" or even "suckers." And her eyes glittered so strangely as she counted the money after each séance that Amy, watching her, almost felt as though Aunt Charlotte was seeing something she wasn't supposed to see. Amy began to wish the summer would end so she could go home to Baltimore.

Amy's funny feelings about the fake séances grew. She felt there was something more wrong in them than just the part about tricking people. It was like the séances were all very dangerous, or something.

As it turned out, Amy was right.

It was during the middle of August, and the sun burned down on the beaches, the sea nettles clogged the surf, and the pavements were almost too hot to walk on with bare feet. The city had been filled with tourists, and Amy didn't even go to the beach, which was so crowded that there was hardly enough room to spread a blanket. Instead, she took her transistor radio and a Coke and some magazines and made herself comfortable out on the grass beside the house where it was shady. From there, she watched the crowds pass by in a never-ending stream.

Amy spent a nice, lazy day there, and eventually, the sun passed overhead and began to melt into the bay behind the island city. Amy gathered up her things and went inside. Aunt Charlotte was flitting around the house, preparing for the evening's séance. Business had become so good that people made appointments in advance.

Taking her seat in the alcove off the parlor, Amy huddled on her stool. Uncomfortable feelings about the séances crowded in on her again, and she guessed she wouldn't be coming back to Ocean City for any more summer vacations. She guessed she would just find things to do around Baltimore instead.

Aunt Charlotte's lilting voice began greeting visitors. Amy peeked out through the curtains and saw people taking their places around the table. More than half the visitors in the parlor were curious tourists. Not too many townspeople came to the séances these days. Most of them had probably caught on to Aunt Charlotte's tricks.

One by one, people drifted into the darkened room until all the seats were filled except Aunt Charlotte's and that of a new customer who had phoned earlier in the day and identified himself as Mr. Arcanus. As the clock struck eight, there was a knock at the door. Aunt Charlotte stepped into the hall to answer it, and Amy heard a slight gasp before the now-familiar words of welcome.

As Mr. Arcanus was led to his chair, a shudder raced through Amy. She could see why Aunt Charlotte had been startled.

The man was very tall, taller than anyone Amy had ever seen, and his shoulders were wide and muscular. He was dressed in a black coat with a turned-up collar. His hands were gloved in black, and a hat with a wide, drooping brim shadowed his face. In the dim light of the candles, there seemed to be only blackness where his face should have been—a featureless pit from which two eyes stared, glowing like lumps of hot charcoal. Mr. Arcanus was a fearful-looking person, and his very presence in the parlor scared Amy.

As Aunt Charlotte sat down, she asked Mr. Arcanus if he would like to remove his hat and coat, but he answered only with a slow shake of his head. Amy found it very peculiar that the man should be wearing such heavy clothing. Even after sunset it was still almost ninety degrees, and the motionless air of the parlor was just about unbearable.

Ruffled though she was by the awesome presence of the stranger, Aunt Charlotte nevertheless began the séance. She asked which of the visitors wished to communicate that evening, and Mrs. Canby raised her hand.

"My brother, Harry," she said. She glanced around the group rather smugly. "He's the one who left us so well—uh, well situated, you know. Do you think—I mean—"

"Indeed, my dear," said Aunt Charlotte. She took in a deep breath. "Let us all now concentrate. Together let us summon the lonely spirit of dear Harry—"

There was silence in the parlor, and in the alcove, Amy tried to remember Mrs. Canby's brother. Wasn't he the one everyone said owned almost all of Factory Row? He was rich as anything, everyone said, but the old houses in Factory Row were all tumbledown and full of rats and he wouldn't do anything to fix them for the people who lived there. Amy's forehead wrinkled as she tried to remember. And there was—was—something about how he killed a child with his great, big car and almost let someone else take the blame. There were other things, too, that the grown-ups whispered about, but she didn't quite understand them all.

How could anybody love someone like Harry! Well, maybe his sister didn't know about all those terrible things. Or maybe she was so glad to get all those buckets of money when he died that she just plain forgave him for being so bad.

Amy's thoughts were interrupted by what was going on in the parlor.

Aunt Charlotte was telling the guests to place their hands on the table, and Amy supposed she was now pushing the button on her chair that would raise the table upward. Suddenly, though, her gaze was caught by the way Mr. Arcanus was staring at Aunt Charlotte. His eyes were shining, red-hot.

The table rose, but not slowly as it usually did when lifted by the machine in the cellar. In a storm of sound as wood tore and snapped, the steel gears ground and shrieked, the table ripped off the floor and sailed upward to the ceiling. Everyone, including Aunt Charlotte, sat frozen in their chairs and stared at the huge table hovering a full five feet above their heads. But Mr. Arcanus remained calm.

In the alcove, behind the curtains, Amy cringed. This was no trick. Something terrible and unknown was happening in the parlor.

Without warning, the table crashed to the floor with a thunderous concussion, narrowly missing the circle of people seated like statues in their chairs.

Visibly shaken, Aunt Charlotte tried to continue her performance. Amy could tell that Aunt Charlotte was disturbed by the intense stare of the dark stranger.

"Ah—very well—" she said nervously. "Harry has answered our call—He is near." Her hands were trembling, and Amy saw that she had difficulty in swallowing after she finished speaking. Her hand moved slightly, to press the button for the spirit wind. But before she could do so, a furious howling filled the room, and a harsh gale of arctic air rushed through the house. Amy shuddered as the wind, carrying the deeply frigid chill of winter, raced through the room. Pictures flew off walls. Lamps and knickknacks crashed to the floor. The candles were extinguished simultaneously.

Gasps and screams came from people at the table, and Aunt Charlotte tried to talk above the wail of the wind. "Please, be calm—It is the spirit wind!" She winced as a vase flew from an end table and splintered against a wall. "It is only Harry, here among us—He grows impatient. We must speak with him."

The only light in the room came from the dark red glow of the eyes of Mr. Arcanus, who continued to remain still and emotionless amid the chaos.

Mrs. Canby was rigid in her chair. Her face, a full one, was streaked with harsh lines as she sat gritting her teeth, her eyes wide with terror. Fear expressed itself on Aunt Charlotte's face, too. What terrible thing was happening?

As though to break the spell of fear that was winding snakelike through everyone's mind, Aunt Charlotte spoke again. "We must speak with Harry now—Can you hear us, Harry?" Her voice cracked under the strain of speaking above the raging scream of the wind that still ripped through the room.

And then the wind stopped.

As abruptly as it had come, it was gone. In its place sounded a long, endless scream that grew in volume until it filled the room. The voice was that of a man shrieking in the most horrible pain imaginable. And still the scream grew louder. Words picked themselves out of the sound. *Help me! Ooooh! Noooo! Make it stop! Make it stop!* Amy had never heard such hopeless terror in a voice before.

Everyone's eyes bulged in terror, except Mr. Arcanus's. He calmly stood up at the table and spoke.

You have summoned the spirit of Harry Patulski. You have heard him. And now you shall see him. Behold! The voice of Mr. Arcanus was deep and heavy, and his words rolled about the room, filling it up, suffocating all the other people. With a gloved hand, he pointed to the center of the table.

A glowing ball of orange light appeared above the table. The color floated there, grew in size, and then turned egg-shaped. Out of this materialized the shape of a man, writhing in a sea of flames.

Mrs. Canby's shriek pierced the room. "Harry!"

The image increased in size and clarity. The utter horror and loathsomeness of the man in the flames was unspeakable. And there was no mistaking the identity of the stranger, Mr. Arcanus.

Amy wanted to run from the house. She tried to move from her stool in the alcove. She could not. Trembling, she tried to shut her eyes and ears to the agony echoing through the parlor.

Now you see, said Arcanus. *Remember this vision for all time.*

He turned and faced the guests, who had left their chairs and cringed in a pack in the corner of the room. *Now leave this place. All of you, except this woman,* he said, pointing to Aunt Charlotte, who was still seated at the table. Her face was blank and white with shock.

Amy opened her mouth to scream as the demon-thing pointed at Aunt Charlotte. No sound came out. After a moment, Amy jumped from the stool and rushed to join the others, who were crowding toward the door.

With a sweep of his hand, Arcanus motioned a dismissal to the huddled group of people. The burning vision of Harry disappeared with a popping sound. And Arcanus spoke once more. *Go from this place. And never again seek something you do not understand nor really wish to see.*

The people pushed through the door in a great wave. Someone grabbed Amy's arm and pulled her along with them. Looking over her shoulder, Amy saw Aunt Charlotte, paralyzed with fright, watching the demon-thing slowly walking toward her.

Clear of the house, everyone ran down the boardwalk, ignoring the laughing crowds, trying to escape the horror they had seen in Aunt Charlotte's parlor. Amy turned and watched the house. For several seconds it was still and quiet. Then suddenly an orange-red glow lit all the windows. The glow brightened. Tongues of flame leaped from the windows. With a thunderous explosion, the little wooden house erupted into one massive pillar of fire. Where the house had stood only seconds before was nothing but a column of heat and yellow flame.

A great crowd of people surrounded Amy. They all watched the house being consumed. In the distance, the wail of a fire engine threaded through the night air. It was all like a hazy dream, and Amy's only thoughts were of Arcanus and Aunt Charlotte, still somewhere within the inferno.

Mario Martin, Jr., is a penname for science fiction writer Thomas F. Montelone, whose first book, Seeds of Change, *was given away as a sales gimmick by its publisher. Born in Maryland in 1946, Montelone was educated at the University of Maryland at College Park. He worked as a psychotherapist at Perkins Hospital Center until his writing begin winning more and more prizes. He has written more than fifty short stories, plays, television scripts, and such novels as the Nebula-winning* The Time-Swept City, Day of the Dragonstar *(with David Bischoff), and horror novels such as* Night-Train.

The Union soldier and Confederate soldier had not met on the battlefield, but now they had a unique assignment.

EIGHT

Little Note Nor Long Remember
Henry T. Parry

"How did you get this detail, Johnny?"

"Just like in the Yankee army, Yank. This sergeant stuck his head in and pointed to me and said I had volunteered. He didn't care much for me because he was from South Carolina and I used to say that the South Carolinians did a lot of big talkin' before the war and then us Virginians had to do a lot of big fightin'."

"It was about that way with me. Seth Perkins, he's our corporal, sent me to see this staff captain."

"Now there's the kind of a job I like. A staff captain. The kind that says you hold this here piece of road, there ain't but ten Yankees for every Reb. Then he gets back out of range of Yankee artillery and writes a report and keeps a copy of it for his mem—ah, memories."

"Yeah, our staff is the same."

"What did he tell you, Yank? Say, what's your name?"

"Ethan Stone, First New Hampshire. What's yours?"

"Mitchell Cummins, Third Virginia."

"How is it you Rebs always have first names like Mitchell or Huger or Page? Not regular names like Pete or Joe or Ezra?"

"They're family names mostly. Seems to me any fellow whose first name is Ethan would be glad to have a different name."

"Maybe so. Anyway, this staff captain said me and somebody else—I guess that's you—were to go down to Weston,

Pennsylvania, and when we got there we'd see what had to be done."

"That's what they told me too, though they did give me some names. I asked why they bothered to assign me duty in a Yankee town and they said that when they wanted to know what a private soldier thought about his details they would look me up. In the meantime I could just shut up and obey orders. Outside of that they didn't tell me anything."

"Me neither. Just do what you see needs doing. You got any ideas?"

"Not me, Yank. A private soldier ain't supposed to have any ideas. Same old story. Hold this here piece of road. Do what you're told even when you ain't been told. Hurry up. Wait."

"Let's drop on down there and see if we can figure out what it is we're supposed to do."

"You bring the money, Willis?"

"I got it, Pricey, but before I turn it over I want some guarantee."

"Well, I want something too, but we'll get to that. Now here's the setup. The plans for the Center Square approach go before the Weston City Council for approval tomorrow morning. There's twelve guys who will vote. Five of them belong to our party and owe their jobs to me. They'll do as I tell them. I made them and I can break them."

"They owe their jobs to you and to the money that some of us raised for their campaigns."

"So we need two votes to approve the plan. A tie vote is the same as a rejection."

"Look, Pricey, are you sure this thing is sewed up? I got a lot of dough riding on this. I got options—or somebody I know's got options—on the square property and on both sides of the street approaching the square. When the approach plans are approved, I'll exercise the options and sell the land to the state for the approach. Then I bid on the highway construction too, of course."

"Now that's where I come in. I want the compensation insurance and all the other insurance on the construction job placed through my insurance office."

"That's hardly news, Pricey, but I guess we can deal on that. But I got to be sure you got the votes tomorrow."

"Willis, I got the votes. I was afraid at first I'd get some heat about that monument that's in the center of the square, something to do with the Civil War. But most of the people of this town don't seem ever to have heard of the Civil War, at least not unless it's on television. And Center Square has been running down for fifty years. Stores closed. Places boarded up. Winos hanging out in abandoned buildings."

"I had Patsy come up from the Chester job and look at the square and the approach street. He says the highway engineers know what they're doing. We'll have to go right through the square and that statue will have to go. No sweat, he says, nothing but a column forty-five feet high with a soldier and a gun standing on top, and around the base they got the names of places that nobody around here ever heard of. Places like Seven Pines, Fredericksburg, Petersburg, and the Wilderness. Patsy says he could bulldoze it down or maybe set some charges that would bring it down neat enough to catch in a paper cup."

"Now, Willis, the other party would normally have seven votes they can count on, enough to stop us. But here's what is going to happen. First of all, you know Mike Ferris in the Eighth Ward. Normally Mike would like to see us all out on the street selling matches in the snow on Christmas Eve. But Mike's sister Mary has a twenty-year-old kid who is building up a rap sheet for himself. Assault, some drug charges. Then three months ago his car hits a kid out near the shopping center and kills him, and he drives away from the scene of the accident without stopping. Somebody gave the license number to the police and they picked him up in twenty minutes. He was stinking drunk. They laid a manslaughter charge on him, along with several others. Now Mike—"

"Get on with it, Pricey."

"Like I was saying, Mike isn't so strong at the county courthouse as he thought and it looked like his sister's kid was going to pull some time. Which, in my opinion, he ought. The kid is a bum. Knowing I would need Mike's help, I called Charley Tolan and told him I wanted the kid's case put on Ike Smith's calendar. Ike will give him a suspended sentence—I've already arranged for that. So that's vote number six."

"Hey, Pricey, this room bugged? You get the feeling we're being listened in on?"

"You're getting jumpy, Willis. Must be all that money you got with you. Seriously, I've had the place—what do they call it?—swept. By Jimmy Haley from the police. He says it's okay. Jimmy wants to make lieutenant if we ever win City Hall back.

"Now for the seventh and winning vote. Homer Castle. Good, upright, honest—well, reasonable, let's say—plain-dealing, conservative Homer. If any ward was going to oppose knocking down Center Square, monument and all, I would expect it to be Homer Castle's ward. You know him, Willis? Tall thin guy, very erect and proper, and shrewd as a fox about his public image. He wears a derby winter and summer and has for thirty years. Some say it's the same derby. He wears a belt and suspenders and he carries an umbrella every day of the year, rain or shine. It's Homer's corny way of appealing to the conservative vote in his ward and I guess he knows what he's doing. They re-elected him five times.

"Now Homer has got two weaknesses, and the first one doesn't matter. It's food. About three times a week Homer goes down to Delcy's Inn on the River Road just below town here and eats enough for a stable of horses. And pays for it too. He's not the petty chiseling type. Stays as thin as a relative's charity. But Homer's big weakness is money. And no small money. No chicken feed for our friend Homer. About once a year the right person—that means someone with a sizeable amount of cash—is able to persuade Homer to see things his way. This year, by virtue of your thirty thousand dollars, it's my great good fortune to be able to persuade Homer to see things my way on the vote for the approach plans. There's vote number seven and that's why I wanted you to bring the money with you this afternoon."

"How do you plan to deliver the cash to Homer?"

"Give cash to an elected official! What are you talking about? I don't give cash to an elected councilman. I give it to the councilman's umbrella."

"Umbrella? What's that? One of those code words?"

117

"No, I mean umbrella. It works this way. This evening Homer will drive down the River Road to Delcy's for dinner. When he walks into the place, complete with derby, umbrella, and that kind of sour look he has, he'll go into the Men's Room. When he comes out he will only have the derby and the sour look, the umbrella will be hanging on a hook in the Men's Room. A couple of minutes later I walk into the Men's Room and I'll drop your thirty-thousand gift into Homer's umbrella, after which I go to the parking lot and drive away. Homer suddenly realizes where he has left his umbrella and rushes to retrieve it and, of course, the dough, which will be lying snugly among the ribs and folds of his bumbershoot."

"How do I know that Homer is getting all thirty thousand, that you aren't holding something out?"

"You don't. And usually I would need something for party expenses. But you don't know Homer. Homer would check around—and he's got some pretty good sources—and if he found I'd been holding anything out, he'd be right down here accusing me of dishonesty—imagine!—and then would begin figuring out how to get even. I don't want to take a chance. I may want to do business again with Homer. Tell you what. You come down there with me and you can drop the envelope in Homer's umbrella yourself. I'll wait outside. He's expecting something in that umbrella tonight."

"Pricey, it's only that I've got to be sure. I'll go along down there but you put the dough in yourself."

"Homer will get there about seven. So let's get started. It gets dark so early now and that River Road isn't the easiest to drive on. Narrow, twisting, and full of holes."

"Nobody will use it once we get the new highway in. Say, when you going to move out of this place? It seems so crowded, even with just the two of us."

"Done me for thirty years, Willis, and it'll do for thirty more. Remember, I'm just a poor insurance broker, not a big highway contractor."

Weston (Pa.) Courier-Journal:
TWO DIE IN ACCIDENT
Mr. Edward Price, 65, and Mr. Willis Brewer, 52,
died as a result of an auto accident when their car

crashed through the guardrail on the River Road and plunged into the LeMoyne River. The body of Mr. Brewer, who was trapped inside the car, was recovered this morning. Mr. Price was thrown clear of the car and was taken to Weston Hospital where he regained consciousness briefly.

Mr. Price was able to tell the police that two long-haired youths wearing military jackets of the type popular with certain hippies stepped out into the road and attempted to flag down his car. Mr. Price said he could not avoid hitting the young men, but was unable to recall any feeling of impact. Mr. Price died of his injuries an hour later.

A police check of local hospitals has not disclosed the admittance of any persons corresponding to the descriptions given by Mr. Price.

"Well, I guess we better be headin' back, Yank. Say, tell me, where did you get it? You ain't such a bad fellow and I wouldn't like to think that maybe I was the one who—you know what I mean? Not that it would be any different now after all these years, but just the same—"

"I know what you mean. I got it on May 5, 1864, in the battle of the Wilderness. It was my twenty-first birthday. What about you?"

"I wasn't at the Wilderness. I got it a month before the war ended. In the trenches before Petersburg. I was sixteen."

"Well, see you again maybe, Johnny."

"Yeah, see you, Yank."

An accountant for a large corporation who writes in his spare time, Henry T. Parry was born in Pennsylvania and graduated from New York University. "The author has told us comparatively little about himself," stated the editor Ellery Queen in the introduction to the first of Parry's twenty-some mystery stories. Parry is obviously a Sherlock Holmes fan—see his ingenious "The Baker Street Irregulars Murder Case." His stories appear largely in Ellery Queen's Mystery Magazine.

Thalia Corson should have died on the Brooklyn Bridge, but her husand's love called her back. Or was it love?

NINE

Clay-Shuttered Doors
Helen R. Hull

For months I have tried not to think about Thalia Corson. Anything may invoke her, with her langorous fragility, thin wrists and throat, her elusive face with its long eyelids. I can't quite remember her mouth. When I try to visualize her sharply I get soft pale hair, the lovely curve from her temple to chin, and eyes blue and intense. Her boy, Fletcher, has eyes like hers.

Today I came back to New York, and my taxi to an up-town hotel was held for a few minutes in Broadway traffic where the afternoon sunlight fused into a dazzle a great expanse of plateglass and elaborate show motor cars. The "Regal Eight"—Winchester Corson's establishment. I huddled as the taxi jerked ahead, in spite of knowledge that Winchester would scarcely peer out of that elegant setting into taxi cabs. I didn't wish to see him, nor would he care to see me. But the glimpse had started the whole affair churning again, and I went through it deliberately, hoping that it might have smoothed out into some rational explanation. Sometimes things do, if you leave them alone, like logs submerged in water that float up later, encrusted thickly. This affair won't add to itself. It stays unique and smooth, sliding through the rest of life without annexing a scrap of seaweed.

I suppose, for an outsider, it all begins with the moment on Brooklyn Bridge; behind that are the years of my friendship with Thalia. Our families had summer cottages on the Cape. She was just enough older, however, so that not until I had finished college did I catch up to any intimacy with her. She had married Winchester Corson, who at that time

120

fitted snugly into the phrase "a rising young man." During those first years, while his yeast sent up preliminary bubbles, Thalia continued to spend her summers near Boston, with Winchester coming for occasional weekends. Fletcher was, unintentionally, born there; he began his difficult existence by arriving as a seven-months baby. Two years later Thalia had a second baby to bring down with her. Those were the summers which gave my friendship for Thalia its sturdy roots. They made me wonder, too, why she had chosen Winchester Corson. He was personable enough; tall, with prominent dark eyes and full mouth under a neat mustache, restless hands, and an uncertain disposition. He could be a charming companion, sailing the catboat with dash, managing lobster parties on the shore; or he would, unaccountably, settle into a foggy grouch, when everyone—children and females particularly—was supposed to approach only on tiptoe, bearing burnt offerings. The last time he spent a fortnight there, before he moved the family to the new Long Island estate, I had my own difficulties with him. There had always been an undertone of sex in his attitude toward me, but I had thought "that's just his male conceit." That summer he was a nuisance, coming upon me with his insistent, messy kisses, usually with Thalia in the next room. They were the insulting kind of kisses that aren't at all personal, and I could have ended them fast enough if there hadn't been the complication of Thalia and my love for her. If I made Winchester angry he'd put an end to Thalia's relation to me. I didn't, anyway, want her to know what a fool he was. Of course she did know, but I thought then that I could protect her.

There are, I have decided, two ways with love. You can hold one love, knowing that, if it is a living thing, it must develop and change. That takes maturity, and care, and a consciousness of the other person. That was Thalia's way. Or you enjoy the beginning of love and, once you're past that, you have to hunt for a new love, because the excitement seems to be gone. Men like Winchester, who use all their brains on their jobs, never grow up; they go on thinking that preliminary stir and snap is love itself. Cut flowers, that was Winchester's idea, while to Thalia love was a tree.

But I said Brooklyn Bridge was the point at which the

affair had its start. It seems impossible to begin there, or anywhere, as I try to account for what happened. Ten years after the summer when Winchester made himself such a nuisance—that last summer the Corsons spent at the Cape—I went down at the end of the season for a week with Thalia and the children at the Long Island place. Winchester drove out for the weekend. The children were mournful because they didn't wish to leave the shore for school; a sharp September wind brought rain and fog down the Sound, and Winchester nourished all that Sunday a disagreeable grouch. I had seen nothing of them for most of the ten intervening years, as I had been first in France and then in China, after feature article stuff. The week had been pleasant: good servants, comfortable house, a half-moon of white beach below the drop of lawn; Thalia a stimulating listener, with Fletcher, a thin, eager boy of twelve, like her in his intensity of interest. Dorothy, a plump, pink child of ten, had no use for stories of French villages or Chinese temples. Nug, the wire-haired terrier, and her dolls were more immediate and convincing. Thalia was thin and noncommittal, except for her interest in what I had seen and done. I couldn't, for all my affection, establish any real contact. She spoke casually of the town house, of dinners she gave for Winchester, of his absorption in business affairs. But she was sheathed in polished aloofness and told me nothing of herself. She did say, one evening, that she was glad I was to be in New York that winter. Winchester, like his daughter Dorothy, had no interest in foreign parts once he had ascertained that I hadn't even seen the Chinese quarters of the motor company in which he was concerned. He had an amusing attitude toward me: careful indifference, no doubt calculated to put me in my place as no longer alluring. Thalia tried to coax him into listening to some of my best stories. "Tell him about the bandits, Mary"—but his sulkiness brought, after dinner, a casual explanation from her, untinged with apology. "He's working on an enormous project, a merging of several companies, and he's so soaked in it he can't come up for a breath."

In the late afternoon the maid set out high tea for us, before our departure for New York. Thalia suggested that perhaps one highball was enough if Winchester intended to drive over the wet roads. Win immediately mixed a second, asking if she had ever seen him in the least affected. "Be better for you than tea before a long damp drive, too." He clinked the ice in his glass. "Jazz you up a bit." Nug was begging for food and Thalia, bending to give him a corner of her sandwich, apparently did not hear Winchester. He looked about the room, a smug, owning look. The fire and candlelight shone in the heavy waxed rafters, made silver beads of the rain on the French windows. I watched him— heavier, more dominant, his prominent dark eyes and his lips sullen, as if the whiskey banked up his temper rather than appeased it.

Then Jim, the gardener, brought the car to the door; the children scrambled in. Dorothy wanted to take Nug, but her father said not if she wanted to sit with him and drive.

"How about chains, sir?" Jim held the umbrella for Thalia.

"Too damned noisy. Don't need them." Winchester slammed the door and slid under the wheel. Thalia and I, with Fletcher between us, sat comfortably in the rear.

"I like it better when Walter drives, don't you, Mother?" said Fletcher as we slid down the drive out to the road.

"Sh—Father likes to drive. And Walter likes Sunday off, too." Thalia's voice was cautious.

"It's too dark to see anything."

"I can see lots," announced Dorothy, whereupon Fletcher promptly turned the handle that pushed up the glass between the chauffeur's seat and the rear.

The heavy car ran smoothly over the wet narrow road, with an occasional rumble and flare of headlights as some car swung past. Not till we reached the turnpike was there much traffic. There Winchester had to slacken his speed for other shiny beetles slipping along through the rain. Sometimes he cut past a car, weaving back into line in the glaring teeth of a car rushing down on him, and Fletcher would turn inquiringly toward his mother. The gleaming, wet darkness and the smooth motion made me drowsy, and I paid little heed until we slowed in a congestion of cars at the approach to the bridge. Far below on the black river, spaced red and white stars suggested slow-moving tugs, and beyond, faint lights splintered in the rain hinted at the city.

"Let's look for the cliff dwellers, Mother."

Thalia leaned forward, her fine, sharp profile dimly out-
lined against the shifting background of arches, and Fletcher
slipped to his feet, his arm about her neck. "There!"

We were reaching the New York end of the bridge, and I
had a swift glimpse of their cliff dwellers—lights in massed
buildings, like ancient camp fires along a receding mountain
side. Just then Winchester nosed out of the slow line, Dorothy screamed, the light from another car tunnelled through
our windows, the car trembled under the sudden grip of
brakes, and like a crazy top spun sickeningly about, with a
final thud against the stone abutment. A shatter of glass, a
confusion of motor horns about us, a moment while the
tautness of shock held me rigid.

Around me that periphery of turmoil—the usual re-
criminations, "what the hell you think you're doing?"—the
shriek of a siren on an approaching motor cycle. Within the
circle I tried to move across the narrow space of the car.
Fletcher was crying; vaguely I knew that the door had
swung open, that Thalia was crouching on her knees, the
rain and the lights pouring on her head and shoulders; her
hat was gone, her wide fur collar looked like a drenched
and lifeless animal. "Hush, Fletcher." I managed to force
movement into my stiff body. "Are you hurt? Thalia—"
Then outside Winchester, with the bristling fury of panic,
was trying to lift her drooping head. "Thalia! My God, you
aren't hurt!" Someone focussed a searchlight on the car as
Winchester got his arms about her and lifted her out
through the shattered door.

Over the springing line of the stone arch I saw the cliff
dwellers' fires and I thought as I scrambled out to follow
Winchester, "She was leaning forward, looking at those,
and that terrific spin of the car must have knocked her head
on the door as it lurched open."

"Lay her down, man!" An important little fellow had
rushed up, a doctor evidently. "Lay her down, you fool!"
Someone threw down a robe, and Winchester, as if Thalia
were a drowned feather, knelt with her, laid her there on the
pavement. I was down beside her and the fussy little man
also. She did look drowned, drowned in that beating sea of
tumult, that terrific honking of motors, unwilling to stop an

instant even for—was it death? Under the white glare of headlights her lovely face had the empty shallowness, the husklikeness of death. The little doctor had his pointed beard close to her breast; he lifted one of her long eyelids. "She's just fainted, eh, doctor?" Winchester's angry voice tore at him.

The little man rose slowly. "She your wife? I'm sorry. Death must have been instantaneous. A blow on the temple."

With a kind of roar Winchester was down there beside Thalia, lifting her, her head lolling against his shoulder, his face bent over her. "Thalia! Thalia! Do you hear? Wake up!" I think he even shook her in his baffled fright and rage. "Thalia, do you hear me? I want you to open your eyes. You weren't hurt. That was nothing." And then, "Dearest, you must!" and more words, frantic, wild words, mouthed close to her empty face. I touched his shoulder, sick with pity, but he staggered up to his feet, lifting her with him. Fletcher pressed shivering against me, and I turned for an instant to the child. Then I heard Thalia's voice, blurred and queer, "You called me, Win?" and Winchester's sudden, triumphant laugh. She was standing against his shoulder, still with that husklike face, but she spoke again, "You did call me?"

"Here, let's get out of this." Winchester was again the efficient, competent man of affairs. The traffic cops were shouting, the lines of cars began to move. Winchester couldn't start his motor. Something had smashed. His card and a few words left responsibility with an officer, and even as an ambulance shrilled up, he was helping Thalia into a taxi. "You take the children, will you?" to me, and "Get her another taxi, will you?" to the officer. He had closed the taxi door after himself, and was gone, leaving us to the waning curiosity of passing cars. As we rode off in a second taxi, I had a glimpse of the little doctor, his face incredulous, his beard wagging, as he spoke to the officer.

Dorothy was, characteristically, tearfully indignant that her father had left her to me. Fletcher was silent as we bumped along under the elevated tracks, but presently he tugged at my sleeve, and I heard his faint whisper. "What is it?" I asked.

"Is my mother really dead?" he repeated.

"Of course not, Fletcher. You saw her get into the cab with your father."

"Why didn't Daddy take us too?" wailed Dorothy, and I had to turn to her, although my nerves echoed her question.

The house door swung open even as the taxi bumped the curb, and the butler hurried out with an umbrella which we were too draggled to need.

"Mr. Corson instructed me to pay the man, madam." He led us into the hall, where a waiting maid popped the children at once into the tiny elevator.

"Will you wait for the elevator, madam? The library is one flight." The butler led me up the stairs, and I dropped into a low chair near the fire, vaguely aware of the long, narrow room, with discreet gold of the walls giving back light from soft lamps. "I'll tell Mr. Corson you have come."

"Is Mrs. Corson—does she seem all right?" I asked.

"Quite, madam. It was a fortunate accident, with no one hurt."

Well, perhaps it had addled my brain! I waited in a kind of numbness for Winchester to come.

Presently he strode in, his feet silent on the thick rugs.

"Sorry," he began, abruptly. "I wanted to look the children over. Not a scratch on them. You're all right, of course?"

"Oh, yes. But Thalia—"

"She won't even have a doctor. I put her straight to bed—she's so damned nervous, you know. Hot-water bottles—she was cold. I think she's asleep now. Said she'd see you in the morning. You'll stay here, of course." He swallowed in a gulp the whiskey he had poured. "Have some, Mary? Or would you like something hot?"

"No, thanks. If you're sure she's all right I'll go to bed."

"Sure?" His laugh was defiant. "Did that damn fool on the bridge throw a scare into you? He gave me a bad minute, I'll say. If that car hadn't cut in on me— I told Walter last week the brakes needed looking at. They shouldn't grab like that. Might have been serious."

"Since it wasn't—" I rose, wearily, watching him pour

amber liquid slowly into his glass—"if you'll have someone show me my room—"

"After Chinese bandits, a little skid ought not to matter to you." His prominent eyes gleamed hostilely at me; he wanted some assurance offered that the skidding wasn't his fault, that only his skill had saved all our lives.

"I can't see Thalia?" I said.

"She's asleep. Nobody can see her." His eyes moved coldly from my face, down to my muddy shoes. "Better give your clothes to the maid for a pressing. You're smeared quite a bit."

I woke early, with clear September sun at the windows of the room, with blue sky behind the sharp city contours beyond the windows. There was none too much time to make the morning train for Albany, where I had an engagement that day, an interview for an article. The maid who answered my ring insisted on serving breakfast to me in borrowed elegance of satin negligee. Mrs. Corson was resting, and would see me before I left. Something—the formality and luxury, the complicated household so unlike the old days at the Cape—accented the queer dread which had filtered all night through my dreams.

I saw Thalia for only a moment. The heavy silk curtains were drawn against the light and in the dimness her face seemed to gather shadows.

"Are you quite all right, Thalia?" I hesitated beside her bed, as if my voice might tear apart the veils of drowsiness in which she rested.

"Why, yes—" as if she wondered. Then she added, so low that I wasn't sure what I heard, "It is hard to get back in."

"What, Thalia?" I bent toward her.

"I'll be myself once I've slept enough." Her voice was clearer. "Come back soon, won't you, Mary?" Then her eyelids closed and her face merged into the shadows of the room. I tiptoed away, thinking she slept.

It was late November before I returned to New York. Freelancing has a way of drawing herrings across your trail and, when I might have drifted back in early November, a younger sister wanted me to come home to Arlington for her marriage. I had written to Thalia, first a note of courtesy for my week with her, and then a letter begging for news. Like many people of charm, she wrote indifferent letters, stiff and childlike, lacking in her personal quality. Her brief reply was more unsatisfactory than usual. The children were away in school, lots of cold rainy weather, everything was going well. At the end, in writing unlike hers, as if she scribbled the line in haste, "I am lonely. When are you coming?" I answered that I'd show up as soon as the wedding was over.

The night I reached Arlington was rainy, too, and I insisted upon a taxi equipped with chains. My brother thought that amusing, and at dinner gave the family an exaggerated account of my caution. I tried to offer him some futile sisterly advice and, to point up my remarks, told about that drive in from Long Island with the Corsons. I had never spoken of it before; I found that an inexplicable inhibition kept me from making much of a story.

"Well, nothing happened, did it?" Richard was triumphant.

"A great deal might have," I insisted. "Thalia was stunned, and I was disagreeably startled."

"Thalia was stunned, was she?" An elderly cousin of ours from New Jersey picked out that item. I saw her fitting it into some pigeon hole, but she said nothing until late that evening when she stopped at the door of my room.

"Have you seen Thalia Corson lately?" she asked.

"I haven't been in New York since September."

She closed the door and lowered her voice, a kind of avid curiosity riding astride the decorous pity she expressed.

"I called there, one day last week. I didn't know what was the matter with her. I hadn't heard of that accident."

I waited, an old antagonism for my proper cousin blurring the fear that shot up through my thoughts.

"Thalia was always *individual*, of course." She used the word like a reproach. "But she had *savoir faire*. But now she's—well—*queer*. Do you suppose her head was affected?"

"How is she queer?"

"She looks miserable, too. Thin and white."

"But how—"

"I am telling you, Mary. She was quite rude. First she didn't come down for ever so long, although I sent up word that I'd come up to her room if she was resting. Then her whole manner—well, I was really offended. She scarcely heard a word I said to her, just sat with her back to a window so I couldn't get a good look at her. When I said, 'You don't look like yourself,' she actually sneered. 'Myself?' she said. 'How do you know?' Imagine! I tried to chatter along as if I noticed nothing. I flatter myself I can manage awkward moments rather well. But Thalia sat there and I am sure she muttered under her breath. Finally I rose to go and I said, meaning well, 'You'd better take a good rest. You look half dead.' Mary, I wish you'd seen the look she gave me! Really I was frightened. Just then their dog came in, you know, Dorothy's little terrier. Thalia used to be silly about him. Well, she actually tried to hide in the folds of the curtain, and I don't wonder! The dog was terrified at her. He crawled on his belly out of the room. Now she must have been cruel to him if he acts like that. I think Winchester should have a specialist. I didn't know how to account for any of it; but of course a blow on the head can affect a person."

Fortunately my mother interrupted us just then, and I didn't, by my probable rudeness, give my cousin reason to suppose that the accident had affected me, too. I sifted through her remarks and decided they might mean only that Thalia found her more of a bore than usual. As for Nug, perhaps he retreated from the cousin! During the next few days the house had so much wedding turmoil that she found a chance only for a few more dribbles: one that Thalia had given up all her clubs—she had belonged to several—the other that she had sent the children to boarding schools instead of keeping them at home. "Just when her husband is doing so well, too!"

I was glad when the wedding party had departed, and I could plan to go back to New York. Personally I think a low-caste Chinese wedding is saner and more interesting than a modern American affair. My cousin "should think I could stay home with the family," and "couldn't we go to New York together, if I insisted upon gadding off?" We couldn't. I saw to that. She hoped that I'd look up Thalia. Maybe I could advise Winchester about a specialist.

I did telephone as soon as I got in. That sentence "I am lonely," in her brief note kept recurring. Her voice sounded thin and remote, a poor connection, I thought. She was sorry. She was giving a dinner for Winchester that evening. The next day?

I had piles of proof to wade through that next day, and it was late afternoon when I finally went to the Corson house. The butler looked doubtful but I insisted, and he left me in the hall while he went off with my card. He returned, a little smug in his message: Mrs. Corson was resting and had left word she must not be disturbed. Well, you can't protest to a perfect butler, and I started down the steps, indignant, when a car stopped in front of the house, a liveried chauffeur opened the door, and Winchester emerged. He glanced at me in the twilight and extended an abrupt hand.

"Would Thalia see you?" he asked.

"No." For a moment I hoped he might convoy me past the butler. "Isn't she well? She asked me to come to-day."

"I hoped she'd see you." Winchester's hand smoothed at his little mustache. "She's just tired from her dinner last night. She overexerted herself, was quite the old Thalia." He looked at me slowly in the dusk, and I had a brief feeling that he was really looking at me, no, *for* me, for the first time in all our meetings, as if he considered me without relation to himself for once. "Come in again, will you?" He thrust away whatever else he thought of saying. "Thalia really would like to see you. Can I give you a lift?"

"No, thanks. I need a walk." As I started off I knew the moment had just missed some real significance. If I had ventured a question—but, after all, what could I ask him? He had said that Thalia was "just tired." That night I sent a note to her, saying I had called and asking when I might see her.

She telephoned me the next day. Would I come in for Thanksgiving? The children would be home, and she wanted an old-fashioned day, everything but the sleigh ride New York couldn't furnish. Dinner would be at six, for the children; perhaps I could come in early. I felt a small grievance at being put off for almost a week, but I promised to come.

That was the week I heard gossip about Winchester, in the curious devious way of gossip. Atlantic City, and a gaudy lady. Someone having an inconspicuous fortnight of convalescence there had seen them. I wasn't surprised, except perhaps that Winchester chose Atlantic City. Thalia was too fine; he couldn't grow up to her. I wondered how much she knew. She must, years ago, with her sensitiveness, have discovered that Winchester was stationary so far as love went and, being stationary himself, was inclined to move the object toward which he directed his passion.

On Thursday, as I walked across Central Park, gaunt and deserted in the chilly afternoon light, I decided that Thalia probably knew more about Winchester's affairs than gossip had given me. Perhaps that was why she had sent the children away. He had always been conventionally discreet, but discretion would be a tawdry coin among Thalia's shining values.

I was shown up to the nursery, with a message from Thalia that she would join me there soon. Fletcher seemed glad to see me, in a shy, excited way, and stood close to my chair while Dorothy wound up her phonograph for a dance record and pirouetted about us with her doll.

"Mother keeps her door tight locked all the time," whispered Fletcher doubtfully. "We can't go in. This morning I knocked and knocked but no one answered."

"Do you like your school?" I asked cheerfully.

"I like my home better." His eyes, so like Thalia's with their long, arched lids, had young bewilderment under their lashes.

"See me!" called Dorothy. "Watch me do this!"

While she twirled I felt Fletcher's thin body stiffen against my arm, as if a kind of panic froze him. Thalia stood in the doorway. Was the boy afraid of her? Dorothy wasn't. She cried, "See me, Mother! Look at me!" and in her lusty confusion, I had a moment to look at Thalia before she greeted me. She was thin, but she had always been that. She did not heed Dorothy's shrieks, but watched Fletcher, a kind of slanting dread on her white, proud face. I had thought, that week on Long Island, that she shut herself away from me, refusing to restore the intimacy of ten years earlier. But now a stiff loneliness hedged her as if she were rimmed in ice and snow. She smiled. "Dear Mary," she said. At the sound of her voice I lost my slightly cherished injury that she had refused earlier to see me. "Let's go down to the library," she went on. "It's almost time for the turkey." I felt Fletcher break his intent watchfulness with a long sigh, and as the children went ahead of us, I caught at Thalia's arm. "Thalia—" She drew away, and her arm, under the soft flowing sleeve of dull blue stuff, was so slight it seemed brittle. I thought suddenly that she must have chosen that gown because it concealed so much beneath its lovely embroidered folds. "You aren't well, Thalia. What is it?"

"Well enough! Don't fuss about me." And even as I stared reproachfully she seemed to gather vitality, so that the dry pallor of her face became smooth ivory and her eyes were no longer hollow and distressed. "Come."

The dinner was amazingly like one of our old holidays. Winchester wore his best mood, the children were delighted and happy. Thalia, under the gold flames of the tall black candles, was a gracious and lovely hostess. I almost forgot my troublesome anxiety, wondering whether my imagination hadn't been playing me tricks.

We had coffee by the library fire and some of Winchester's old Chartreuse. Then he insisted upon exhibiting his new radio. Thalia demurred, but the children begged for a concert. "This is their party, Tally!" Winchester opened the doors of the old teakwood cabinet which housed the apparatus. Thalia sank back into the shadows of a wing chair, and I watched her over my cigarette. Off guard, she had relaxed into strange apathy. Was it the firelight or my unaccustomed Chartreuse? Her features seemed blurred as if a clumsy hand trying to trace a drawing made uncertain outlines. Strange groans and whirrs from the radio.

"Win, I can't stand it!" Her voice dragged from some great distance. "Not tonight." She swayed to her feet, her hands restless under the loose sleeves.

"Static," growled Winchester. "Wait a minute."

"No!" Again it was as if vitality flowed into her. "Come, children. You have had your party. Time to go upstairs. I'll go with you."

They were well trained, I thought. Kisses for their father, a curtsy from Dorothy for me, and a grave little hand extended by Fletcher. Then Winchester came toward the fire as the three of them disappeared.

"You're good for Thalia," he said, in an undertone. "She's—well, what do you make of her?"

"Why?" I fenced, unwilling to indulge him in my vague anxieties.

"You saw how she acted about the radio. She has whims like that. Funny, she was herself at dinner. Last week she gave a dinner for me, important affair, pulled it off brilliantly. Then she shuts herself up and won't open her door for days. I can't make it out. She's thin—"

"Have you had a doctor?" I asked, banally.

"That's another thing. She absolutely refuses. Made a fool of me when I brought one here. Wouldn't unlock her door. Says she just wants to rest. But—" he glanced toward the door—"do you know that fool on the bridge—that little runt? The other night, I swear I saw him rushing down the steps as I came home. Thalia just laughed when I asked about it."

Something clicked in my thoughts, a quick suspicion, drawing a parallel between her conduct and that of people I had seen in the East. Was it some drug? That lethargy, and the quick spring into vitality? Days behind a closed door—

"I wish you'd persuade her to go off for a few weeks. I'm frightfully pressed just now, in an important business matter, but if she'd go off—maybe you'd go with her?"

"Where, Winchester?" We both started, with the guilt of conspirators. Thalia came slowly into the room. "Where shall I go? Would you suggest—Atlantic City?"

"Perhaps. Although some place farther south this time of year—" Winchester's imperturbability seemed to me far worse than some slight sign of embarrassment; it marked him as so rooted in successful deceit whether Thalia's inquiry were innocent or not. "If Mary would go with you. I can't get away just now."

"I shall not go anywhere until your deal goes through. Then—" Thalia seated herself again in the wing chair. The hand she lifted to her cheek, fingers just touching her temple beneath the soft drift of hair, seemed transparent against the firelight. "Have you told Mary about your deal? Winchester plans to be the most important man on Automobile Row." Was there mockery in her tone? "I can't tell you the details, but he's buying out all the rest."

"Don't be absurd. Not all of them. It's a big merging of companies, that's all."

"We entertain the lords at dinner, and in some mysterious way that smooths the merging. It makes a wife almost necessary."

"Invite Mary to the next shebang, and let her see how well you do it." Winchester was irritated. "For all your scoffing, there's as much politics to being president of such a concern as of the United States."

"Yes, I'll invite Mary. Then she'll see that you don't really want to dispense with me—yet."

"Good God, I meant for a week or two."

As Winchester, lighting a cigarette, snapped the head from several matches in succession, I moved my chair a little backward, distressed. There was a thin wire of significance drawn so taut between the two that I felt at any moment it might splinter in my face.

"It's so lucky—" malice flickered on her thin face—"that you weren't hurt in that skid on the bridge, Mary. Winchester would just have tossed you in the river to conceal your body."

"If you're going over that again!" Winchester strode out of the room. As Thalia turned her head slightly to watch him, her face and throat had the taut rigidity of pain so great that it congeals the nerves.

I was silent. With Thalia I had never dared intrude except when she admitted me. In another moment she too had risen. "You'd better go home, Mary," she said, slowly. "I might tell you things you wouldn't care to live with."

I tried to touch her hand, but she retreated. If I had been wiser or more courageous, I might have helped her. I shall always have that regret, and that can't be much better to live with than whatever she might have told me. All I could say was stupidly, "Thalia, if there's anything I can do! You know I love you."

"Love? That's a strange word," she said, and her laugh in the quiet room was like the shrilling of a grasshopper on a hot afternoon. "One thing I will tell you." (She stood now on the stairway above me.) "Love has no power. It never shouts out across great space. Only fear and self-desire are strong."

Then she had gone, and the butler appeared silently, to lead me to the little dressing room.

"The car is waiting for you, madam," he assured me, opening the door. I didn't want it, but Winchester was waiting, too, hunched angrily in a corner.

"That's the way she acts," he began. "Now you've seen her I'll talk about it. Thalia never bore grudges, you know that."

"It seems deeper than a grudge," I said cautiously.

"That reference to the—the accident. That's a careless remark I made. I don't even remember just what I said. Something entirely inconsequential. Just that it was damned lucky no one was hurt when I was putting this merger across. You know if it'd got in the papers it would have queered me. Wrecking my own car—there's always a suspicion you've been drinking. She picked it up and won't drop it. It's like a fixed idea. If you can suggest something. I want her to see a nerve specialist. What does she do behind that locked door?"

"What about Atlantic City?" I asked, abruptly. I saw his dark eyes bulge, trying to ferret out my meaning, there in the dusky interior of the car.

"A week there with you might do her good." That was all he would say, and I hadn't courage enough to accuse him, even in Thalia's name.

"At least you'll try to see her again," he said, as the car stopped in front of my apartment house.

I couldn't sleep that night. I felt that just over the edge of my squirming thoughts there lay clear and whole the meaning of it all, but I couldn't reach past thought. And then, stupidly enough, I couldn't get up the next day. Just a feverish cold, but the doctor insisted on a week in bed and subdued me with warnings about influenza.

I had begun to feel steady enough on my feet to consider venturing outside my apartment when the invitation came, for a formal dinner at the Corson's. Scrawled under the engraving was a line, "Please come. T." I sent a note, explaining that I had been ill, and that I should come—the dinner was a fortnight away—unless I stayed too wobbly.

I meant that night to arrive properly with the other guests, but my watch, which had never before done anything except lose a few minutes a day, had gained an unsuspected hour. Perhaps the hands stuck—perhaps— Well, I was told I was early, Thalia was dressing, and only the children, home for the Christmas holidays, were available. So I went again to the nursery. Dorothy was as plump and unconcerned as ever, but Fletcher had a strained, listening effect and he looked too thin and white for a little boy. They were having their supper on a small table, and Fletcher kept going to the door, looking out into the hall. "Mother promised to come up," he said.

The maid cleared away their dishes, and Dorothy, who was in a beguiling mood, chose to sit on my lap and entertain me with stories. One was about Nug the terrier; he had been sent out to the country because Mother didn't like him any more.

"I think," interrupted Fletcher, "she likes him, but he has a queer notion about her."

"She doesn't like him," repeated Dorothy. Then she dismissed that subject, and Fletcher too, for curiosity about the old silver chain I wore. I didn't notice that the boy had slipped away, but he must have gone down stairs; for presently his fingers closed over my wrist, like a frightened bird's claw, and I turned to see him, trembling, his eyes dark with terror. He couldn't speak but he clawed at me, and I shook Dorothy from my knees and let him pull me out to the hall.

"What is it, Fletcher?" He only pointed down the stairway, toward his mother's door, and I fled down those stairs. *What* had the child seen?

"The door wasn't locked—" he gasped behind me—"I opened it very still and went in—"

I pushed it ajar. Thalia sat before her dressing table, with the threefold mirrors reiterating like a macabre symphony her rigid, contorted face. Her gown, burnished blue and green like peacock's feathers, sheathed her gaudily, and silver, blue, and green chiffon clouded her shoulders. Her hands clutched at the edge of the dressing table. For an instant I could not move, thrust through with a terror like the

136

boy's. Then I stumbled across the room. Before I reached her, the mirrors echoed her long shudder, her eyelids dragged open, and I saw her stare at my reflection wavering toward her. Then her hands relaxed, moved quickly toward the crystal jars along the heavy glass of the table and, without a word, she leaned softly forward, to draw a scarlet line along her white lips.

"How cold it is in here," I said, stupidly, glancing toward the windows, where the heavy silk damask, drawn across, lay in motionless folds. "Fletcher said—" I was awkward, an intruder.

"He startled me." Her voice came huskily. She rouged her hollow cheeks. It was as if she drew another face for herself. "I didn't have time to lock the door." Then turning, she sought him out, huddled at the doorway, like a moth on a pin of fear. "It wasn't nice of you, Son. It's all right now. You see?" She rose, drawing her lovely scarf over her shoulders. "You should never open closed doors." She blew him a kiss from her finger tips. "Now run along and forget you were so careless."

The icy stir of air against my skin had ceased. I stared at her, my mind racing back over what I knew of various drugs and the stigmata of their victims. But her eyes were clear and undilated, a little piteous. "This," she said, "is the last time. I can't endure it." And then, with that amazing flood of vitality, as if a sudden connection had been made and current flowed again, "Come, Mary. It is time we were down stairs."

I thought Fletcher peered over the railing as we went down. But a swift upward glance failed to detect him.

The dinner itself I don't remember definitely except that it glittered and sparkled, moving with slightly alcoholic wit through elaborate courses, while I sat like an abashed poor relation at a feast, unable to stop watching Thalia, wondering whether my week of fever had given me a tendency to hallucinations. At the end a toast was proposed, to Winchester Corson and his extraordinary success. "It's done, then?" Thalia's gaiety had sudden malice—as she looked across at Winchester, seating himself after a slightly pompous speech. "Sealed and cemented forever?"

"Thanks to his charming wife, too," cried a plump, bald man, waving his glass. "A toast to Mrs. Corson!"

Thalia rose, her rouge like flecked scarlet on white paper. One hand drew her floating scarf about her throat, and her painted lips moved without a sound. There was an instant of agitated discomfort, as the guests felt their mood broken so abruptly, into which her voice pierced, thin, high. "I—deserve—such a toast—"

I pushed back my chair and reached her side.

"I'll take her—" I saw Winchester's face, wine-flushed, angry rather than concerned. "Come, Thalia."

"Don't bother. I'll be all right—now." But she moved ahead of me so swiftly that I couldn't touch her. I thought she tried to close her door against me, but I was too quick for that. The silver candelabra still burned above the mirrors. "Mary!" Her voice was low again as she spoke a telephone number. "Tell him *at once*." She stood away from me, her face a white mask with spots of scarlet, her peacock dress ashimmer. I did as I was bid and when I had said, "Mrs. Corson wishes you at once," there was an emptiness where a man's voice had come which suggested a sudden leap out of a room somewhere.

"I can never get in again!" Her fingers curled under the chiffon scarf. "Never! The black agony of fighting back— If he—" She bent her head, listening. "Go down to the door and let him in," she said.

I crept down the stairs. Voices from the drawing-room. Winchester was seeing the party through. Almost as I reached the door and opened it I found him there: the little doctor with the pointed beard. He brushed past me up the stairs. He knew the way, then! I was scarcely surprised to find Thalia's door fast shut when I reached it. Behind it came not a sound. Fletcher, like an unhappy sleepwalker, his eyes heavy, slipped down beside me, clinging to my hand. I heard farewells, churring of taxis and cars. Then Winchester came up the stairs.

"She's shut you out?" He raised his fist and pounded on the door. "I'm going to stop this nonsense!"

"I sent for a doctor," I said. "He's in there."

"Is it—" his face was puffy and gray—"that same fool?"

Then the door opened, and the man confronted us.

138

"It is over," he said.

"What have you done to her?" Winchester lunged toward the door, but the little man's lifted hand had dignity enough somehow to stop him.

"She won't come back again." He spoke slowly. "You may look if you care to."

"She's dead?"

"She died—months ago. There on the bridge. But you called to her, and she thought you wanted—*her.*"

Winchester thrust him aside and strode into the room. I dared one glance and saw only pale hair shining on the pillow. Then Fletcher flung himself against me, sobbing, and I knelt to hold him close against the fear we both felt.

What Winchester saw I never knew. He hurled himself past us, down the stairs. And Thalia was buried with the coffin lid fast closed under the flowers.

A publisher's granddaughter, Helen Hull said she can't "remember when I did not intend to write." Born in Michigan in about 1889, she was educated at Michigan State College, the University of Michigan, and the University of Chicago. Her mystery novel, A Tapping on the Wall, *won a college writing prize in 1960. Her best known work is the story "Clay-Shuttered Doors."*

Warburg Tantavul had refused to permit his son to marry cousin Arabella. So why did his will promise such a great reward for the birth of their first child?

TEN

The Jest of Warburg Tantavul

Seabury Quinn

Warburg Tantavul was dying. Little more than skin and bones, he lay propped up with pillows in the big sleigh bed and smiled as though he found the thought of dissolution faintly amusing.

Even in comparatively good health the man was never prepossessing. Now, wasted with disease, that smile of self-sufficient satisfaction on his wrinkled face, he was nothing less than hideous. The eyes, which nature had given him, were small, deep-set and ruthless. The mouth, which his own thoughts had fashioned through the years, was wide and thin-lipped, almost colorless, and even in repose was tightly drawn against his small and curiously perfect teeth. Now, as he smiled, a flickering light, lambent as the quick reflection of an unseen flame, flared in his yellowish eyes, and a hard white line of teeth showed on his lower lip, as if he bit it to hold back a chuckle.

"You're still determined that you'll marry Arabella?" he asked his son, fixing his sardonic, mocking smile on the young man.

"Yes, Father, but—"

"No buts, my boy"—this time the chuckle came, low and muted, but at the same time glassy-hard—"no buts. I've told you I'm against it, and you'll rue it to your dying day if you should marry her; but"—he paused, and breath rasped in his wizened throat—"but go ahead and marry her, if your heart's set on it. I've said my say and warned you—heh, boy, never say your poor old father didn't warn you!"

He lay back on his piled-up pillows for a moment, swallowing convulsively, as if to force the fleeting life-breath back, then, abruptly: "Get out," he ordered. "Get out and stay out, you poor fool; but remember what I've said."

"Father," young Tantavul began, stepping toward the bed, but the look of sudden concentrated fury in the old man's tawny eyes halted him in midstride.

"Get—out—I—said," his father snarled, then, as the door closed softly on his son:

"Nurse—hand—me—that—picture." His breath was coming slowly, now, in shallow labored gasps, but his withered fingers writhed in a gesture of command, pointing to the silver-framed photograph of a woman which stood upon a little table in the bedroom windowbay.

He clutched the portrait as if it were some precious relic, and for a minute let his eyes rove over it. "Lucy," he whispered hoarsely, and now his words were thick and indistinct, "Lucy, they'll be married, 'spite of all that I have said. They'll be married, Lucy, d'ye hear?" Thin and high-pitched as a child's, his voice rose to a piping treble as he grasped the picture's silver frame and held it level with his face. "They'll be married, Lucy dear, and they'll have—"

Abruptly as a penny whistle's note is stilled when no more air is blown in it, old Tantavul's cry hushed. The picture, still grasped in his hands, fell to the tufted coverlet, the man's lean jaw relaxed and he slumped back on his pillows with a shadow of the mocking smile still in his glazing eyes.

Etiquette requires that the nurse await the doctor's confirmation at such times, so, obedient to professional dictates, Miss Williamson stood by the bed until I felt the dead man's pulse and nodded; then with the skill of years of practice she began her offices, bandaging the wrists and jaws and ankles that the body might be ready when the representative of Martin's Funeral Home came for it.

My friend de Grandin was annoyed. Arms akimbo, knuckles on his hips, his black-silk kimono draped round him like a mourning garment, he voiced his plaint in no uncertain terms. In fifteen little so small minutes he must leave for the theatre, and that son and grandson of a filthy swine who was the florist had not delivered his gardenia. And was it not a fact that he could not go forth without a fresh gardenia for his lapel? But certainly. Why did that *sale chameau* procrastinate? Why did he delay delivering that unmentionable flower till this unspeakable time of night? He was Jules de Grandin, he, and not to be oppressed by any species of a goat who called himself a florist. But no. It must not be. It should not be, by blue! He would—

"Axin' yer pardon, sir," Nora McGinnis broke in from the study door, "there's a Miss an' Mr. Tantavul to see ye, an'—"

"Bid them be gone, *ma charmeuse*. Request that they jump in the bay—*Grand Dieu*"—he cut his oratory short—*"les enfants dans le bois!"*

Truly, there was something reminiscent of the Babes in the Wood in the couple who had followed Nora to the study door. Dennis Tantavul looked even younger and more boyish than I remembered him, and the girl beside him was so childish in appearance that I felt a quick, instinctive pity for her. Plainly they were frightened, too, for they clung hand to hand like frightened children going past a graveyard, and in their eyes was that look of sick terror I had seen so often when the X-ray and blood test confirmed preliminary diagnosis of carcinoma.

"Monsieur, Mademoiselle!" The little Frenchman gathered his kimono and his dignity about him in a single sweeping gesture as he struck his heels together and bowed stiffly from the hips. "I apologize for my unseemly words. Were it not that I have been subjected to a terrible, calamitous misfortune, I should not so far have forgotten myself—"

The girl's quick smile cut through his apology. "We understand," she reassured. "We've been through trouble, too, and have come to Dr. Trowbridge—"

"Ah, then I have permission to withdraw?" he bowed again and turned upon his heel, but I called him back.

"Perhaps you can assist us," I remarked as I introduced the callers.

"The honor is entirely mine, Mademoiselle," he told her as he raised her fingers to his lips. "You and Monsieur your brother—"

"He's not my brother," she corrected. "We're cousins. That's why we've called on Dr. Trowbridge."

De Grandin tweaked the already needle-sharp points of his small blond mustache. *"Pardonnez-moi?"* he begged. "I have resided in your country but a little time; perhaps I do not understand the language fluently. It is because you and Monsieur are cousins that you come to see the doctor? Me, I am dull and stupid like a pig; I fear I do not comprehend."

Dennis Tantavul replied: "It's not because of the relationship, Doctor—not entirely, at any rate, but—"

He turned to me: "You were at my father's bedside when he died; you remember what he said about marrying Arabella?"

I nodded.

"There was something—some ghastly, hidden threat concealed in his warning, Doctor. It seemed as if he jeered at me—dared me to marry her, yet—"

"Was there some provision in his will?" I asked.

"Yes, sir," the young man answered. "Here it is." From his pocket he produced a folded parchment, opened it and indicated a paragraph:

> "To my son Dennis Tantavul I give, devise and be-
> queath all my property of every kind and sort, real,
> personal and mixed, of which I may die seized and
> possessed, or to which I may be entitled, in the
> event of his marrying Arabella Tantavul, but should
> he not marry the said Arabella Tantavul, then it is
> my will that he receive only one half of my estate,
> and that the residue thereof go to the said Arabella
> Tantavul, who has made her home with me since
> childhood and occupied the relationship of daugh-
> ter to me."

"H'm," I returned the document, "this looks as if he really wanted you to marry your cousin, even though—"

"And see here, sir," Dennis interrupted, "here's an envelope we found in Father's papers."

Sealed with red wax, the packet of heavy, opaque parchment was addressed:

"To my children, Dennis and Arabella Tantavul, to
be opened by them upon the occasion of the birth
of their first child."

De Grandin's small blue eyes were snapping with the
flickering light they showed when he was interested.
"Monsieur Dennis," he took the thick envelope from the
caller, "Dr. Trowbridge has told me something of your father's death-bed scene. There is a mystery about this business. My suggestion is you read the message now—"

"No, sir. I won't do that. My father didn't love me—
sometimes I think he hated me—but I never disobeyed a
wish that he expressed, and I don't feel at liberty to do so
now. It would be like breaking faith with the dead. But"—
he smiled a trifle shamefacedly—"Father's lawyer Mr.
Bainbridge is out of town on business, and it will be his duty
to probate the will. In the meantime I'd feel better if the will
and this envelope were in other hands than mine. So we
came to Dr. Trowbridge to ask him to take charge of them till
Mr. Bainbridge gets back, meanwhile—"

"Yes, Monsieur, meanwhile?" de Grandin prompted as
the young man paused.

"You know human nature, Doctor," Dennis turned to
me; "no one can see farther into hidden meanings than the
man who sees humanity with its mask off, the way a doctor
does. D'ye think Father might have been delirious when he
warned me not to marry Arabella, or—" His voice trailed
off, but his troubled eyes were eloquent.

"H'm," I shifted uncomfortably in my chair, "I can't see
any reason for hesitating, Dennis. That bequest of all your
father's property in the event you marry Arabella seems to
indicate his true feelings." I tried to make my words convincing, but the memory of old Tantavul's dying words
dinned in my ears. There had been something gloating in
his voice as he told the picture that his son and niece would
marry.

De Grandin caught the hint of hesitation in my tone.
"Monsieur," he asked Dennis, "will not you tell us of the
antecedents of your father's warning? Dr. Trowbridge is
perhaps too near to see the situation clearly. Me, I have no

144

knowledge of your father or your family. You and Mademoiselle are strangely like. The will describes her as having lived with you since childhood. Will you kindly tell us how it came about?"

The Tantavuls were, as he said, strangely similar. Anyone might easily have taken them for twins. Like as two plaster portraits from the same mold were their small straight noses, sensitive mouths, curling pale-gold hair.

Now, once more hand in hand, they sat before us on the sofa, and as Dennis spoke I saw the frightened, haunted look creep back into their eyes.

"Do you remember us as children, Doctor?" he asked me.

"Yes, it must have been some twenty years ago they called me out to see you youngsters. You'd just moved into the old Stephens house, and there was a deal of gossip about the strange gentleman from the West with his two small children and Chinese cook, who greeted all the neighbors' overtures with churlish rebuffs and never spoke to anyone."

"What did you think of us, sir?"

"H'm; I thought you and your sister—as I thought her then—had as fine a case of measles as I'd ever seen."

"How old were we then, do you remember?"

"Oh, you were something like three; the little girl was half your age, I'd guess."

"Do you recall the next time you saw us?"

"Yes, you were somewhat older then; eight or ten, I'd say. That time it was the mumps. You were queer, quiet little shavers. I remember asking if you thought you'd like a pickle, and you said, 'No, thank you, sir, it hurts.'"

"It did, too, sir. Every day Father made us eat one; stood over us with a whip till we'd chewed the last morsel."

"What?"

The young folks nodded solemnly as Dennis answered, "Yes, sir; every day. He said he wanted to check up on the progress we were making."

For a moment he was silent, then: "Dr. Trowbridge, if anyone treated you with studied cruelty all your life—if you'd never had a kind word or gracious act from that person in all your memory, then suddenly that person offered you a favor—made it possible for you to gratify your dearest wish, and threatened to penalize you if you failed to do so, wouldn't you be suspicious? Wouldn't you suspect some sort of dreadful practical joke?"

"I don't think I quite understand."

"Then listen: in all my life I can't remember ever having seen my father smile, not really smile with friendliness, humor or affection, I mean. My life—and Arabella's, too—was one long persecution at his hands. I was two years or so old when we came to Harrisonville, I believe, but I still have vague recollections of our Western home, of a house set high on a hill overlooking the ocean, and a wall with climbing vines and purple flowers on it, and a pretty lady who would take me in her arms and cuddle me against her breast and feed me ice cream from a spoon, sometimes. I have a sort of recollection of a little baby sister in that house, too, but these things are so far back in babyhood that possibly they were no more than childish fancies which I built up for myself and which I loved so dearly and so secretly they finally came to have a kind of reality for me.

"My real memories, the things I can recall with certainty, begin with a hurried train trip through hot, dry, uncomfortable country with my father and a strangely silent Chinese servant and a little girl they told me was my cousin Arabella.

"Father treated me and Arabella with impartial harshness. We were beaten for the slightest fault, and we had faults a-plenty. If we sat quietly we were accused of sulking and asked why we didn't go and play. If we played and shouted we were whipped for being noisy little brats.

"As we weren't allowed to associate with any of the neighbors' children we made up our own games. I'd be Geraint and Arabella would be Enid of the dovewhite feet, or perhaps I'd be King Arthur in the Castle Perilous, and she'd be the kind Lady of the Lake who gave him back his magic sword. And though we never mentioned it, both of us knew that whatever the adventure was, the false knight or giant I contended with was really my father. But when actual trouble came I wasn't an heroic figure.

"I must have been twelve or thirteen when I had my last thrashing. A little brook ran through the lower part of our land, and the former owners had widened it into a lily pond. The flowers had died out years before, but the outlines of the pool remained, and it was our favorite summer play place. We taught ourselves to swim—not very well, of course, but well enough—and as we had no bathing suits we used to go in in our underwear. When we'd finished swimming we'd lie in the sun until our underthings were dry, then slip into our outer clothing. One afternoon as we were splashing in the water, happy as a pair of baby otters, and nearer to shouting with laughter than we'd ever been before, I think, my father suddenly appeared on the bank.

" 'Come out o' there!' he shouted to me, and there was a kind of sharp, dry hardness in his voice I'd never heard before. "So this is how you spend your time?' he asked as I climbed up the bank. 'In spite of all I've done to keep you decent, you do a thing like this!'

" 'Why, Father, we were only swimming—' I began, but he struck me on the mouth.

" 'Shut up, you little rake!' he roared. 'I'll teach you!' He cut a willow switch and thrust my head between his knees; then while he held me tight as in a vice he flogged me with the willow till the blood came through my skin and stained my soaking cotton shorts. Then he kicked me back into the pool as a heartless master might a beaten dog.

"As I said, I wasn't an heroic figure. It was Arabella who came to my rescue. She helped me up the slippery bank and took me in her arms. 'Poor Dennie,' she said. 'Poor, poor Dennie. It was my fault, Dennie, dear, for letting you take me into the water!' Then she kissed me—the first time anyone had kissed me since the pretty lady of my half-remembered dreams. 'We'll be married on the very day that Uncle Warburg dies,' she promised, 'and I'll be so sweet and good to you, and you'll love me so dearly that we'll both forget these dreadful days.'

"We thought my father'd gone, but he must have stayed to see what we would say, for as Arabella finished he stepped from behind a rhododendron bush, and for the first time I heard him laugh. 'You'll be married, will you?' he asked. 'That would be a good joke—the best one of all. All right, go ahead—see what it gets you.'

"That was the last time he ever actually struck me, but from that time on he seemed to go out of his way to invent mental tortures for us. We weren't allowed to go to school,

147

but he had a tutor, a little rat-faced man named Ericson, come in to give us lessons, and in the evening he'd take the book and make us stand before him and recite. If either of us failed a problem in arithmetic or couldn't conjugate a French or Latin verb he'd wither us with sarcasm, and always as a finish to his diatribe he'd jeer at us about our wish to be married, and threaten us with something dreadful if we ever did it.

"So, Dr. Trowbridge, you see why I'm suspicious. It seems almost as if this provision in the will is part of some horrible practical joke my father prepared deliberately—as if he's waiting to laugh at us from the grave."

"I can understand your feelings, boy," I answered, "but—"

"'But' be damned and roasted on the hottest griddle in hell's kitchen!" Jules de Grandin interrupted. "The wicked dead one's funeral is at two tomorrow afternoon, *n'est-ce-pas?*

"*Très bien.* At eight tomorrow evening—or earlier, if it will be convenient—you shall be married. I shall esteem it a favor if you permit that I be best man; Dr. Trowbridge will give the bride away, and we shall have a merry time, by blue! You shall go upon a gorgeous honeymoon and learn how sweet the joys of love can be—sweeter for having been so long denied! And in the meantime we shall keep the papers safely till your lawyer returns.

"You fear the so unpleasant jest? *Mais non,* I think the jest is on the other foot, my friends, and the laugh on the other face!"

Warburg Tantavul was neither widely known nor popular, but the solitude in which he had lived had invested him with mystery; now the bars of reticence were down and the walls of isolation broken, upward of a hundred neighbors, mostly women, gathered in the Martin funeral chapel as the services began. The afternoon sun beat softly through the stained glass windows and glinted on the polished mahogany of the casket. Here and there it touched upon bright spots of color that marked a woman's hat or a man's tie. The solemn hush was broken by occasional whispers: "What'd he die of? Did he leave much? Were the two young folks his only heirs?"

Then the burial office: "Lord, Thou hast been our refuge from one generation to another . . . for a thousand years in Thy sight are but as yesterday . . . Oh teach us to number our days that we may apply our hearts unto wisdom. . . ."

As the final Amen sounded one of Mr. Martin's frock-coated young men glided forward, paused beside the casket, and made the stereotyped announcement: "Those who wish to say goodbye to Mr. Tantavul may do so at this time."

The grisly rite of the passing by the bier dragged on. I would have left the place; I had no wish to look upon the man's dead face and folded hands; but de Grandin took me firmly by the elbow, held me till the final curiosity-impelled female had filed past the body, then steered me quickly toward the casket.

He paused a moment at the bier, and it seemed to me there was a hint of irony in the smile that touched the corners of his mouth as he leant forward. *"Eh bien,* my old one; we know a secret, thou and I, *n'est-ce-pas?"* he asked the silent form before us.

I swallowed back an exclamation of dismay. Perhaps it was a trick of the uncertain light, perhaps one of those ghastly, inexplicable things which every doctor and embalmer meets with sometimes in his practice—the effect of desiccation from formaldehyde, the pressure of some tissue gas within the body, or something of the sort—at any rate, as Jules de Grandin spoke the corpse's upper lids drew back the fraction of an inch, revealing slits of yellow eye which seemed to glare at us with mingled hate and fury.

"Good heavens; come away!" I begged. "It seemed as if he *looked* at us, de Grandin!"

"Et puis—and if he did? I damn think I can trade him look for look, my friend. He was clever, that one, I admit it; but do not be mistaken, Jules de Grandin is nobody's imbecile."

The wedding took place in the rectory of St. Chrysostom's. Robed in stole and surplice, Dr. Bentley glanced benignly from Dennis to Arabella, then to de Grandin and me as he began: "Dearly beloved, we are gathered together here in the sight of God and in the face of this company to join together this man and this woman in holy matrimony. . . ." His round and ruddy face grew slightly stern as he admonished, "If any man can show just cause why they should not lawfully be joined together, let him now speak or else hereafter for ever hold his peace."

He paused the customary short, dramatic moment, and I thought I saw a hard, grim look spread on de Grandin's face. Very faint and far-off seeming, so faint that we could scarcely hear it, but gaining steadily in strength, there came a high, thin, screaming sound. Curiously, it seemed to me to resemble the long-drawn, wailing shriek of a freight train's whistle heard miles away upon a still and sultry summer night, weird, wavering and ghastly. Now it seemed to grow in shrillness, though its volume was no greater.

I saw a look of haunted fright leap into Arabella's eyes, saw Dennis' pale face go paler as the strident whistle sounded shriller and more shrill; then, as it seemed I could endure the stabbing of that needle sound no longer, it ceased abruptly, giving way to blessed, comforting silence. But through the silence came a burst of chuckling laughter, half breathless, half hysterical, wholly devilish: *Huh—hu-u-uh—hu-u-u-uh!* the final syllable drawn out until it seemed almost a groan.

"The wind, *Monsieur le Curé;* it was nothing but the wind," de Grandin told the clergyman sharply. "Proceed to marry them, if you will be so kind."

"Wind?" Dr. Bentley echoed. "I could have sworn I heard somebody laugh, but—"

"It is the wind, Monsieur; it plays strange tricks at times," the little Frenchman insisted, his small blue eyes as hard as frozen iron. "Proceed, if you will be so kind. We wait on you."

"Forasmuch as Dennis and Arabella have consented to be joined together in holy wedlock, I pronounce them man and wife," concluded Dr. Bentley, and de Grandin, ever gallant, kissed the bride upon the lips, and before we could restrain him, planted kisses on both Dennis' cheeks.

"*Cordieu,* I thought that we might have the trouble, for a time," he told me as we left the rectory.

"What *was* that awful shrieking noise we heard?" I asked.

"It was the wind, my friend," he answered in a hard, flat, toneless voice. "The ten times damned, but wholly ineffectual wind."

*   *   *

"So, then, little sinner, weep and wail for the burden of mortality you have assumed. Weep, wail, cry and breathe, my small and wrinkled one! Ha, you will not? *Pardieu,* I say you shall!"

Gently, but smartly, he spanked the small red infant's small red posterior with the end of a towel wrung out in hot water, and as the smacking impact sounded the tiny toothless mouth opened and a thin, high, piping squall of protest sounded. "Ah, that is better, *mon petit ami,*" he chuckled. "One cannot learn too soon that one must do as one is told, not as one wishes, in this world which you have just entered. Look to him, Mademoiselle," he passed the wriggling, bawling morsel of humanity to the nurse and turned to me as I bent over the table where Arabella lay. "How does the little mother, Friend Trowbridge?" he asked.

"U'm'mp," I answered noncommittally. "Bear a hand, here, will you? The perineum's pretty badly torn—have to do a quick repair job—"

"But in the morning she will have forgotten all the pain," laughed de Grandin as Arabella, swathed in blankets, was trundled from the delivery room. "She will gaze upon the little monkey-thing which I just caused to breathe the breath of life and vow it is the loveliest of all God's lovely creatures. She will hold it at her tender breast and smile on it, she will—*Sacré nom d'un rat vert,* what is that?"

From the nursery where, ensconced in wire trays, a score of newborn fragments of humanity slept or squalled, there came a sudden frightened scream—a woman's cry of terror.

We raced along the corridor, reached the glass-walled room and thrust the door back, taking care to open it no wider than was necessary, lest a draft disturb the carefully conditioned air of the place.

Backed against the farther wall, her face gone gray with fright, the nurse in charge was staring at the skylight with terror-widened eyes, and even as we entered she opened her lips to emit another scream.

"Desist, *ma bonne,* you are disturbing your small charges!" de Grandin seized the horrified girl's shoulder and administered a shake. Then: "What is it, Mademoiselle?" he whispered. "Do not be afraid to speak; we shall respect your confidence—but speak softly."

151

"It—it was up there!" she pointed with a shaking finger toward the black square of the skylight. "They'd just brought Baby Tantavul in, and I had laid him in his crib when I thought I heard somebody laughing. Oh"—she shuddered at the recollection—"it was awful! not really a laugh, but something more like a long-drawn-out hysterical groan. Did you ever hear a child tickled to exhaustion—you know how he moans and gasps for breath, and laughs, all at once? I think the fiends in hell must laugh like that!"

"Yes, yes, we understand," de Grandin nodded, "but tell us what occurred next."

"I looked around the nursery, but I was all alone here with the babies. Then it came again, louder, this time, and seemingly right above me. I looked up at the skylight, and—there it was!"

"It was a face, sir—just a face, with no body to it, and it seemed to float above the glass, then dip down to it, like a child's balloon drifting in the wind, and it looked right past me, down at Baby Tantavul, and laughed again."

"A face, you say, Mademoiselle—"

"Yes, sir, yes! The awfullest face I've ever seen. It was thin and wrinkled—all shriveled like a monkey—and as it looked at Baby Tantavul its eyes stretched open till their whites glared all around the irises, and the mouth opened, not widely, but as if it were chewing something it relished—and it gave that dreadful, cackling, jubilating laugh again. That's it! I couldn't think before, but it seemed as if that bodiless head were laughing with a sort of evil triumph, Dr. de Grandin!"

"H'm," he tweaked his tightly waxed mustache, "I should not wonder if it did, Mademoiselle." To me he whispered, "Stay with her, if you will, my friend, I'll see the supervisor and have her send another nurse to keep her company. I shall request a special watch for the small Tantavul. At present I do not think the danger is great, but mice do not play where cats are wakeful."

"Isn't he just lovely?" Arabella looked up from the small bald head that rested on her breast, and ecstasy was in her eyes. "I don't believe I ever saw so beautiful a baby!"

"*Tiens*, Madame, his voice is excellent, at any rate," de

Grandin answered with a grin, "and from what one may observe his appetite is excellent, as well."

Arabella smiled and patted the small creature's back. "You know, I never had a doll in my life," she confided. "Now I've got this dear little mite, and I'm going to be so happy with him. Oh, I wish Uncle Warburg were alive. I know this darling baby would soften even his hard heart.

"But I mustn't say such things about him, must I? He really wanted me to marry Dennis, didn't he? His will proved that. You think he wanted us to marry, Doctor?"

"I am persuaded that he did, Madame. Your marriage was his dearest wish, his fondest hope," the Frenchman answered solemnly.

"I felt that way, too. He was harsh and cruel to us when we were growing up, and kept his stony-hearted attitude to the end, but underneath it all there must have been some hidden stratum of kindness, some lingering affection for Dennis and me, or he'd never have put that clause in his will—"

"Nor have left this memorandum for you," de Grandin interrupted, drawing from an inner pocket the parchment envelope Dennis had entrusted to him the day before his father's funeral.

She started back as if he menaced her with a live scorpion, and instinctively her arms closed protectively around the baby at her bosom. "The—that—letter?" she faltered, her breath coming in short, smothered gasps. "I'd forgotten all about it. Oh, Dr. de Grandin, burn it. Don't let me see what's in it. I'm afraid!"

It was a bright May morning, without sufficient breeze to stir the leaflets on the maple trees outside the window, but as de Grandin held the letter out I thought I heard a sudden sweep of wind around the angle of the hospital, not loud, but shrewd and keen, like wind among the graveyard evergreens in autumn, and, curiously, there seemed a note of soft malicious laughter mingled with it.

The little Frenchman heard it, too, and for an instant he looked toward the window, and I thought I saw the flicker of an ugly sneer take form beneath the waxed ends of his mustache.

153

"Open it, Madame," he bade. "It is for you and Monsieur Dennis, and the little *Monsieur Bébé* here."

"I—I daren't—"

"Tenez, then Jules de Grandin does!" With his penknife he slit the heavy envelope, pressed suddenly against its ends so that its sides bulged, and dumped its contents on the counterpane. Ten fifty-dollar bills dropped on the coverlet. And nothing else.

"Five hundred dollars!" Arabella gasped. "Why—"

"A birthday gift for *petit Monsieur Bébé,* one surmises," laughed de Grandin. *"Eh bien,* the old one had a sense of humor underneath his ugly outward shell, it seems. He kept you on the tenterhooks lest the message in this envelope contained dire things, while all the time it was a present of congratulation."

"But such a gift from Uncle Warburg—I can't understand it!"

"Perhaps that is as well, too, Madame. Be happy in the gift and give your ancient uncle credit for at least one act of kindness. *Au 'voir.*"

"Hanged if I can understand it, either," I confessed as we left the hospital. "If that old curmudgeon had left a message berating them for fools for having offspring, or even a new will that disinherited them both, it would have been in character, but such a gift—well, I'm surprised."

Amazingly, he halted in midstep and laughed until the tears rolled down his face. *"You* are surprised!" he told me when he managed to regain his breath, *"Cordieu,* my friend, I do not think that you are half as much surprised as Monsieur Warburg Tantavul!"

Dennis Tantavul regarded me with misery-haunted eyes. "I just can't understand it," he admitted. "It's all so sudden, so utterly—"

"Pardonnez-moi," de Grandin interrupted from the door of the consulting room, "I could not help but hear your voice, and if it is not an intrusion—"

"Not at all, sir," the young man answered. "I'd like the benefit of your advice. It's Arabella, and I'm terribly afraid she's—"

"Non, do not try it, *mon ami,"* de Grandin warned. "Do you give us the symptoms, let us make the diagnosis. He who acts as his own doctor has a fool for a patient, you know."

"Well, then, here are the facts: this morning Arabella woke me up, crying as if her heart would break. I asked her what the trouble was, and she looked at me as if I were a stranger—no, not exactly that, rather as if I were some dreadful thing she'd suddenly found at her side. Her eyes were positively round with horror, and when I tried to take her in my arms to comfort her she shrank away as if I were infected with the plague.

" 'Oh, Dennie, don't!' she begged and positively cringed away from me. Then she sprang out of bed and drew her kimono around her as if she were ashamed to have me see her in her pajamas, and ran out of the room.

"Presently I heard her crying in the nursery, and when I followed her in there—" He paused and tears came to his eyes. "She was standing by the crib where little Dennis lay, and in her hand she held a long sharp steel letter-opener. 'Poor little mite, poor little flower of unpardonable sin,' she said. 'We've got to go, Baby darling; you to limbo, I to hell—oh, God wouldn't, *couldn't* be so cruel as to damn you for our sin!—but we'll all three suffer torment endlessly, because we didn't know!'

"She raised the knife to plunge it in the little fellow's heart, and he stretched out his hands and laughed and cooed as the sunlight shone on the steel. I was on her in an instant, wrenching the knife from her with one hand and holding her against me with the other, but she fought me off.

" 'Don't touch me, Dennie, please, *please* don't,' she begged. I know it's mortal sin, but I love you so, my dear, that I just can't resist you if I let you put your arms about me.'

"I tried to kiss her, but she hid her face against my shoulder and moaned as if in pain when she felt my lips against her neck. Then she went limp in my arms, and I carried her, unconscious but still moaning piteously, into her sitting room and laid her on the couch. I left Sarah the nursemaid with her, with strict orders not to let her leave the room. Can't you come over right away?"

De Grandin's cigarette had burned down till it threatened his mustache, and in his little round blue eyes there was a look of murderous rage. *"Bête!"* he murmured savagely. *"Sale chameau;* species of a stinking goat! This is his doing, undoubtlessly. Come, my friends, let us rush, hasten, fly. I would talk with Madame Arabella."

"No, sir, she's done gone," the portly nursemaid told us when we asked for Arabella. "The baby started squealing something awful right after Mister Dennis left, and I knew it was time for his breakfast, so Miss Arabella was laying nice and still on the sofa, and I said, 'You lay still there, honey, whilst I see after your baby;' so I went to the nursery, and fixed him all up, and carried him back to the setting room where Miss Arabella was, and she ain't there no more. No, sir."

"I thought I told you—" Dennis began furiously, but de Grandin laid a hand upon his arm.

"Do not upbraid her, *mon ami,* she did wisely, though she knew it not; she was with the small one all the while, so no harm came to him. Was it not better so, after what you witnessed in the morning?"

"Ye-es," the other grudgingly admitted, "I suppose so. But Arabella—"

"Let us see if we can find a trace of her," the Frenchman interrupted. "Look carefully, do you miss any of her clothing?"

Dennis looked about the pretty chintz-hung room. "Yes," he decided as he finished his inspection, "her dress was on that lounge and her shoes and stockings on the floor beneath it. They're all gone."

"So," de Grandin nodded. "Distracted as she seemed, it is unlikely she would have stopped to dress had she not planned on going out. Friend Trowbridge, will you kindly call police headquarters and inform them of the situation? Ask to have all exits to the city watched."

As I picked up the telephone he and Dennis started on a room-by-room inspection of the house.

"Find anything?" I asked as I hung up the 'phone after talking with the missing persons bureau.

"Corbleu, but I should damn say yes!" de Grandin an-

swered as I joined them in the upstairs living room. "Look yonder, if you please, my friend."

The room was obviously the intimate apartment of the house. Electric lamps under painted shades were placed beside deep leather-covered easy chairs, ivory-enameled bookshelves lined the walls to a height of four feet or so, upon their tops was a litter of gay, unconsidered trifles—cinnabar cigarette boxes, bits of hammered brass. Old china, blue and red and purple, glowed mellowly from open spaces on the shelves, its colors catching up and accenting the muted blues and reds of antique Hamadan carpet. A Paisley shawl was draped scarfwise across the baby grand piano in one corner.

Directly opposite the door a carven crucifix was standing on the bookcase top. It was an exquisite bit of Italian work, the cross of ebony, the corpus of old ivory, and so perfectly executed that though it was a scant six inches high, one could note the tense, tortured muscles of the pendent body, the straining throat which overfilled with groans of agony, the brow all knotted and bedewed with the cold sweat of torment. Upon the statue's thorn-crowned head, where it made a bright iridescent halo, was a band of gem-encrusted platinum, a woman's diamond-studded wedding ring.

"*Hélas*, it is love's crucifixion!" whispered Jules de Grandin.

Three months went by, and though the search kept up unremittingly, no trace of Arabella could be found. Dennis Tantavul installed a fulltime highly-trained and recommended nurse in his desolate house, and spent his time haunting police stations and newspaper offices. He aged a decade in the ninety days since Arabella left; his shoulders stooped, his footsteps lagged, and a look of constant misery lay in his eyes. He was a prematurely old and broken man.

"It's the most uncanny thing I ever saw," I told de Grandin as we walked through West Forty-second Street toward the West Shore Ferry. We had gone over to New York for some surgical supplies, and I do not drive my car in the metropolis. Truck drivers there are far too careless and repair bills for wrecked mudguards far too high. "How a full-grown woman would evaporate this way is something I can't understand. Of course, she may have done away with herself, dropped off a ferry, or—"

"*S-s-st,*" his sibilated admonition cut me short. "That woman there, my friend, observe her, if you please." He nodded toward a female figure twenty feet or so ahead of us.

I looked, and wondered at his sudden interest at the draggled hussy. She was dressed in tawdry finery much the worse for wear. The sleazy silken skirt was much too tight, the cheap fur jaquette far too short and snug, and the high heels of her satin shoes were shockingly run over. Makeup was fairly plastered on her cheeks and lips and eyes, and short black hair bristled untidily beneath the brim of her abbreviated hat. Written unmistakably upon her was the nature of her calling, the oldest and least honorable profession known to womanhood.

"Well," I answered tartly, "what possible interest can you have in a—"

"Do not walk so fast," he whispered as his fingers closed upon my arm, "and do not raise your voice. I would that we should follow her, but I do not wish that she should know."

The neighborhood was far from savory, and I felt uncomfortably conspicuous as we turned from Forty-second Street into Eleventh Avenue in the wake of the young strumpet, followed her provocatively swaying hips down two malodorous blocks, finally pausing as she slipped furtively into the doorway of a filthy, unkempt "rooming house."

We trailed her through a dimly lighted barren hall and up a flight of shadowy stairs, then up two further flights until we reached a sort of oblong foyer bounded on one end by the stairwell, on the farther extremity by a barred and very dirty window, and on each side by sagging, paint-blistered doors. On each of these was pinned a card, handwritten with the many flourishes dear to the chirography of the professional card-writer who still does business in the poorer quarters of our great cities. The air was heavy with the odor of cheap whiskey, bacon rind and fried onions.

We made a hasty circuit of the hall, studying the cardboard labels. On the farthest door the notice read *Miss Sieglinde.*

"Mon Dieu," he exclaimed as he read it, *"c'est le mot propre!"*

"Eh?" I returned.

"Sieglinde, do not you recall her?"

"No-o, can't say I do. The only Sieglinde I remember is the character in Wagner's *Die Walküre* who unwittingly became her brother's paramour and bore him a son—"

"Précisément. Let us enter, if you please." Without pausing to knock he turned the handle of the door and stepped into the squalid room.

The woman sat upon the unkempt bed, her hat pushed back from her brow. In one hand she held a cracked tea-cup, with the other she poised a whiskey bottle over it. She had kicked her scuffed and broken shoes off; we saw that she was stockingless, and her bare feet were dark with long-accumulated dirt and black-nailed as a miner's hands. "Get out!" she ordered thickly. "Get out o' here. I ain't receivin'—" a gasp broke her utterance, and she turned her head away quickly. Then: "Get out o' here, you lousy bums!" she screamed. "Who d'ye think you are, breakin' into a lady's room like this? Get out, or—"

De Grandin eyed her steadily, and as her strident command wavered: "Madame Arabella, we have come to take you home," he announced softly.

"Good God, man, you're crazy!" I exclaimed. "Arabella? This—"

"Precisely, my old one; this is Madame Arabella Tantavul whom we have sought these many months in vain." Crossing the room in two quick strides he seized the cringing woman by the shoulders and turned her face up to the light. I looked, and felt a sudden swift attack of nausea.

He was right. Thin to emaciation, her face already lined with the deep-bitten scars of evil living, the woman on the bed was Arabella Tantavul, though the shocking change wrought in her features and the black dye in her hair had disguised her so effectively that I should not have known her.

"We have come to take you home, *ma pauvre,"* he repeated. "Your husband—"

159

"My husband!" her reply was half a scream. "Dear God, as if I had a husband—"

⌣"And the little one who needs you," he continued. "You cannot leave them thus, Madame."

"I can't? Ah, that's where you're wrong, Doctor, I can never see my baby again, in this world or the next. Please go away and forget you've seen me, or I shall have to drown myself—I've tried it twice already, but the first time I was rescued, and the second time my courage failed. But if you try to take me back, or if you tell Dennis you saw me—"

"Tell me, Madame," he broke in, "was not your flight caused by a visitation from the dead?"

Her faded brown eyes—eyes that had been such a startling contrast to her pale-gold hair—widened. "How did you know?" she whispered.

"*Tiens,* one may make surmises. Will not you tell us just what happened? I think there is a way out of your difficulties."

"No, no, there isn't; there can't be!" Her head drooped listlessly. "He planned his work too well; all that's left for me is death—and damnation afterward."

"But if there were a way—if I could show it to you?"

"Can you repeal the laws of God?"

"I am a very clever person, Madame. Perhaps I can accomplish an evasion, if not an absolute repeal. Now tell us, how and when did Monsieur your late but not at all lamented uncle come to you?"

"The night before—before I went away. I woke about midnight, thinking I heard a cry from Dennie's nursery. When I reached the room where he was sleeping I saw my uncle's face glaring at me through the window. It seemed to be illuminated by a sort of inward hellish light, for it stood out against the darkness like a jack-o'-lantern, and it smiled an awful smile at me. 'Arabella,' it said, and I could see its thin dead lips writhe back as if all the teeth were burning-hot, 'I've come to tell you that your marriage is a mockery and a lie. The man you married is your brother, and the child you bore is doubly illegitimate. You can't continue living with them, Arabella. That would be an even greater sin. You must leave them right away, or'—once more his lips crept back until his teeth were bare—'or I shall come to visit

160

you each night, and when the baby has grown old enough to understand I'll tell him who his parents really are. Take your choice, my daughter. Leave them and let me go back to the grave, or stay and see me every night and know that I will tell your son when he is old enough to understand. If I do it he will loathe and hate you; curse the day you bore him.'

"'And you'll promise never to come near Dennis or the baby if I go?' I asked.

"He promised, and I staggered back to bed, where I fell fainting.

"Next morning when I wakened I was sure it had been a bad dream, but when I looked at Dennis and my own reflection in the glass I knew it was no dream, but a dreadful visitation from the dead.

"Then I went mad. I tried to kill my baby, and when Dennis stopped me I watched my chance to run away, came over to New York and took to this." She looked significantly around the miserable room. "I knew they'd never look for Arabella Tantavul among the city's whores; I was safer from pursuit right here than if I'd been in Europe or China."

"But, Madame," de Grandin's voice was jubilant with shocked reproof, "that which you saw was nothing but a dream; a most unpleasant dream, I grant, but still a dream. Look in my eyes, if you please!"

She raised her eyes to his, and I saw his pupils widen as a cat's do in the dark, saw a line of white outline the cornea, and, responsive to his piercing gaze, beheld her brown eyes set in a fixed stare, first as if in fright, then with a glaze almost like that of death.

"Attend me, Madame Arabella," he commanded softly. "You are tired—*grand Dieu,* how tired you are! You have suffered greatly, but you are about to rest. Your memory of that night is gone; so is all memory of the things which have transpired since. You will move and eat and sleep as you are bidden, but of what takes place around you till I bid you wake you will retain no recollection. Do you hear me, Madame Arabella?"

"I hear," she answered softly in a small tired voice.

"*Très bon.* Lie down, my little poor one. Lie down to rest and dreams of love. Sleep, rest, dream and forget.

"Will you be good enough to 'phone to Dr. Wyckoff?" he asked me. "We shall place her in his sanitorium, wash this *sacré* dye from her hair and nurse her back to health; then when all is ready we can bear her home and have her take up life and love where she left off. No one shall be the wiser. This chapter of her life is closed and sealed for ever.

"Each day I'll call upon her and renew hypnotic treatments that she may simulate the mild but curable mental case which we shall tell the good Wyckoff she is. When finally I release her from hypnosis her mind will be entirely cleared of that bad dream that nearly wrecked her happiness."

Arabella Tantavul lay on the sofa in her charming boudoir, an orchid negligée about her slender shoulders, an eiderdown rug tucked around her feet and knees. Her wedding ring was once more on her finger. Pale with a pallor not to be disguised by the most skillfully applied cosmetics, and with deep violet crescents underneath her amber eyes, she lay back listlessly, drinking in the cheerful warmth that emanated from the fire of apple-logs that snapped and crackled on the hearth. Two months of rest at Dr. Wyckoff's sanitorium had cleansed the marks of dissipation from her face, and the ministrations of beauticians had restored the pale-gold luster to her hair, but the listlessness that followed her complete breakdown was still upon her like the weakness from a fever.

"I can't remember anything about my illness, Dr. Trowbridge," she told me with a weary little smile, "but vaguely I connect it with some dreadful dream I had. And"—she wrinkled her smooth forehead in an effort at remembering—"I think I had a rather dreadful dream last night, but—"

"Ah-*ha?*" de Grandin leant abruptly forward in his chair. "What was it that you dreamed, Madame?"

"I—don't—know," she answered slowly. "Odd, isn't it, how you can remember that a dream was so unpleasant, yet not recall its details? Somehow, I connect it with Uncle Warburg; but—"

"*Parbleu,* do you say so? Has he returned? *Ah bah,* he makes me to be so mad, that one!"

162

*   *   *

"It is time we went, my friend," de Grandin told me as the tall clock in the hall beat out its tenth deliberate stroke; "we have important duties to perform."

"For goodness' sake," I protested, "at this hour o' night?"

"Precisely. At Monsieur Tantavul's I shall expect a visitor tonight, and—we must be ready for him.

"Is Madame Arabella sleeping?" he asked Dennis as he answered our ring at the door.

"Like a baby," answered the young husband. "I've been sitting by her all evening, and I don't believe she even turned in bed."

"And you did keep the window closed, as I requested?"

"Yes, sir; closed and latched."

"*Bien*. Await us here, *mon brave;* we shall rejoin you presently."

He led the way to Arabella's bedroom, removed the wrappings from a bulky parcel he had lugged from our house, and displayed the object thus disclosed with an air of inordinate pride. "Behold him," he commanded gleefully. "Is he not magnificent?"

"Why—what the devil?—it's nothing but an ordinary window screen," I answered.

"A window screen, I grant, my friend; but not an ordinary one. Can not you see it is of copper?"

"Well—"

"*Parbleu,* but I should say it is well," he grinned. "Observe him, how he works."

From his kit bag he produced a roll of insulated wire, an electrical transformer, and some tools. Working quickly he passe-patouted the screen's wooden frame with electrician's tape, then plugged a wire in a nearby lamp socket, connected it with the transformer, and from the latter led a double strand of cotton-wrapped wire to the screen. This he clipped firmly to the copper meshes and led a third strand to the metal grille of the heat register. Last of all he filled a bulb syringe with water and sprayed the screen, repeating the performance till it sparkled like a cobweb in the morning sun. "And now, *Monsieur le Revenant,*" he chuckled as he finished, "I damn think all is ready for your warm reception!"

163

For something like an hour we waited, then he tiptoed to the bed and bent over Arabella.

"Madame!"

The girl stirred slightly, murmuring some half-audible response, and:

"In half an hour you will rise," he told her. "You will put your robe on and stand by the window, but on no account will you go near it or lay hands on it. Should anyone address you from outside you will reply, but you will not remember what you say or what is said to you."

He motioned me to follow, and we left the room, taking station in the hallway just outside.

How long we waited I have no accurate idea. Perhaps it was an hour, perhaps less; at any rate the silent vigil seemed unending, and I raised my hand to stifle back a yawn when:

"Yes, Uncle Warburg, I can hear you," we heard Arabella saying softly in the room beyond the door.

We tiptoed to the entry: Arabella stood before the window, and from beyond it glared the face of Warburg Tantavul.

It was dead, there was no doubt about that. In sunken cheek and pinched-in nose and yellowish-gray skin there showed the evidence of death and early putrefaction, but dead though it was, it was also animated with a dreadful sort of life. The eyes were glaring horribly, the lips were red as though they had been painted with fresh blood.

"You hear me, do you?" it demanded. "Then listen, girl; you broke your bargain with me, now I'm come to keep my threat: every time you kiss your husband"—a shriek of bitter laughter cut his words, and his staring eyes half closed with hellish merriment—"or the child you love so well, my shadow will be on you. You've kept me out thus far, but some night I'll get in, and—"

The lean dead jaw dropped, then snapped up as if lifted by sheer will-power, and the whole expression of the corpse-faced changed. Surprise, incredulous delight, anticipation as before a feast were pictured on it. "Why"—its cachinnating laughter sent a chill up my spine—"why your window's open! You've changed the screen and I can enter!"

Slowly, like a child's balloon stirred by a vagrant wind, the awful thing moved closer to the window. Closer to the screen it came, and Arabella gave ground before it and put up her hands to shield her eyes from the sight of its hellish grin of triumph.

"*Sapristi,*" swore de Grandin softly. "Come on, my old and evil one, come but a little nearer—"

The dead thing floated nearer. Now its mocking mouth and shriveled, pointed nose were almost pressed against the copper meshes of the screen; now they began to filter through the meshes like a wisp of fog—

There was a blinding flash of blue-white flame, the sputtering gush of fusing metal, a wild, despairing shriek that ended ere it fairly started in a sob of mortal torment, and the sharp and acrid odor of burned flesh!

"Arabella—darling—is she all right?" Dennis Tantavul came charging up the stairs. "I thought I heard a scream—"

"You did, my friend," de Grandin answered, "but I do not think that you will hear its repetition unless you are unfortunate enough to go to hell when you have died."

"What was it?"

"*Eh bien,* one who thought himself a clever jester pressed his jest too far. Meantime, look to Madame your wife. See how peacefully she lies upon her bed. Her time for evil dreams is past. Be kind to her, *mon jeune.* Do not forget, a woman loves to have a lover, even though he is her husband." He bent and kissed the sleeping girl upon the brow. "*Au 'voir,* my little lovely one," he murmured. Then, to me:

"Come, Trowbridge, my good friend. Our work is finished here. Let us leave them to their happiness."

An hour later in the study he faced me across the fire. "Perhaps you'll deign to tell me what it's all about now?" I asked sarcastically.

"Perhaps I shall," he answered with a grin. "You will recall that this annoying Monsieur Who Was Dead Yet Not Dead appeared and grinned most horrifyingly through windows several times? Always from the outside, please remember. At the hospital, where he nearly caused the *guarde-malade* to have a fit, he laughed and mouthed at her through the glass skylight. When he first appeared and

165

threatened Madame Arabella he spoke to her through the window—"

"But her window was open," I protested.

"Yes, but screened," he answered with a smile. "Screened with iron wire, if you please."

"What difference did that make? Tonight I saw him almost force his features through—"

"A copper screen," he supplied. "Tonight the screen was copper; me, I saw to that."

Then, seeing my bewilderment: "Iron is the most earthy of all metals," he explained. "It and its derivative, steel, are so instinct with the earth's essence that creatures of the spirit cannot stand its nearness. The legends tell us that when Solomon's Temple was constructed no tool of iron was employed, because even the friendly *jinn* whose help he had enlisted could not perform their tasks in close proximity to iron. The witch can be detected by the pricking of an iron pin—never by a pin of brass.

"Very well. When first I thought about the evil dead one's reappearances I noted that each time he stared outside the window. Glass, apparently, he could not pass—and glass contains a modicum of iron. Iron window-wire stopped him. 'He are not a true ghost, then,' I inform me. 'They are things of spirit only, they are thoughts made manifest. This one is a thing of hate, but also of some physical material as well; he is composed in part of emanations from the body which lies putrefying in the grave. *Voilà,* if he have physical properties he can be destroyed by physical means.'

"And so I set my trap. I procured a screen of copper through which he could effect an entrance, but I charged it with electricity. I increased the potential of the current with a step-up transformer to make assurance doubly sure, and then I waited for him like the spider for the fly, waited for him to come through that charged screen and electrocute himself. Yes, certainly."

"But is he really destroyed?" I asked dubiously.

"As the candle flame when one has blown it out. He was—how do you say it?—short-circuited. No malefactor in the chair of execution ever died more thoroughly than that one, I assure you."

"It seems queer, though, that he should come back from

the grave to haunt those poor kids and break up their marriage when he really wanted it," I murmured wonderingly.

"Wanted it? Yes, as the trapper wants the bird to step within his snare."

"But he gave them such a handsome present when little Dennis was born—"

"*La la,* my good, kind, trusting friend, you are *naif.* The money I gave Madame Arabella was my own. I put it in that envelope."

"Then what was the real message?"

"It was a dreadful thing, my friend; a dreadful, wicked thing. The night that Monsieur Dennis left that package with me I determined that the old one meant to do him injury, so I steamed the cover open and read what lay within. It made plain the things which Dennis thought that he remembered.

"Long, long ago Monsieur Tantavul lived in San Francisco. His wife was twenty years his junior, and a pretty, joyous thing she was. She bore him two fine children, a boy and girl, and on them she bestowed the love which he could not appreciate. His surliness, his evil temper, his constant fault-finding drove her to distraction, and finally she sued for divorce.

"But he forestalled her. He spirited the children away, then told his wife the plan of his revenge. He would take them to some far off place and bring them up believing they were cousins. Then when they had attained full growth he would induce them to marry and keep the secret of their relationship until they had a child, then break the dreadful truth to them. Thereafter they would live on, bound together by their fear of censure, or perhaps of criminal prosecution, but their consciences would cause them endless torment, and the very love they had for each other would be like fetters forged of white-hot steel, holding them in odious bondage from which there was no escape. The sight of their children would be a reproach to them, the mere thought of love's sweet communion would cause revulsion to the point of nausea.

"When he had told her this his wife went mad. He thrust her into an asylum and left her there to die while he came with his babies to New Jersey, where he reared them together, and by guile and craftiness nurtured their love, knowing that when finally they married he would have his so vile revenge."

"But, great heavens, man, they're brother and sister!" I exclaimed in horror.

"Perfectly," he answered coolly. "They are also man and woman, husband and wife, and father and mother."

"But—but—" I stammered, utterly at loss for words.

"But me no buts, good friend. I know what you would say. Their child? *Ah bah,* did not the kings of ancient times repeatedly take their own sisters to wife, and were not their offspring usually sound and healthy? But certainly cross-breeding produces inferior progeny only when defective recessive genes are matched. Look at little Monsieur Dennis. Were you not blinded by your silly, unrealistic training and tradition—did you not know his parents' near relationship—you would not hesitate to pronounce him an unusually fine, healthy child.

"Besides," he added earnestly, "they love each other, not as brother and sister, but as man and woman. He is her happiness, she is his, and little Monsieur Dennis is the happiness of both. Why destroy this joy—*le bon Dieu* knows they earned it by a joyless childhood—when I can preserve it for them by simply keeping silent?"

For a quarter of a century, Seabury Quinn's ghostly tales were almost always ranked first by the readers of Weird Tales, *where nearly all of his more than 160 stories appeared. Born in Washington, D.C., in 1889, Quinn graduated from the Law School of the Washington, D.C. Bar, saw military service in World War I, became the editor of trade journals for mortuary directors, and was an expert on mortuary law and science. He is best known, however, as the creator of Dr. Jules De Grandin, the dapper blond ghosthunter whose best cases are collected in* The Phantom-Fighter, *His best non-de Grandin tales appear in* Is the Devil a Gentleman?

Myrtle Meriwether was determined to remain a beauty pageant contestant for-ever. . . .

ELEVEN

Remember My Name

Edward D. Hoch

I don't get a great deal of fan mail in my business. I under-stand that some science fiction and horror writers receive letters from readers almost daily, but for most mystery writ-ers—especially short story writers—it's different. One or two letters a month drift in, often critical of some technical error in your latest work, and that's about it.

So I was especially surprised one morning in September when my wife brought in the mail and handed me a small padded mailing bag with the address hand-printed with a thick black pen. It was from someone named Keith Web-ster, a name that churned up half-forgotten memories. The package was postmarked from a town in Delaware.

Keith Webster. Someone I'd known a long time ago, in my youth. Why was he sending me this package, which seemed about the size of a paperbound book?

"You could just open it and see," my wife suggested.

"It's a video tape," I said, pulling the familiar plastic con-tainer from inside the padded bag.

"Is there a note?"

"No, just the tape. I suppose we'll have to play it."

Much as I liked receiving mail, I was annoyed that some-one was interrupting my work day, especially since I was well into a new story that had a deadline only a week away. I slid the tape into the slot on the VCR, turned on the televi-sion and pushed the *play* button. Almost at once the scene from the afternoon soap opera was replaced by a medium long shot of a stool placed against a blank yellow wall. A middle-aged man with a short, neatly trimmed beard and glasses walked into the scene from the left and sat on the stool, addressing the camera.

"Hi, Buddy! This is Keith Webster. Remember my name? We were in the army together at Fort Dix, during basic training back in the Korean War. I often wondered what happened to you, and last month I saw your name on the cover of a magazine. I know you wanted to write even then, and I'm glad to see you've been successful. I went to the library and found your address in a reference book, and I thought you might be interested in hearing from me after all these years.

"Did you ever get to Korea? I didn't, of course. After that trouble I was discharged. Then—"

"What trouble?" my wife asked. "Fill me in."

I stopped the tape for a moment and sat staring at the screen. It was difficult to connect this bearded face I was seeing with the bright, clean-shaven boy I'd known for those few short weeks at Fort Dix. He'd been a non-conformist even then. "He met a girl down in Atlantic City and went AWOL with her. They sort of busted up the town and the army tossed him out." I turned the tape back on.

"—I drifted around New York and finally got a job. Cathy had given me the name of someone in the stagehands' union, and he got me in. I started working Broadway shows and made a career of it. Now I work the big casino shows in Atlantic City. The work is pretty much the same, changing sets and raising curtains. I'm sending you this tape because I'll probably be retiring in another year or two and I'd love to see you while I'm still here. Do you ever get down to Atlantic City? I live over in Delaware, just outside Wilmington, but this would be the best place to get together. There's a lot of action here. I work the main showroom at the Ali Baba Hotel."

There was a bit more on the tape, talk of the old days and finally phone numbers where he could be reached in Atlantic City and in Delaware. I rewound it and my wife said, "It would give us a good excuse for a couple of days in Atlantic City."

"I suppose so." I'd never been very excited about gambling, though on occasion I'd risked a few dollars at black jack or in the slot machines. Still, Atlantic City was only a

170

five-hour drive from our home in Albany, New York, and the early September weather was still delightful.

The next day I phoned Keith Webster at the number he'd given on the tape. The phone rang several times and when he answered I had the impression I might have wakened him. "Hello?"

"Is this Keith? Keith Webster?"

"Buddy! I still recognize your voice after all these years! How the hell are you?"

"Not bad. How about you? On the video you looked great."

"I can't complain. Life's been pretty good."

"So, you married?"

"Not now. I was for ten years, but she walked out on me. I guess I wasn't cut out for marriage. But we can talk about that when I see you. Are you coming down to Atlantic City?"

"Yeah, this writing for a living has its advantages. I can take a long weekend whenever I want. My wife and I are thinking of driving down next Saturday and staying till Monday."

"That's great! The Miss America Pageant is next week."

"Is the Ali Baba a good place to stay?"

"One of the best. Maybe I can even get them to comp you."

"There's no danger of encountering those forty thieves, is there?"

He chuckled. "The only thieves here are the one-armed bandits, and there's more like four thousand of them."

So the following Saturday my wife and I set out for Atlantic City. She'd always done most of the driving in our household, but at the last minute there'd been a change in plans. Her elderly uncle in Philadelphia was quite ill and not expected to live. Since she was to be so close to the city she felt she should stop there for a day, then go on to Atlantic City by bus to meet me. As I'd arranged to meet Webster for dinner on our first night there, this seemed to be the best plan. If I stopped in Philadelphia with her, it would necessitate changing all our Atlantic City plans.

I dropped her at a hotel in midtown Philadelphia, then headed over the Ben Franklin Bridge to New Jersey. It was only an hour to Atlantic City, but I felt odd driving the car even that distance. I was glad when the city came into view and I headed directly for the Ali Baba, one of the newer casino hotels at the east end of the Boardwalk.

The room Keith had reserved for us was certainly impressive, with thick shag carpeting and a pedestal-mounted television that seemed to be growing out of the floor. A fancy bowl of fruit sat on a table near the window, tied with a red ribbon and tagged, *Compliments of the Management.* I walked to the window and saw that the room overlooked the Boardwalk and the ocean.

Almost at once the phone rang, and when I picked it up I heard Keith's familiar voice, sounding just as he had on the videotape. "I'm glad you could make it! Did they give you a decent room?"

"It's a beauty, Keith. Thanks a lot."

"Don't mention it. Stop by the casino once or twice so they'll believe me when I tell them you're a high roller."

"The quarter slots are about my speed, Keith. When will I see you?"

"How about dinner? Is your wife with you?"

"She stopped off in Phily to visit an elderly uncle who's ill. I drove in alone and she's taking the bus tomorrow."

"I'm looking forward to meeting her. But let's get together tonight anyway. There's someone I want you to meet."

I glanced at my watch and saw that it was already after five. "Fine. Where and when?"

"The Cave Room downstairs. I'll see you there at seven."

I reached the lobby a half-hour early, after a vigorous shower to wash off some of the road sweat. It seemed as good a time as any to put in an appearance at the casino so I wandered over to the blackjack tables and finally took a seat at the five-dollar one. A young woman with curly hair and a tight dress was dealing for the house, and demonstrating a remarkable run of luck. I lost thirty dollars within five minutes and decided that was my limit for the present.

I drifted into the Cave Room and sat at the bar, ordering a rum and Coke. After about ten minutes Keith Webster appeared. I recognized him at once from the videotape, but what really riveted my eyes was the woman at his side. She was as lovely as I remembered her, and the straight blond hair still reached to her hips. It was Cathy Meriwether, exactly as she'd been forty years earlier.

Keith grinned when he saw my amazed expression. "This is Cathy's daughter, Sandra. Looks a lot like her mother, doesn't she?"

"It's amazing!" I acknowledged, shaking the young woman's hand. "I'd have sworn it was Cathy."

"My mother's old friends always say that," Sandra Meriwether told me. Even her voice was the one I remembered from so long ago.

"Sandra's here for the Miss America Pageant," Keith explained. "She's covering it for a magazine."

"You should be one of the contestants," I told her seriously.

"Thanks, but I'm too old."

We went in to dinner together and I noticed how my old army buddy fawned over her. It was like the past all over again. "How's your mother doing?" I asked at one point, after we'd ordered.

"All right." That was all. No details.

"Cathy used to come here for the pageant," Keith explained, taking a sip of his cocktail. "Then Sandra started coming. Seeing them every year is one of the delights of my job."

I frowned at a random memory. "Wasn't this the week you two—?"

Keith Webster laughed. "Ran off together? You can say it. Sandra knows the whole story. Yes, it was in September of '51. I went AWOL from Fort Dix and we drove down here together. I remember it was the final night of the Miss America Pageant. That was quite a time." His eyes glowed at the memory. "The next morning Cathy was gone and I was alone. That just about drove me crazy. I chased after her in my car and that was when I lost control and went through the window of a hardware store. I was court-martialed and got tossed out of the army."

"I always thought they were too hard on you," I said.

"Oh, it worked out well in the long run. When I heard from Cathy again she gave me the name of a guy who helped get me into the stagehands' union. It's the closest I ever came to show business, I guess. I moved down here so I could see more of her."

"You said you were living in Delaware."

He nodded. "Outside Wilmington. It's an easy commute, across the Memorial Bridge and straight down Route 40. I like the location because it's about halfway."

"Halfway between what?"

He and Sandra exchanged quick glances. "Well, Cathy lives in southern Delaware—a place called Rehoboth Beach. I drive down to see her sometimes."

"My mother's still a lively woman," Sandra volunteered. "She's always at work on something."

After dinner Keith gave us a backstage tour, where leggy showgirls in various states of undress were preparing for the next performance. "I'll be retiring soon," he told me. "Don't think I won't miss all this."

Since he'd been responsible for my room I felt he deserved an invitation. The three of us ended the evening up there, looking out at the ocean. Keith snapped on the television so we could watch the Miss America finals being televised from just down the Boardwalk. I had some drinks sent up, although by that time we'd all had enough.

Somewhere during the middle of the pageant Keith departed quietly. "I'm staying at the hotel tonight," he mumbled. "Too drunk to drive home."

Sandra was seated on the big bed, her back against the padded headboard. "Aren't they lovely?" she asked, watching the flickering images on the television screen.

I turned out the rest of the lights and joined her with another drink. "You're the one who's lovely, just like your mother."

"Tell me something. Did you ever sleep with her?"

"Me? No, no—she was always Keith's girl then."

She rolled over on the bed. "Would you like to sleep with me?"

"I—"

"I'm not Keith's girl now."

I tried to comprehend what she meant by that, but my mind was foggy with drink. We rolled around on the bed for a while, and I remember light from the television screen reflecting on her face as she asked, "Do you know who I am?"

"Cathy. No, you're Sandra. But you really are Cathy, aren't you? Just like you were forty years ago."

"I am Myrtle," she whispered into my ear. "Myrtle Meriwether. Remember my name."

"Myrtle—What kind of a name is that? No wonder you changed it!"

Then I slept, and remembered no more.

By the time I awakened, with a dull headache, the morning sun was beginning to appear at the corners of the shrouded windows. I was alone in the big bed. Sandra, or whoever she was, had gone. I went into the bathroom and splashed cold water on my face, then returned to sit on the edge of the bed and dial the hotel operator. I only hoped Keith hadn't tried to drive after he left my room.

"Operator."

"Keith Webster's room, please."

"One moment."

I heard it ringing. On the fifth ring he picked it up. " 'Lo?"

"Keith, it's me. Where is she? Where's Sandra?"

Silence. I repeated my question and he replied with, "Do you know what time it is?"

"What's your room number, Keith? I'm coming down."

"Six twenty-seven. Give me five minutes."

I was there in four. He answered my knock on his door, still groggy from sleep, and I repeated my question. "Where is she?"

"Who? Sandra? I left her with you."

"She was gone when I woke up."

"Forget her. She's bad news."

"It's Cathy, isn't it? There's no Sandra."

He merely shook his head. "I told you, forget her."

"She told me her name was Myrtle. Myrtle Meriwether."

"She told you that?"

"Keith, I have to see her again!"

He sighed and steadied himself against the door frame. "She's gone back to Rehoboth Beach, Buddy. The pageant is over."

"Then that's where I'm going! I have to find her."

I spun around and started down the hall, but he grabbed me by the shoulder. "If you're really going, I'm tagging along."

"What's the fastest way? All the way up to Wilmington?"

He glanced at his watch. "There's a car ferry to Lewes from Cape May. If we hurry we can catch the first morning run."

The weather had turned suddenly cooler overnight, resulting in a heavy mist that hung over the entire shoreline as we drove south toward Cape May. There was little traffic early Sunday morning and we made good time on the Garden State Parkway. Still, we might have missed the ferry except that it had been held up until the fog lifted a little.

We landed in Delaware just five miles north of Rehoboth Beach. When I pulled into the big parking lot there were no other cars in sight and the mist still hung over the shoreline as it had on the Jersey side. "Where to now?" I asked Keith.

I noticed he'd grown pale during the crossing and wondered if the choppy waters had been too much for his stomach. "You really want to do this, Buddy?"

"I want to see her."

"Come on, then. She'll be along the beach."

We started through the damp sand, and almost at once the place took on a mystic, dream-like quality. I was surrounded by giant sand castles, some reaching above my head, all of them wrapped in mist and in various states of ruin. "What is this place?" I asked Keith.

"They have a big sand castle contest every August. It takes a while for the kids to knock them all down."

I walked slower now as the sand tugged at my shoes, seeing these elaborate castles spread out on all sides.

Then, through the mist, I heard someone calling my name.

She was standing there, about fifty feet ahead of us, perched on the ruined tower of a castle, her long hair blowing gently though there was no hint of a breeze.

That was when I was suddenly afraid.

"Come here," she called. "I'm waiting for you."

"Cathy!"

"I am Myrtle. Remember my name."

I broke into a run then, heading straight for her. Keith shouted and dove for my feet, tackling me in the sand. I landed on my face.

"Keith, damn it! Let me go!"

"Not there, Buddy. You don't want to go there."

I rubbed the sand from my face and eyes, and by that time she was gone. I lay there gasping for breath, choking and sobbing all at once. "Where is she, Keith?"

"Gone, Buddy. Gone until the next beauty pageant. What's that? Miss U.S.A., Miss Universe?"

"What do you mean, gone? It was Cathy, wasn't it?"

"It was Cathy," he agreed. "And Sandra. But really Myrtle."

"How could she look exactly the same after forty years?"

Keith Webster got up and started brushing the damp sand from his clothes. "Do you really want to know, Buddy? Myrtle Meriwether won the first beauty contest ever held in America, right here at Rehoboth Beach. She was Miss United States." He paused and stared off into the mist, as if trying to see her one more time. "That was in the summer of 1880."

Edward D. Hoch was born in New York in 1930, educated at the University of Rochester, served in the army, and worked as an editor for Pocket Books and for an advertising company before becoming a full time writer. He has written more than 700 short stories, creating such series detectives as Captain Leopold of Homicide (Leopold's Way); Dr. Sam Hawthorne, a specialist in impossible crimes; professional thief Nick Velvet; Simon Ark, who may be two thousand years old (The Quests of Simon Ark); and others. In 1968 he won the Mystery Writers of America's prestigious award for best short story for "The Oblong Room." In 1982 he was elected president of the Mystery Writers of America.

The characters a writer creates can become so realistic that they seem alive—
some more than others.

TWELVE

Author, Author!

Isaac Asimov

It occurred to Graham Dorn, and not for the first time, either, that there was one serious disadvantage in swearing you'll go through fire and water for a girl, however beloved. Sometimes she takes you at your miserable word.

This is one way of saying that he had been waylaid, shanghaied and dragooned by his fiancée into speaking at her maiden aunt's Literary Society. Don't laugh! It's not funny from the speaker's rostrum. Some of the faces you have to look at!

To race through the details, Graham Dorn had been jerked onto a platform and forced upright. He had read a speech on "The Place of the Mystery Novel in American Literature" in an appalled tone. Not even the fact that his own eternally precious June had written it (part of the bribe to get him to speak in the first place) could mask the fact that it was essentially tripe.

And then when he was weltering, figuratively speaking, in his own mental gore, the harpies closed in, for lo, it was time for the informal discussion and assorted feminine gush.

—Oh, Mr. Dorn, do you work from inspiration? I mean do you just sit down and then an idea strikes you—all at once? And you must sit up all night and drink black coffee to keep you awake till you get it down?

—Oh, yes. Certainly. (His working hours were two to four in the afternoon every other day, and he drank milk.)

—Oh, Mr. Dorn, you must do the most awful research to get all those bizarre murders. About how much must you do before you can write a story?

—About six months, usually. (The only reference books he ever used were a six-volume encyclopedia and year-before-last's World Almanac.)

—Oh, Mr. Dorn, did you make up your Reginald de Meister from a real character? You must have. He's oh, so convincing in his every detail.

—He's modeled after a very dear boyhood chum of mine. (Dorn had never known *anyone* like de Meister. He lived in continual fear of meeting someone like him. He had even a cunningly fashioned ring containing a subtle Oriental poison for use just in case he did. So much for de Meister.)

Somewhere past the knot of women June Billings sat in her seat and smiled with sickening and proprietary pride.

Graham passed a finger over his throat and went through the pantomime of choking to death as unobtrusively as possible. June smiled, nodded, threw him a delicate kiss, and did nothing.

Graham decided to pass a stern, lonely, woman-less life and to have nothing but villainesses in his stories forever after.

He was answering in monosyllables, alternating yesses and noes. Yes, he did take cocaine on occasion. He found it helped the creative urge. No, he didn't think he could allow Hollywood to take over de Meister. He thought movies weren't true expressions of real Art. Besides they were just a passing fad. Yes, he would read Miss Crum's manuscripts if she brought them. Only too glad to. Reading amateur manuscripts was such fun, and editors are really such brutes.

And then refreshments were announced, and there was a sudden vacuum. It took a split second for Graham's head to clear. The mass of femininity had coalesced into a single specimen. She was four feet ten and about eighty-five pounds in weight. Graham was six-two and two hundred ten worth of brawn. He could probably have handled her without difficulty, especially since both her arms were occupied with a pachyderm of a purse. Still, he felt a little delicate, to say nothing of queasy, about knocking her down. It didn't seem quite the thing to do.

She was advancing, with admiration and fervor disgustingly clear in her eyes, and Graham felt the wall behind him. There was no doorway within armreach on either side.

"Oh, Mr. de Meister—do, do please let me call you Mr. de Meister. Your creation is so real to me, that I can't think of you as simply Graham Dorn. You don't mind, do you?"

"No, no, of course not," gargled Graham, as well as he could through thirty-two teeth simultaneously set on edge. "I often think of myself as Reginald in my more frivolous moments."

"Thank you. You can have no idea, *dear* Mr. de Meister, how I have looked *forward* to meeting you. I have read *all* your works, and I think they are wonderful."

"I'm glad you think so." He went automatically into the modesty routine. "Really nothing, you know. Ha, ha, ha! Like to please the readers, but lots of room for improvement. Ha, ha, ha!"

"But you really are, you know." This was said with intense earnestness. "I mean good, *really* good. I think it is wonderful to be an author like you. It must be almost like being God."

Graham stared blankly. "Not to editors, sister."

Sister didn't get the whisper. She continued, "To be able to create living characters out of nothing; to unfold souls to all the world; to put thoughts into words; to build pictures and create worlds. I have often thought that an author was the most gloriously gifted person in creation. Better an inspired author starving in a garret than a king upon his throne. Don't you think so?"

"Definitely," lied Graham.

"What are the crass material goods of the world to the wonders of weaving emotions and deeds into a little world of its own?"

"What, indeed?"

"And posterity, think of posterity!"

"Yes, yes. I often do."

She seized his hand. "There's only one little request. You might," she blushed faintly, "you might give poor Reginald—if you will allow me to call him that just once—a chance to marry Letitia Reynolds. You make her just a little too cruel to him. I'm sure I weep over it for hours together sometimes. But then he is too, too real to me."

And from somewhere, a lacy frill of handkerchief made its appearance, and went to her eyes. She removed it, smiled bravely, and scurried away. Graham Dorn inhaled, closed his eyes, and gently collapsed into June's arms.

His eyes opened with a jerk. "You may consider," he said severely, "our engagement frazzled to the breaking point. Only my consideration for your poor, aged parents prevents your being known henceforward as the ex-fiancée of Graham Dorn."

"Darling, you are so noble." She massaged his sleeve with her cheek. "Come, I'll take you home and bathe your poor wounds."

"All right, but you'll have to carry me. Has your precious, loveable aunt got an axe?"

"But why?"

"For one thing she had the gall to introduce me as the brain-father, God help me, of the famous Reginald de Meister."

"And aren't you?"

"Let's get out of this creep-joint. And get this. I'm no relative, by brain or otherwise, of that character. I disown him. I cast him into the darkness. I spit upon him. I declare him an illegitimate son, a foul degenerate, and the offspring of a hound, and I'll be damned if he ever pokes his lousy patrician nose into my typewriter again."

They were in the taxi, and June straightened his tie. "All right, Sonny, let's see the letter."

"What letter?"

She held out her hand. "The one from the publishers."

Graham snarled and flipped it out of his jacket pocket. "I've thought of inviting myself to his house for tea, the damned flintheart. He's got a rendezvous with a pinch of strychnine."

"You may rave later. What does he say? Hmm—uh-huh—'doesn't quite come up to what is expected—feel that de Meister isn't in his usual form—a little revision perhaps towards—feel sure the novel can be adjusted—are returning under separate cover—'"

She tossed it aside. "I told you you shouldn't have killed off Sancha Rodriguez. She was what you needed. You're getting skimpy on the love interest."

"*You* write it! I'm through with de Meister. It's getting so club-women call me Mr. de Meister, and my picture is printed in newspapers with the caption Mr. de Meister. I have no individuality. No one ever heard of Graham Dorn. I'm always: Dorn, Dorn, you know, the guy who writes the de Meister stuff, *you* know."

June squealed, "Silly! You're jealous of your own detective."

"I am not jealous of my own character. Listen! I hate detective stories. I never read them after I got into the two-syllable words. I wrote the first as a clever, trenchant, biting satire. It was to blast the entire false school of mystery writers. That's why I invented this de Meister. He was the detective to end all detectives. The Compleat Ass, by Graham Dorn.

"So the public, along with snakes, vipers, and ungrateful children, takes this filth to its bosom. I wrote mystery after mystery trying to convert the public—"

Graham Dorn drooped a little at the futility of it all.

"Oh, well." He smiled wanly, and the great soul rose above adversity. "Don't you see? I've got to write other things. I can't waste my life. But who's going to read a serious novel by Graham Dorn, now that I'm so thoroughly identified with de Meister."

"You can use a pseudonym."

"I will not use a pseudonym. I'm proud of my name."

"But you can't drop de Meister. Be sensible, dear."

"A normal fiancée," Graham said bitterly, "would want her future husband to write something really worthwhile and become a great name in literature."

"Well, I do want you to, Graham. But just a little de Meister once in a while to pay the bills that accumulate."

"Ha!" Graham knocked his hat over his eyes to hide the sufferings of a strong spirit in agony. "Now you say that I can't reach prominence unless I prostitute my art to that unmentionable. Here's your place. Get out. I'm going home and write a good scorching letter on asbestos to our senile Mr. MacDunlap."

"Do exactly as you want to, cookie," soothed June. "And tomorrow when you feel better, you'll come and cry on my shoulder, and we'll plan a revision of *Death on the Third Deck* together, shall we?"

"The engagement," said Graham, loftily, "is broken."

"Yes, dear. I'll be home tomorrow at eight."

"That is of no possible interest to me. Good-bye!"

Publishers and editors are untouchables, of course. Theirs is a heritage of the outstretched hand and the well-toothed smile; the nod of the head and the slap of the back.

But perhaps somewhere, in the privacy of the holes to which authors scurry when the night falls, a private revenge is taken. There phrases may be uttered where no one can overhear, and letters may be written that need not be mailed, and perhaps a picture of an editor, smiling pensively, is enshrined above the typewriter to act the part of bulls-eye in an occasional game of darts.

Such a picture of MacDunlap, so used, enlightened Graham Dorn's room. And Graham Dorn himself, in his usual writing costume (street clothes and typewriter), scowled at the fifth sheet of paper in his typewriter. The other four were draped over the edge of the waste basket, condemned for their milk-and-watery mildness.

He began:

"Dear Sir—" and added slowly and viciously, "or Madam, as the case may be."

He typed furiously as the inspiration caught him, disregarding the faint wisp of smoke curling upward from the overheated keys:

"You say you don't think much of de Meister in this story. Well, I don't think much of de Meister, period. You can handcuff your slimy carcass to his and jump off the Brooklyn Bridge. And I hope they drain the East River just before you jump.

"From now on, my works will be aimed higher than your scurvy press. And the day will come when I can look back on this period of my career with the loathing that is its just—"

Someone had been tapping Graham on the shoulder during the last paragraph. Graham twitched it angrily and ineffectively at intervals.

Now he stopped, turned around, and addressed the stranger in his room courteously: "Who the devilish damnation are you? And you can leave without bothering to answer. I won't think you rude."

The newcomer smiled graciously. His nod wafted the delicate aroma of some unobtrusive hair-oil toward Graham. His lean hard-bitten jaw stood out keenly, and he said in a well-modulated voice:

"De Meister is the name. Reginald de Meister."

Graham rocked to his mental foundations and heard them creak.

"Glub," he said.

"Pardon?"

Graham recovered. "I said, 'glub,' a little code word meaning *which* de Meister."

"*The* de Meister," explained de Meister, kindly.

"My character? My detective?"

De Meister helped himself to a seat and his finely-chiseled features assumed that air of well-bred boredom so admired in the best circles. He lit a Turkish cigarette, which Graham at once recognized as his detective's favorite brand, tapping it slowly and carefully against the back of his hand first, a mannerism equally characteristic.

"Really, old man," said de Meister. "This is really excruciatin'ly funny. I suppose I am your character, y'know, but let's not work on that basis. It would be so devastatin'ly awkward."

"Glub," said Graham again, by way of rejoinder.

His mind was feverishly setting up alternatives. He didn't drink, more, at the moment, was the pity, so he wasn't drunk. He had a chrome-steel digestion and he wasn't overheated, so it wasn't a hallucination. He never dreamed, and his imagination—as befitted a paying commodity—was under strict control. And since, like all authors, he was widely considered more than half a screwball, insanity was out of the question.

Which left de Meister simply an impossibility, and Graham felt relieved. It's a very poor author indeed who hasn't learned the fine art of ignoring impossibilities in writing a book.

He said smoothly, "I have here a volume of my latest

work. Do you mind naming your page and crawling back into it. I'm a busy man and God knows I have enough of you in the tripe I write."

"But I'm here on business, old chap. I've got to come to a friendly arrangement with you first. Things are deucedly uncomfortable as they are."

"Look, do you know you're bothering me? I'm not in the habit of talking to mythical characters. As a general thing, I don't pal around with them. Besides which, it's time your mother told you that you really don't exist."

"My dear fellow, I always existed. Existence is such a subjective thing. What a mind thinks exists, *does* exist. I existed in your mind, for instance, ever since you first thought of me."

Graham shuddered. "But the question is, what are you doing *out* of my mind. Getting a little narrow for you? Want elbow room?"

"Not at all. Rather satisfact'ry mind in its way, but I achieved a more concrete existence only this afternoon, and so I seize the opportunity to engage you face to face in the aforementioned business conversation. You see, that thin sentimental lady of your society—"

"What society?" questioned Graham hollowly. It was all awfully clear to him now.

"The one at which you made a speech—" de Meister shuddered in his turn—"on the detective novel. She believed in my existence, so, naturally, I exist."

He finished his cigarette and flicked it out with a negligent twist of the wrist.

"The logic," declared Graham, "is inescapable. Now what do you want and the answer is no."

"Do you realize, old man, that if you stop writing de Meister stories, my existence will become that dull, wraithlike one of all superannuated fictional detectives. I'd have to gibber through the gray mists of Limbo with Holmes, Lecocq, and Dupin."

"A very fascinating thought, I think. A very fitting fate."

Reginald de Meister's eyes turned icy, and Graham suddenly remembered the passage on page 123 of *The Case of the Broken Ashtray:*

His eyes, hitherto lazy and unattentive, hardened into twin pools of blue ice and transfixed the butler, who staggered back, a stifled cry on his lips.

Evidently, de Meister lost none of his characteristics out of the novels he adorned.

Graham staggered back, a stifled cry on his lips.

De Meister said menacingly, "It would be better for you if the de Meister mysteries continue. Do you understand?"

Graham recovered and summoned a feeble indignation. "Now wait a while. You're getting out of hand. Remember, in a way, I'm your father. That's right. Your mental father. You can't hand me ultimatums or make threats. It isn't filial. It's lacking in the proper respect and love."

"And another thing," said de Meister, unmoved. "We've got to straighten out this business of Letitia Reynolds. It's gettin' deucedly borin', y'know."

"Now you're getting silly. My love scenes have been widely heralded as miracles of tenderness and sentiment not found in one murder mystery out of a thousand. — Wait, I'll get you a few reviews. I don't mind your attempts to dictate my actions so much, but I'm damned if you'll criticize my writing."

"Forget the reviews. Tenderness and all that rot is what I don't want. I've been driftin' after the fair lady for five volumes now, and behavin' the most insufferable ass. This has got to stop."

"In what way?"

"I've got to marry her in your present story. Either that, or make her a good, respectable mistress. And you'll have to stop making me so damned Victorian and gentlemanly towards ladies. I'm only human, old man."

"Impossible!" said Graham, "and that includes your last remark."

De Meister grew severe. "Really, old chap, for an author, you display the most appallin' lack of concern for the well-bein' of a character who has supported you for a good many years."

Graham choked eloquently. "Supported me? In other words, you think I couldn't sell real novels, hey? Well, I'll show you. I wouldn't write another de Meister story for a million dollars. Not even for a fifty percent royalty and all television rights. How's that?"

De Meister frowned and uttered those words that had been the sound of doom to so many criminals: "We shall see, but you are not yet done with me."

With firmly jutting jaw, he vanished.

Graham's twisted face straightened out, and slowly— very slowly—he brought his hands up to his cranium and felt carefully.

For the first time in a long and reasonably ribald mental life, he felt that his enemies were right and that a good dry cleaning would not hurt his mind at all.

The *things* that existed in it!

Graham Dorn shoved the doorbell with his elbow a second time. He distinctly remembered her saying she would be home at eight.

The peep hole shoved open. "Hello!"

"Hello!"

Silence!

Graham said plaintively, "It's raining outside. Can't I come in to dry?"

"I don't know. Are we engaged, Mr. Dorn?"

"If I'm not," was the stiff reply, "then I've been turning down the frenzied advances of a hundred passion-stricken girls—beautiful ones, all of them—for no apparent reason."

"Yesterday, you said—"

"Ah, but who listens to what I say? I'm just quaint that way. Look, I brought you posies." He flourished roses before the peep hole.

June opened the door. "Roses! How plebeian. Come in, cookie, and sully the sofa. Whoa, whoa, before you move a step, what have you got under the other arm? Not the manuscript of *Death on the Third Deck*?"

"Correct. Not that excrescence of a manuscript. This is something different."

June's tone chilled. "That isn't your precious novel, is it?"

Graham flung his head up, "How did you know about it?"

"You slobbered the plot all over me at MacDunlap's silver anniversary party."

"I did not. I couldn't unless I were drunk."

"Oh, but you were. Stinking is the term. And on two cocktails too."

"Well, if I was drunk, I couldn't have told you the right plot."

"Is the setting a coal-mine district?"

"—uh—yes."

"And are the people concerned real, earthy, unartificial, down-to-earth characters, speaking and thinking just like you and me? Is it a story of basic economic forces? Are the human characters lifted up and thrown down and whirled around, all at the mercy of the coal mine and mechanized industry of today?"

"—uh—yes."

She nodded her head retrospectively. "I remember distinctly. First, you got drunk and were sick. Then you got better, and told me the first few chapters. Then I got sick."

She approached the glowering author. "Graham." She leant her golden head upon his shoulder and cooed softly. "Why don't you continue with the de Meister stories? You get such pretty checks out of them."

Graham writhed out of her grasp. "You are a mercenary wretch, incapable of understanding an author's soul. You may consider our engagement broken."

He sat down hard on the sofa, and folded his arms. "Unless you will consent to read the script of my novel and give me the usual story analysis."

"May I give you my analysis of *Death on the Third Deck* first?"

"No."

"Good! In the first place, your love interest is becoming sickening."

"It is not." Graham pointed his finger indignantly. "It breathes a sweet and sentimental fragrance, as of an older day. I've got the review here that says it." He fumbled in his wallet.

"Oh, bullfeathers. Are you going to start quoting that guy in the Pillsboro (Okla.) Clarion? He's probably your second cousin. You know that your last two novels were completely below par in royalties. And *Third Deck* isn't even being sold."

"So much the better—Ow!" He rubbed his head violently. "What did you do that for?"

"Because the only place I could hit as hard as I wanted to, without disabling you, was your head. Listen! The public is tired of your corny Letitia Reynolds. Why don't you let her soak her 'gleaming golden crown of hair' in kerosene and get familiar with a match?"

"But June, that character is drawn from life. From you!"

"Graham Dorn! I am not here to listen to insults. The mystery market today is swinging towards action and hot, honest love and you're still in the sweet, sentimental stickiness of five years ago."

"But that's Reginald de Meister's character."

"Well, change his character. Listen! You introduce Sancha Rodriguez. That's fine. I approve of her. She's Mexican, flaming, passionate, sultry, and in love with him. So what do you do? First he behaves the impeccable gentleman, and then you kill her off in the middle of the story."

"Hmm, I see— You really think it would improve things to have de Meister forget himself. A kiss or so—"

June clenched her lovely teeth and her lovely fists. "Oh, darling, how glad I am love is blind! If it ever peeked one tiny little bit, I couldn't stand it. Look, you squirrel's blue plate special, you're going to have de Meister and Rodriguez fall in love. They're going to have an affair through the entire book and you can put your horrible Letitia into a nunnery. She'd probably be happier there from the way you make her sound."

"That's all *you* know about it, my sweet. It so happens that Reginald de Meister is in love with Letitia Reynolds and wants *her,* not this Rodriguez person."

"And what makes you think that?"

"He told me so."

"Who told you so?"

"Reginald de Meister."

"What Reginald de Meister?"

"*My* Reginald de Meister."

"What do you mean, your Reginald de Meister?"

"My *character,* Reginald de Meister."

June got up, indulged in some deep-breathing and then said in a very calm voice, "Let's start all over."

She disappeared for a moment and returned with an aspirin. "Your Reginald de Meister from your books, told you in person, he was in love with Letitia Reynolds?"

"That's right."

June swallowed the aspirin.

"Well, I'll explain, June, the way he explained it to me. All characters really exist—at least, in the minds of the authors. But when people really begin to believe in them, they begin to exist in reality because what people believe in, is so as far as they're concerned and what is existence anyway?"

June's lips trembled. "Oh, Gramie, please don't. Mother will never let me marry you if they put you in an asylum."

"Don't call me Gramie, June, for God's sake. I tell you he was there, trying to tell me what to write and how to write it. He was almost as bad as you. Aw, come on, Baby, don't cry."

"I can't help it. I always thought you were crazy, but I never thought you were *crazy!*"

"All right, what's the difference? Let's not talk about it, anymore. I'm never going to write another mystery novel. After all—" (he indulged in a bit of indignation)—"when it gets so that my own character—my *own* character—tries to tell me what to do, it's going too far."

June looked over her handkerchief. "How do you know it was really de Meister?"

"Oh golly. As soon as he tapped his Turkish cigarette on the back of his hand and started dropping g's like snowflakes in a blizzard, I knew the worst had come."

The telephone rang. June leaped up. "Don't answer, Graham. It's probably from the asylum. I'll tell them you're not here. Hello. Hello. Oh, Mr. MacDunlap." She heaved a sigh of relief, then covered the mouthpiece and whispered hoarsely, "It might be a trap."

"Hello, Mr. MacDunlap? . . . No, he's not here. . . . Yes, I think I can get in touch with him. . . . At Martin's tomorrow, noon. . . . I'll tell him. . . . With who? . . . With who???" She hung up suddenly.

"Graham, you're to lunch with MacDunlap tomorrow."

"At his expense! Only at his expense!"

Her great blue eyes got greater and bluer, "And Reginald de Meister is to dine with you."

"What Reginald de Meister."

"Your Reginald de Meister."

"*My* Reg—"

"Oh, Gramie, *don't.*" Her eyes misted, "Don't you see, Gramie, now they'll put us both in an insane asylum—and Mr. MacDunlap, too. And they'll probably put us all in the same padded cell. Oh, Gramie, three is such a dreadful crowd."

And her face crumpled into tears.

Grew S. MacDunlap (that the S. stands for "Some" is a vile untruth spread by his enemies) was alone at the table when Graham Dorn entered. Out of this fact, Graham extracted a few fleeting drops of pleasure.

It was not so much, you understand, the presence of MacDunlap that did it, as the absence of de Meister.

MacDunlap looked at him over his spectacles and swallowed a liver pill, his favorite sweetmeat.

"Aha. You're here. What is this corny joke you're putting over on me? You had no right to mix me up with a person like de Meister without warning me he was real. I might have taken precautions. I could have hired a bodyguard. I could have bought a revolver."

"He's *not* real. God damn it! Half of him was *your* idea."

"That," returned MacDunlap with heat, "is libel. And what do you mean, he's not real? When he introduced himself, I took three liver pills at once and he didn't disappear. Do you know what three pills are? Three pills, the kind I've got (the doctor should only drop dead), could make an elephant disappear—if he weren't real. I *know.*"

Graham said wearily, "Just the same, he exists only in my mind."

"In your mind, I know he exists. Your mind should be investigated by the Pure Food and Drugs Act."

The several polite rejoinders that occurred simultaneously to Graham were dismissed almost immediately as containing too great a proportion of pithy Anglo-Saxon expletives. After all—ha, ha—a publisher is a publisher however Anglo-Saxony he may be.

Graham said, "The question arises then how we're to get rid of de Meister."

"Get rid of de Meister?" MacDunlap jerked the glasses off his nose in his sudden start, and caught them in one hand. His voice thickened with emotion. "Who wants to get rid of him?"

"Do you want him around?"

"God forbid," MacDunlap said between shudders. "Next to him, my brother-in-law is an angel."

"He has no business outside my books."

"For my part, he has no business inside them. Since I started reading your manuscripts, my doctor added kidney pills and cough syrups to my medicines." He looked at his watch, and took a kidney pill. "My worst enemy should be a book publisher only a year."

"Then why," asked Graham patiently, "don't you want to get rid of de Meister?"

"Because he is publicity."

Graham stared blankly.

"Look! What other writer has a real detective. All the others are fictional. Everyone knows that. But yours—*yours* is real. We can let him solve cases and have big newspaper writeups. He'll make the Police Department look silly. He'll make—"

"That," interrupted Graham, categorically, "is by all odds the most obscene proposal I have ever had my ears manured with."

"It will make money."

"Money isn't everything."

"Name one thing it isn't.—Shh!" He kicked a near-fracture into Graham's left ankle and rose to his feet with a convulsive smile, "Mr. de Meister!"

"Sorry, old dear," came a lethargic voice. "Couldn't quite make it, you know. Loads of engagements. Must have been most borin' for you."

Graham Dorn's ears quivered spasmodically. He looked over his shoulder and reeled backward as far as a person could reel while in a sitting position. Reginald de Meister had sprouted a monocle since his last visitation, and his monocular glance was calculated to freeze blood.

De Meister's greeting was casual. "My dear Watson! So glad to meet you. Overjoyed deucedly."

"Why don't you go to hell?" Graham asked curiously.

"My dear fellow. Oh, my dear fellow."

MacDunlap cackled, "That's what I like. Jokes! Fun! Makes everything pleasant to start with. Now shall we get down to business?"

"Certainly. The dinner is on the way, I trust? Then I'll just order a bottle of wine. The usual, Henry." The waiter ceased hovering, flew away, and skimmed back with a bottle that opened and gurgled into a glass.

De Meister sipped delicately, "So nice of you, old chap, to make me a habitué of this place in your stories. It holds true even now and it is most convenient. The waiters all know me. Mr. MacDunlap, I take it you have convinced Mr. Dorn of the necessity of continuing the de Meister stories."

"Yes," said MacDunlap.

"No," said Graham.

"Don't mind him," said MacDunlap. "He's temperamental. You know these authors."

"Don't mind him," said Graham. "He's microcephalic. You know these publishers."

"Look, old chappie. I take it MacDunlap hasn't pointed out to you the unpleasanter side of acting stubborn."

"For instance what, old stinkie?" asked Graham, courteously.

"Well, have you ever been haunted?"

"Like coming behind me and saying, Boo!"

"My dear fellow, I say. I'm much more subtle than that. I can really haunt one in modern, up-to-date methods. For instance, have you ever had your individuality submerged?"

He snickered.

There was something familiar about that snicker. Graham suddenly remembered. It was on page 103 of *Murder Rides the Range:*

> His lazy eyelids flicked down and up. He laughed lightly and melodiously, and though he said not a word, Hank Marslowe cowered. There was hidden

193

menace and hidden power in that light laugh, and somehow the burly rancher did not dare reach for his guns.

To Graham it still sounded like a nasty snicker, but he cowered, and did not dare reach for his guns.

MacDunlap plunged through the hole the momentary silence had created.

"You see, Graham. Why play around with ghosts? Ghosts aren't reasonable things. They're not *human!* If it's more royalties you want—"

Graham fired up. "Will you refrain from speaking of money? From now on I write only great novels of tearing human emotions."

MacDunlap's flushed face changed suddenly.

"No," he said.

"In fact, to change the subject just a moment—" and Graham's tone became surpassingly sweet, as the words got all sticky with maple syrup—"I have a manuscript here for you to look at."

He grasped the perspiring MacDunlap by the lapel firmly. "It is a novel that is the work of five years. A novel that will grip you with its intensity. A novel that will shake you to the core of your being. A novel that will open a new world. A novel that will—"

"No," said MacDunlap.

"A novel that will blast the falseness of this world. A novel that pierces to the truth. A novel—"

MacDunlap, being able to stretch his hand no higher, took the manuscript.

"No," he said.

"Why the bloody hell don't you read it?" inquired Graham.

"Now?"

"Well, start it."

"Look, supposing I read it tomorrow, or even the next day. I have to take my cough syrup now."

"You haven't coughed once since I got here."

"I'll let you know immediately—"

"This," said Graham, "is the first page. Why don't you begin it? It will grip you instantly."

MacDunlap read two paragraphs and said, "Is this laid in a coal-mining town?"

"Yes."

"Then I can't read it. I'm allergic to coal dust."

"But it's not real coal dust, MacIdiot."

"That," pointed out MacDunlap, "is what you said about de Meister."

Reginald de Meister tapped a cigarette carefully on the back of his hand in a subtle manner which Graham immediately recognized as betokening a sudden decision.

"That is all devastatin'ly borin', you know. Not quite gettin' to the point, you might say. Go ahead, MacDunlap, this is no time for half measures."

MacDunlap girded his spiritual loins and said, "All right, Mister Dorn, with you it's no use being nice. Instead of de Meister, I'm getting coal dust. Instead of the best publicity in fifty years, I'm getting social significance. All right, Mister Smartaleck Dorn, if in one week you don't come to terms with me, *good* terms, you will be blacklisted in every reputable publishing firm in the United States and foreign parts." He shook his finger and added in a shout, "Including Scandinavian."

Graham Dorn laughed lightly, "Pish," he said, "tush. I happen to be an officer of the Author's Union, and if you try to push me around I'll have *you* blacklisted. How do you like that?"

"I like it fine. Because supposing I can prove you're a plagiarist."

Graham Dorn nearly died laughing. MacDunlap waited patiently.

"Me," gasped Graham recovering narrowly from merry suffocation. "Me, the most original writer of the decade."

"Is that so? And maybe you don't remember that in each case you write up, you casually mention de Meister's notebooks on previous cases."

"So what?"

"So he has them. Reginald, my boy, show Mister Dorn your notebook of your last case —You see that. That's *Mystery of the Milestones* and it has, in detail, every incident in your book—and dated the year before the book was published. Very authentic."

195

"Again so what?"

"Have you maybe got the right to copy his notebook and call it an original murder mystery?"

"Why, you case of mental poliomyelitis, that notebook is my invention."

"Who says so? It's in de Meister's handwriting, as any expert can prove. And maybe you have a piece of paper, some little contract or agreement, you know, that gives you the right to use his notebooks?"

"How can I have an agreement with a mythical personage?"

"What mythical personage?"

"You and I know de Meister doesn't exist."

"Ah, but does the jury know? When I testify that I took three strong liver pills and he didn't disappear, what twelve men will say he doesn't exist?"

"This is blackmail."

"Certainly. I'll give you a week. Or in other words, seven days."

Graham Dorn turned desperately to de Meister. "You're in on this, too. In my books I give you the keenest sense of honor. Is this honorable?"

De Meister shrugged. "My dear fellow. All this—and haunting, too."

Graham rose.

"Where are you going?"

"Home to write you a letter." Graham's brows beetled defiantly. "And this time I'll mail it. I'm not giving in. I'll fight to the last ditch. And, de Meister, you let loose with one single little haunt and I'll rip your head out of its socket and spurt the blood all over MacDunlap's new suit."

He stalked out, and as he disappeared through the door, de Meister disappeared through nothing at all.

MacDunlap let out a soft yelp and then took a liver pill, a kidney pill, and a tablespoon of cough syrup in rapid succession.

Graham Dorn sat in June's front parlor, and having long since consumed his fingernails, was starting on the first knuckles.

June, at the moment, was not present, and this Graham

felt was just as well. A dear girl; in fact, a dear, sweet girl. But his mind was not on her.

It was concerned instead with a miasmic series of flashbacks over the preceding six days:

—Say, Graham, I met your side-kick at the club yesterday. You know, de Meister. Got an awful shock. I always had the idea he was a sort of Sherlock Holmes that didn't exist. That's one on me, boy. Didn't know—Hey, where are you going?

—Hey, Dorn, I hear your boss de Meister is back in town. Ought to have material for more stories soon. You're lucky you've got someone to grind out your plots ready-made— Huh? Well, goodbye."

—Why, Graham, darling, wherever were you last night? Ann's affair didn't get *anywhere* without you; or at least, it wouldn't have, if it hadn't been for Reggie de Meister. He asked after you; but then, I guess he felt lost without his Watson. It must feel wonderful to Watson for such—*Mister* Dorn! And the same to you, sir!

—You put one over on me. I thought you made up those wild things. Well, truth is stranger than fiction, ha, ha!

—Police officials deny that the famous amateur criminologist Reginald de Meister has interested himself in this case. Mr. de Meister himself could not be reached by our reporters for comment. Mr. de Meister is best known to the public for his brilliant solutions to over a dozen crimes, as chronicled in fiction form by his so-called "Watson," Mr. Grayle Doone.

Graham quivered and his arms trembled in an awful desire for blood. De Meister was haunting him—but good. He was losing his individuality, exactly as had been threatened.

It gradually dawned upon Graham that the monotonous ringing noise he heard was not in his head, but, on the contrary, from the front door.

Such seemed likewise the opinion of Miss June Billings whose piercing call shot down the stairs and biffed Graham a sharp uppercut to the eardrums.

"Hey, dope, see who's at the front door, before the vibration tears the house down. I'll be down in half an hour."

"Yes, dear!"

Graham shuffled his way to the front door and opened it.

197

"Ah, there. Greetin's," said de Meister, and brushed past.

Graham's dull eyes stared, and then fired high, as an animal snarl burst from his lips. He took up that gorilla posture, so comforting to red-blooded American males at moments like this, and circled the slightly-confused detective.

"My dear fellow, are you ill?"

"I," explained Graham, "am not ill, but you will soon be past all interest in that, for I am going to bathe my hands in your heart's reddest blood."

"But I say, you'll only have to wash them afterwards. It would be such an obvious clue, wouldn't it?"

"Enough of this gay banter. Have you any last words?"

"Not particularly."

"It's just as well. I'm not interested in your last words."

He thundered into action, bearing down upon the unfortunate de Meister like a bull elephant. De Meister faded to the left, shot out an arm and a foot, and Graham described a parabolic arc that ended in the total destruction of an end table, a vase of flowers, a fish-bowl, and a five-foot section of wall.

Graham blinked, and brushed away a curious goldfish from his left eyebrow.

"My dear fellow," murmured de Meister, "oh, my dear fellow."

Too late, Graham remembered that passage in *Pistol Parade:*

> De Meister's arms were whipcord lightning, as with sure rapid thrusts, he rendered the two thugs helpless. Not by brute force, but by his expert knowledge of judo, he defeated them easily without hastening his breath. The thugs groaned in pain.

Graham groaned in pain.

He lifted his right thigh an inch or so to let his femur slip back into place.

"Hadn't you better get up, old chap?"

"I will stay here," said Graham with dignity, "and contemplate the floor in profile view, until such time as it suits me or until such time as I find myself capable of moving a muscle. I don't care which. And now, before I proceed to take further measures with you, what the hell do you want?"

Reginald de Meister adjusted his monocle to a nicety. "You know, I suppose, that MacDunlap's ultimatum expires tomorrow?"

"And you and he with it, I trust."

"You will not reconsider."

"Ha!"

"Really," de Meister sighed, "this is borin' no end. You have made things comfortable for me in this world. After all, in your books, you've made me well-known in all the clubs and better restaurants, the bosom friend, y'know, of the mayor and commissioner of police, the owner of a Park Avenue penthouse and a magnificent art collection. And it all lingers over, old chap. Really quite affectin'."

"It is remarkable," mused Graham, "the intensity with which I am not listening and the distinctness with which I do not hear a word you say."

"Still," said de Meister, "there is no denyin' my book world suits me better. It is somehow more fascinatin', freer from dull logic, more apart from the necessities of the world. In short, I must go back, and to active participation. You have till tomorrow!"

Graham hummed a gay little tune with flat little notes.

"Is this a new threat, de Meister?"

"It is the old threat intensified. I'm going to rob you of every vestige of your personality. And eventually public opinion will force you to write as, to paraphrase you, de Meister's Compleat Stooge. Did you see the name the newspaper chappies pinned on you today, old man?"

"Yes, Mr. Filthy de Meister, and did you read a half-column item on page ten in the same paper. I'll read it *for* you: 'Noted Criminologist in 1-A. Will be inducted shortly, draft board says.'"

For a moment, de Meister said and did nothing. And then one after another, he did the following things: removed his monocle slowly, sat down heavily, rubbed his chin abstractedly, and lit a cigarette after long and careful tamping. Each of these, Graham Dorn's trained authorial eye recognized as singly representing perturbation and distress on the part of his character.

And never, in any of his books, did Graham remember a time when de Meister had gone through all four consecutively.

Finally, de Meister spoke. "Why you had to bring up draft registrations in your last book, I really don't know. This urge to be topical; this fiendish desire to be up to the minute with the news is the curse of the mystery novel. A true mystery is timeless; should have no relation to current events; should—"

"There is one way," said Graham, "to escape induction—"

"You might at least have mentioned a deferred classification on some vital ground."

"There is one way," said Graham, "to escape induction—"

"Criminal negligence," said de Meister.

"Look! Go back to the books and you'll never be filled with lead."

"Write them and I'll do it."

"Think of the war."

"Think of your ego."

Two strong men stood face to face (or would have, if Graham weren't still horizontal) and neither flinched.

Impasse!

And the sweet, feminine voice of June Billings interrupted and snapped the tension:

"May I ask, Graham Dorn, what you are doing on the floor. It's been swept today and you're not complimenting me by attempting to improve the job."

"I am not sweeping the floor. If you looked carefully," replied Graham gently, "you would see that your own adored fiancé is lying here a mass of bruises and a hotbed of pains and aches."

"You've ruined my end table!"

"I've broken my leg."

"And my best lamp."

"And two ribs."

"And my fishbowl."

"And my Adam's apple."

"And you haven't introduced your friend."

"And my cervical verte—What friend?"

"This friend."

"Friend! Ha!" And a mist came over his eyes. She was so young, so fragile to come into contact with hard, brutal facts of life. "This," he muttered brokenly, "is Reginald de Meister."

De Meister at this point broke a cigarette sharply in two, a gesture pregnant with the deepest emotion.

June said slowly, "Why—why, you're different from what I had thought."

"How had you expected me to look?" asked de Meister, in soft, thrilling tones.

"I don't know. Differently than you do,—from the stories I heard."

"You remind me, somehow, Miss Billings, of Letitia Reynolds."

"I think so. Graham said he drew her from me."

"A very poor imitation, Miss Billings. Devastatin'ly poor."

They were six inches apart now, eyes fixed with a mutual glue, and Graham yelled sharply. He sprang upright as memory smote him a nasty smite on the forehead.

A passage from *Case of the Muddy Overshoe* occurred to him. Likewise one from *The Primrose Murders*. Also one from *The Tragedy of Hartley Manor, Death of a Hunter, White Scorpion* and, to put it in a small nutshell, from *every* one of the others.

The passage read:

> There was a certain fascination about de Meister that appealed irresistibly to women.

And June Billings was—as it had often, in Graham's idler moments, occurred to him—a woman.

And fascination simply gooed out of her ears and coated the floor six inches deep.

"Get out of this room, June," he ordered.

"I will not."

"There is something I must discuss with Mr. de Meister man to man. I demand that you leave this room."

"Please go, Miss Billings," said de Meister.

June hesitated, and in a very small voice said, "Very well."

"Hold on," shouted Graham. "Don't let him order you about. I demand that you stay."

She closed the door very gently behind her.

The two men faced each other. There was that in either pair of eyes that indicated a strong man brought to bay. There was stubborn, undying antagonism; no quarter; no compromise. It was exactly the sort of situation Graham Dorn always presented his readers with, when two strong men fought for one hand, one heart, one girl.

The two said simultaneously, "Let's make a deal!"

Graham said, "You have convinced me, Reggie. Our public needs us. Tomorrow I shall begin another de Meister story. Let us shake hands and forget the past."

De Meister struggled with his emotion. He laid his hand on Graham's lapel, "My dear fellow, it is I who have been convinced by your logic. I can't allow you to sacrifice yourself for me. There are great things in you that must be brought out. Write your coal-mining novels. They count, not I."

"I couldn't, old chap. Not after all you've done for me, and all you've meant to me. Tomorrow we start anew."

"Graham, my—my spiritual father, I couldn't allow it. Do you think I have no feelings, *filial* feelings—in a spiritual sort of way."

"But the war, think of the war. Mangled limbs. Blood. All that."

"I must stay. My country needs me."

"But if I stop writing, eventually you will stop existing. I can't allow that."

"Oh, that!" De Meister laughed with a careless elegance. "Things have changed since. So many people believe in my existence now that my grip upon actual existence has become too firm to be broken. I don't have to worry about Limbo any more."

"Oh." Graham clenched his teeth and spoke in searing sibilants: "So that's your scheme, you snake. Do you suppose I don't see you're stuck on June?"

"Look here, old chap," said de Meister haughtily. "I can't permit you to speak slightingly of a true and honest love. I love June and she loves me—I know it. And if you're going to be stuffy and Victorian about it, you can swallow some nitroglycerine and tap yourself with a hammer."

"I'll nitroglycerine you! Because I'm going home tonight and beginning another de Meister story. You'll be part of it and you'll get back into it, and what do you think of that?"

"Nothing, because you can't write another de Meister story. I'm too real now, and you can't control me just like *that*. And what do you think of that?"

It took Graham Dorn a week to make up his mind what to think of that, and then, his thoughts were completely and startlingly unprintable.

In fact, it was impossible to write.

That is, startling ideas occurred to him for great novels, emotional dramas, epic poems, brilliant essays—but he couldn't write anything about Reginald de Meister.

The typewriter was simply fresh out of Capital R's.

Graham wept, cursed, tore his hair, and anointed his finger tips with liniment. He tried typewriter, pen, pencil, crayon, charcoal, and blood.

He could not write.

The doorbell rang, and Graham threw it open.

MacDunlap stumbled in, falling over the first drifts of torn paper directly into Graham's arms.

Graham let him drop. "Hah!" he said, with frozen dignity.

"My heart!" said MacDunlap, and fumbled for his liver pills.

"Don't die there," suggested Graham, courteously. "The management won't permit me to drop human flesh into the incinerator."

"Graham, my boy," MacDunlap said, emotionally, "no more ultimatums! No more threats! I come now to appeal to your finer feelings, Graham—" he went through a slight choking interlude—"I love you like a son. This skunk, de Meister must disappear. You must write more de Meister stories for my sake. Graham—I will tell you something in private. My wife is in love with this detective. She tells me I am not romantic. I! Not romantic! Can you understand it?"

"I can," was the tragic response. "He fascinates all women."

"With that face? With that monocle?"

"It says so in all my books."

MacDunlap stiffened. "Ah ha. You again. Dope! If only you ever stopped long enough to let your mind know what your typewriter was saying."

"You insisted. Feminine trade." Graham didn't care any more. Women! He snickered bitterly. Nothing wrong with any of them that a blockbuster wouldn't fix.

MacDunlap hemmed. "Well, feminine trade. Very necessary. —But Graham, what shall I do? It's not only my wife. She owns fifty shares in MacDunlap, Inc. in her own name. If she leaves me, I lose control. Think of it, Graham. The catastrophe to the publishing world."

"Grew, old chap," Graham sighed a sigh so deep, his toenails quivered sympathetically. "I might as well tell you. June, my fiancée, you know, loves this worm. And he loves her because she is the prototype of Letitia Reynolds."

"The what of Letitia?" asked MacDunlap, vaguely suspecting an insult.

"Never mind. My life is ruined." He smiled bravely and choked back the unmanly tears, after the first two had dripped off the end of his nose.

"My poor boy!" The two gripped hands convulsively.

"Caught in a vise by this foul monster," said Graham.

"Trapped like a German in Russia," said MacDunlap.

"Victim of an inhuman fiend," said Graham.

"Exactly," said MacDunlap. He wrung Graham's hand as if he were milking a cow. "You've got to write de Meister stories and get him back where, next to Hell, he most belongs. Right?"

"Right! But there's one little catch."

"What?"

"I can't write. He's so real now, I *can't* put him into a book."

MacDunlap caught the significance of the massed drifts of used paper on the floor. He held his head and groaned, "My corporation! My wife!"

"There's always the army," said Graham.

MacDunlap looked up. "What about *Death on the Third Deck,* the novel I rejected three weeks ago."

"That doesn't count. It's past history. It's already affected him."

"Without being published?"

"Sure. That's the story I mentioned his draft board in. The one that put him in 1-A."

"I could think of better places to put him."

"MacDunlap!" Graham Dorn jumped up, and grappled MacDunlap's lapel. "Maybe it can be revised."

MacDunlap coughed hackingly, and stifled out a dim grunt.

"We can put anything we want into it."

MacDunlap choked a bit.

"We can fix things up."

MacDunlap turned blue in the face.

Graham shook the lapel and everything thereto attached, "Say something, won't you?"

MacDunlap wrenched away and took a tablespoon of cough syrup. He held his hand over his heart and patted it a bit. He shook his head and gestured with his eyebrows.

Graham shrugged. "Well, if you just want to be sullen, go ahead. I'll revise it without you."

He located the manuscript and tried his fingers gingerly on the typewriter. They went smoothly, with practically no creaking at the joints. He put on speed, more speed, and then went into his usual race, with the portable jouncing along merrily under the accustomed head of steam.

"It's working," he shouted. "I can't write new stories, but I can revise old, unpublished ones."

MacDunlap watched over his shoulder. He breathed only at odd moments.

"Faster," said MacDunlap, "faster!"

"Faster than thirty-five?" said Graham, sternly. "OPA* forbid! Five more minutes."

"Will he be there?"

"He's always there. He's been at her house every evening this week." He spat out the fine ivory dust into which he had ground the last inch of his incisors. "But God help you if your secretary falls down on the job."

"My boy, on my secretary you can depend."

"She's got to read that revision by nine."

*The Office of Price Administration was in charge of gasoline rationing at this period. Remember "A" stickers?

"If she doesn't drop dead."

"With my luck, she will. Will she believe it?"

"Every word. She's seen de Meister. She *knows* he exists."

Brakes screeched, and Graham's soul cringed in sympathy with every molecule of rubber frictioned off the tires.

He bounded up the stairs, MacDunlap hobbling after.

He rang the bell and burst in at the door. Reginald de Meister standing directly inside received the full impact of a pointing finger, and only a rapid backward movement of the head kept him from becoming a one-eyed mythical character.

June Billings stood aside, silent and uncomfortable.

"Reginald de Meister," growled Graham, in sinister tones, "prepare to meet your doom."

"Oh, boy," said MacDunlap, "are you going to get it."

"And to what," asked de Meister, "am I indebted for your dramatic but unilluminatin' statement. Confusin', don't you know." He lit a cigarette with a fine gesture and smiled.

"Hello, Gramie," said June, tearfully.

"Scram, vile woman."

June sniffed. She felt like a heroine out of a book, torn by her own emotions. Naturally, she was having the time of her life.

So she let the tears dribble and looked forlorn.

"To return to the subject, what is this all about?" asked de Meister, wearily.

"I have rewritten *Death on the Third Deck.*"

"Well?"

"The revision," continued Graham, "is at present in the hands of MacDunlap's secretary, a girl on the style of Miss Billings, my fiancée that was. That is, she is a girl who aspires to the status of a moron, but has not yet quite attained it. She'll believe every word."

"Well?"

Graham's voice grew ominous, "You remember, perhaps, Sancha Rodriguez?"

For the first time, Reginald de Meister shuddered. He caught his cigarette as it dropped. "She was killed by Sam Blake in the sixth chapter. She was in love with me. Really, old fellow, what messes you get me into."

"Not half the mess you're in now, old chap. Sancha Rodriguez did *not* die in the revision."

"Die!" came a sharp, but clear female voice, "I'll show him if I died. And where have *you* been this last month, you two-crosser?"

De Meister did not catch his cigarette this time. He didn't even try. He recognized the apparition. To an unprejudiced observer, it might have been merely a svelte Latin girl equipped with dark, flashing eyes, and long, glittering fingernails, but to de Meister, it was Sancha Rodriguez—*undead!*

MacDunlap's secretary had read and believed.

"Miss Rodriguez," throbbed de Meister, charmingly, "how fascinatin' to see you."

"Mrs. de Meister to you, you double-timer, you two-crosser, you scum of the ground, you scorpion of the grass. And who is this woman?"

June retreated with dignity behind the nearest chair.

"*Mrs.* de Meister," said Reginald pleadingly, and turned helplessly to Graham Dorn.

"Oh, you have forgotten, have you, you smooth talker, you low dog. I'll show you what it means to deceive a weak woman. I'll make you mincemeat with my fingernails."

De Meister back-pedaled furiously. "But darling—"

"Don't you make sweet talk. What are you doing with this woman?"

"But, darling—"

"Don't give me any explanations. What are you doing with this woman?"

"But darling—"

"Shut up! What are you doing with this woman?"

Reginald de Meister was up in a corner, and Mrs. de Meister shook her fists at him. "Answer me!"

De Meister disappeared.

Mrs. de Meister disappeared right after him.

June Billings collapsed into real tears.

Graham Dorn folded his arms and looked sternly at her.

MacDunlap rubbed his hands and took a kidney pill.

"It wasn't my fault, Gramie," said June. "You said in your books he fascinated all women, so I couldn't help it. Deep inside, I hated him all along. You believe me, don't you?"

"A likely story!" said Graham, sitting down next to her on the sofa. "A likely story. But I forgive you, maybe."

MacDunlap said tremulously, "My boy, you have saved my stocks. Also, my wife, of course. And remember—you promised me one de Meister story each year."

Graham gritted, "Just one, and I'll henpeck him to death, and keep one unpublished story forever on hand, just in case. And you're publishing my novel, aren't you, Grew, old boy?"

"Glug," said MacDunlap.

"Aren't you?"

"Yes, Graham. Of course, Graham. Definitely, Graham. Positively, Graham."

"Then leave us now. There are matters of importance I must discuss with my fiancée."

MacDunlap smiled and tiptoed out the door.

Ah, love, love, he mused, as he took a liver pill and followed it up by a cough syrup chaser.

Born in Russia in 1920, Isaac Asimov was brought to the United States at the age of three. Perhaps the most famous science fiction writer alive, Dr. Asimov was educated at Columbia University and has been a teacher of biochemistry, a chemist for the U.S. Navy, an Army man, and a writer. His two most noted series are Foundation *and the* I, Robot *series. In the 1960s he began a nonfiction series of books explaining science for the general public; his latest series is the Black Widowers mystery stories. He has won six Hugos, two Nebulas, and the James T. Grady Award from the American Association for the Advancement of Science. His more than 400 books are characteristically imaginative, stimulating, and civilized.*